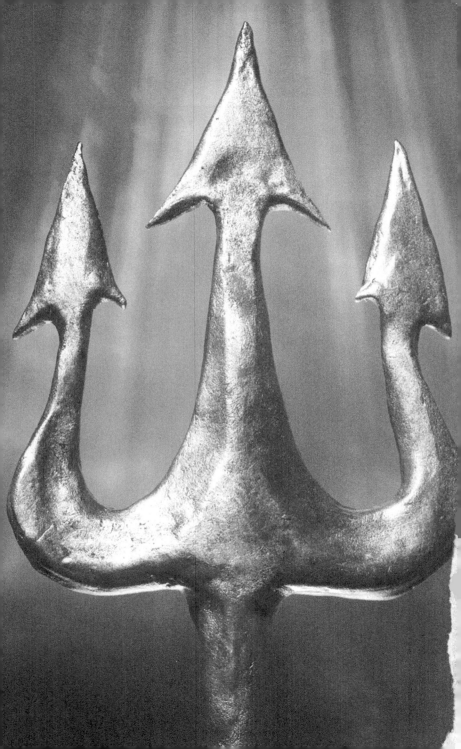

HIS ANGEL

Trident Security Book 2

Samantha A. Cole

His Angel
Copyright © 2015 Samantha Cole
All Rights Reserved.
Suspenseful Seduction Publishing

His Angel is a work of fiction. Names, characters, businesses, organizations, places, events, and incidents either are the product of the author's imagination or are used fictitiously. Any resemblance to actual persons, living or dead, events, or locales is entirely coincidental.

Cover by Samantha A. Cole
Editing by Eve Arroyo—www.evearroyo.com

AI RESTRICTION: The author expressly prohibits any entity from using any part of this publication, including text and graphics, for purposes of training artificial intelligence (AI) technologies to generate text or graphics, including without limitation technologies that are capable of generating works in the same style or genre as this publication. The author reserves all rights to license uses of this work for generative AI training and the development of machine learning language models.

No part of this book may be reproduced, scanned or distributed in any printed or electronic form without permission. Please do not participate in or encourage piracy of copyrighted materials in violation of the author's rights. Purchase only authorized editions.

ACKNOWLEDGEMENTS

Just want to take a brief moment to thank all the people who had a hand in helping with this book as well as the Trident Security Series.

Charla and Abby for being my beta-readers, and Abby's husband for taking a look a technical look at a few scenes!

To my editor, Eve Arroyo, for all her fine tuning!

To my family and friends who don't get offended when I whip out a pen and piece of paper, or napkin, and start jotting down notes when an idea comes to me in the middle of a meal or other event. Thanks for putting up with me!

And lastly, to the fans of Book 1, who loved it and let me know they were anxiously awaiting Book 2. I hope you enjoyed it!

NOTE FROM THE AUTHOR

The story within these pages is completely fictional but the concepts of BDSM are real. If you do choose to participate in the BDSM lifestyle, please research it carefully and take all precautions to protect yourself. Fiction is based on real life but real life is *not* based on fiction. Remember—Safe, Sane and Consensual!

Any information regarding persons or places has been used with creative literary license so there may be discrepancies between fiction and reality. The Navy SEALs missions and personal qualities within have been created to enhance the story and, again, may be exaggerated and not coincide with reality.

The author has full respect for the members of the United States military and the varied members of law enforcement and thanks them for their continuing service to making this country as safe and free as possible.

WHO'S WHO AND THE HISTORY OF
TRIDENT SECURITY & THE COVENANT

***While not every character is in every book, these are the ones with the most mentions throughout the series. This guide will help keep readers straight about who's who.

Trident Security (TS) is a private investigative and military agency, co-owned by Ian and Devon Sawyer. With governmental and civilian contracts, the company got its start when the brothers and a few of their teammates from SEAL Team Four retired to the private sector. The company is located on a guarded compound, which was a former import/export company cover for a drug trafficking operation in Tampa, Florida. Three warehouses on the property were converted into large apartments, the TS offices, gym, and bunk rooms.

In addition to the security business, there is a fourth warehouse that now houses an elite BDSM club, co-owned by Devon, Ian, and their cousin, Mitch Sawyer, who is the manager. A lot of time and money has gone into making The Covenant the most sought after membership in the Tampa/St. Petersburg area and beyond. Members are thoroughly vetted before being granted access to the elegant club.

WHO'S WHO AND THE HISTORY OF TRIDENT SECURIT...

There are currently over twenty Doms who have been appointed Dungeon Masters (DMs), and they rotate two or three shifts each throughout the month. At least four DMs are on duty at all times at various posts in the pit and play-rooms, with an additional one roaming around. Their job is to ensure the safety of all the submissives in the club. They step in if a sub uses their safeword and the Dom in the scene doesn't hear or heed it, and make sure the equipment used in scenes isn't harming the subs.

The Covenant's security team takes care of everything else that isn't scene-related, and provides safety for all members and are essentially the bouncers. The current total membership is just over 350. The fire marshal had approved them for 500 when the warehouse-turned-kink club first opened, but the cousins had intentionally kept that number down to maintain an elite status.

Between Trident Security and The Covenant there's plenty of romance, suspense, and steamy encounters. Come meet the Sexy Six-Pack, their friends, family, and teammates.

The Sexy Six-Pack (Alpha Team) and Their Significant Others

- Ian "Boss-man" Sawyer: Devon and Nick's brother; retired Navy SEAL; co-owner of Trident Security and The Covenant; Dom.
- Devon "Devil Dog" Sawyer: Ian and Nick's brother; retired Navy SEAL; co-owner of Trident Security and The Covenant; Dom/fiancé of Kristen,

- Ben "Boomer" Michaelson: retired Navy SEAL; explosives and ordnance specialist; son of Rick and Eileen.
- Jake "Reverend" Donovan: retired Navy SEAL; Dom and Whip Master at The Covenant.
- Brody "Egghead" Evans: retired Navy SEAL; computer specialist; Dom.
- Marco "Polo" DeAngelis: retired Navy SEAL; communications specialist and back up helicopter pilot; Dom.
- Nick Sawyer: Ian and Devon's brother; current Navy SEAL.
- Kristen "Ninja-girl" Sawyer: author of romance/suspense novels; fiancée/submissive of Devon.
- Angelina "Angie/Angel" Sawyer: graphic artist.

Extended Family, Friends, and Associates of the Sexy Six-Pack

- Mitch Sawyer: Cousin of Ian, Devon, and Nick; co-owner/manager of The Covenant, Dom.
- T. Carter: US spy and assassin; works for covert agency Deimos; Dom.
- Shelby Whitman: human resources clerk; two-time cancer survivor; submissive.
- Curt Bannerman: retired Navy SEAL; owner of Halo Customs, a motorcycle repair and detail shop.
- Jenn "Baby-girl" Mullins: college student; goddaughter of Ian; "niece" of Devon, Brody, Jake, Boomer, and Marco; father was a Navy SEAL; parents murdered.

- Mike Donovan: owner of the Irish pub, Donovan's; brother of Jake.
- Charlotte "Mistress China" Roth: Parole officer; Domme and Whip Master at The Covenant.
- Travis "Tiny" Daultry: former professional football player; head of security at The Covenant and Trident compound; occasional bodyguard for TS.
- Rick and Eileen Michaelson: Boomer's parents. Rick is a retired Navy SEAL.
- Charles "Chuck" and Marie Sawyer: Ian, Devon, and Nick's parents. Charles is a self-made real estate billionaire. Marie is a plastic surgeon involved with Operation Smile.
- Will Anders: Assistant Curator of the Tampa Museum of Art Kristen Anders's cousin.
- Dr. Roxanne London: pediatrician; Domme/wife (Mistress Roxy) of Kayla.
- Kayla London: social worker; submissive/wife of Roxanne.
- Chase Dixon: retired Marine Raider; owner of Blackhawk Security; associate of TS.
- Doug Henderson: retired Marine; bodyguard.
- Reggie Helm: lawyer for TS and The Covenant; Dom/boyfriend of Colleen.
- Colleen McKinley: office manager of TS; girlfriend/submissive of Reggie.
- Carl Talbot: college professor; Dom and Whip Master at The Covenant.

Members of Law Enforcement

- Larry Keon: Assistant Director of the FBI.

WHO'S WHO AND THE HISTORY OF TRIDENT SECURIT...

- Frank Stonewall: Special Agent in Charge of the Tampa FBI.

The K9s of Trident

- Beau: An orphaned Lab/Pit mix, rescued by Ian. Now a trained K9 who has more than earned his spot on the Alpha Team.

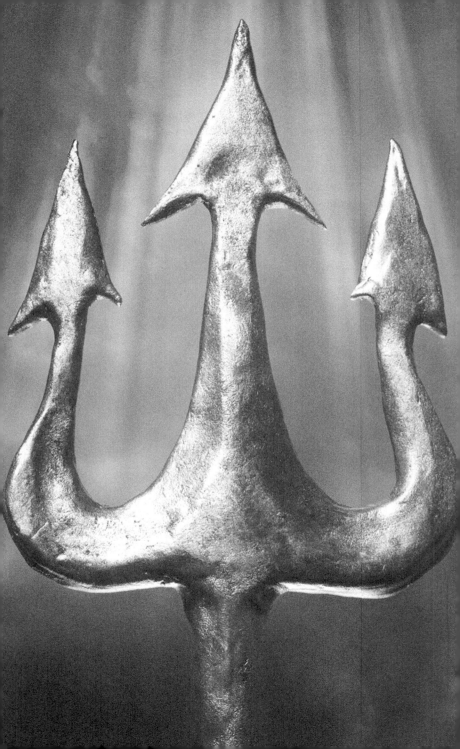

CHAPTER ONE

"Come on, Beau," Ian Sawyer called to his lab-pit bull mix as he walked up the driveway to Brody Evans' new house. The large, black dog finished a quick call to nature on Brody's curbside mailbox before running to his owner's side. Ian often wondered if the mutt had some Great Dane in its pedigree because he was tall enough that Ian, at six-foot-three, could almost pat the dog's head without bending over. It hadn't always been the case. When Ian found the six-week-old pup shivering and crying beside its dying mother outside his front door, Beau couldn't have weighed more than seven or eight pounds.

Ian recalled the night he'd heard the intruder alert go off on his phone a little over a year and a half ago. He'd been in his apartment watching the eleven o'clock news. The residence was located within his business compound, surrounded by a security fence to keep out unexpected visitors. At least it did until the furry duo broke in.

When the alert went off, he switched the TV channel to bring up the compound's multiple CCTV camera angles. Expecting to see a guard, his brother, or one of his team members walking around, he'd been surprised to see an animal limping toward his front door. Zooming in, he saw it was a badly injured dog carrying a small puppy in her mouth.

By the time he'd gotten outside, the mother had expended the last of her energy and collapsed a few feet away. The pup was dirty, a little malnourished, and covered in fleas but in good health. The mother, though, had been torn to shreds by another dog or some other animal. When Ian cautiously approached the pair, she'd nudged her baby closer to the human she was entrusting him to and then passed away without a sound.

After rushing the puppy to a nearby veterinary clinic open at all hours, Ian returned, followed the path the mother dog had taken, and found she'd dug under the fence line to get to his door. He'd followed drag marks leading into the woods on the other side of the fence. A little way into the brush, he'd discovered two additional puppies, which had both died several hours earlier. Ian retrieved a shovel and the mother dog's body, then buried the three of them under a tree at one o'clock in the morning before heading back to the compound to fill in the hole under the fence.

The pup had been bathed, neutered, chipped, and received his shots, then Ian took him home. The six men who made up the primary core team of Trident Security were all retired Navy SEALs, and for the first few weeks, the poor dog had gone by the name "FNG" for "'fucking new guy." But that changed as soon as Ian's goddaughter met the little guy for the first time and gave him a new name. Jenn had been reading *Beau Geste* in school and dubbed the pit bull mix with the same moniker.

When Beau was three months old, Ian had an old Navy

friend begin training him like military working dogs at a nearby facility. The pup had taken to the training as if he'd been bred for it. And although he now was a full-fledged protection and tracking dog, when he wasn't on duty, the big guy was an even bigger goofball who just wanted to get belly rubs or play fetch until he dropped. The dog was a well-loved addition to Trident Security and had full access to the business facilities and the residential apartments within the compound.

Ian and his brother, Devon, lived at the company compound they owned. As for the other four men of the Trident Security team, they all resided within ten minutes of the facilities. Brody was one of their teammates and had purchased his place about two months earlier. Tonight, Ian brought the dog to a last-minute barbecue since the house had a fenced-in backyard. Beau would have plenty of green grass to roll around in, something he didn't have at the paved compound.

The door was unlocked, so Ian let himself in, with Beau making a beeline to the kitchen to greet the rest of his favorite humans. Brody was the first person to reach down and pet him. The tall, broad man, also known as "Egghead," was the team's computer geek and master hacker. He'd designed and/or programmed the team's security and tracking systems, computers, and gadgets. He was also the team flirt and joker and rarely without his signature smile and quick wit.

The rest of the crew in attendance were Jake "Reverend" Donovan, team sniper, Marco "Polo" DeAngelis, communication specialist, and Ben "Boomer" Michaelson, demolition and explosives expert. Last but not least, Ian's younger brother, Devon "Devil Dog" Sawyer, was their breacher and lead climber. Ian was their team leader and interrogator, the same position he'd held in SEAL Team Four. While each man had their specialties, they could take over each other's positions if needed. They worked so well together that they could almost read each other's minds.

When Ian entered the kitchen, everyone paused long enough to greet him before resuming their conversations. He leaned down and gave Kristen a quick peck on the cheek as she smiled at him.

Kristen Anders was the only non-team member in Brody's house at the moment. She was Ian's future sister-in-law, an author of erotic romance novels, and the love of Devon's life. The guy had popped the question three months ago between Thanksgiving and Christmas, and after crying for several minutes, she'd said yes. They'd been in Nepal at the time, visiting Ian and Devon's parents while their mother was performing surgery at a clinic there for Operation Smile. The two had spent about ten days helping Chuck Sawyer, the brothers' father, and many other volunteers build a school in a nearby village.

The proposal hadn't surprised anyone but their parents since Devon had collared his submissive eight weeks earlier in a ceremony at The Covenant. It was the BDSM club which the brothers' also owned along with their cousin and club manager, Mitch Sawyer.

While Brody prepared boneless chicken breasts for the grill, Kristen patted ground beef into hamburger patties. When Beau plopped down on the floor next to her, she slid off a flip-flop and raised her foot to scratch his underbelly, much to the dog's delight. She glanced back at Ian. "Where's Jenn? Didn't she come with you?"

Ian leaned against the counter beside her, crossed his arms over his sculpted chest, and grumbled, "Nope. She

HIS ANGEL

went shopping with some friends from college this afternoon. Apparently, she has a date tonight."

Her eyes lit up with the opposite reaction he'd had after learning his goddaughter was going on a date. With a guy. Who probably wasn't any good for her. Who probably only wanted to get into the pretty girl's pants. He'd kill the bastard if he knew who he was.

Before Kristen could respond, Brody's eyes narrowed from where he stood a few feet away in front of the opened refrigerator door. "Jenn's going on a date?" His loud voice was filled with shocked annoyance. "With whom?"

The hush which fell over the room was interrupted by a short squeal of delight as five pairs of curious, angry eyes and one pair of elated ones stared at Ian. He let out a loud sigh. "I have no idea. She refused to tell me because she knew I'd have you investigate him."

The big, protective men all scowled, but Brody responded, "If she doesn't give you his name, tell Baby-girl she can't go. It's as simple as that."

A loud groan sounded, and everyone turned toward Kristen, who was rolling her eyes as if she was in the presence of six idiots. "Guys, come on. Your niece is nineteen years old and will be twenty in three months. She's an adult whether you like it or not. She's smart and can hold her own if she needs to. You can't ground her for refusing to let you harass some poor kid who wants to take her out."

The men were all Jennifer Mullins' surrogate uncles. Her father had been their lieutenant in the SEALs, and the team spent many off-hours at the man's family home near their base. The once-little girl had grown up with over forty "uncles," who she still kept in touch with through emails and phone calls. But she'd always been closest to these six men. When she was born, her parents had asked Jeff's best

5

friend, Ian, to be her godfather and legal guardian if anything ever happened to them. Ian had been happy to do it but never thought he would need to take their place so early in her life. Later this month would be the first anniversary of her parents' murders.

The team had found out this past September their deaths weren't the result of a burglary gone wrong but, instead, were part of a larger plot to kill several former members of SEAL Team Four. A Texas senator with bigger aspirations had hired a hit-man to take out Jeff Mullins, Ian, Devon, Jake, Brody, and two others. He'd realized they had been on a fact-finding mission years earlier and may have recognized him as a man who'd met with their target.

The senator's distant cousin was a Colombian drug lord with whom he'd developed a clandestine relationship in exchange for the financial backing to climb out of poverty into college and law school. In return, the senator became Ernesto Diaz's asset in Dallas. Besides being the head of a lucrative drug cartel, Diaz had been involved in the sex trade and arms dealing.

The FBI and Navy investigators had made the connection between the deaths of Jeff and Lisa Mullins, Eric Prichard, and Quincy Dale. The men of Trident security had been tapped to sort through boxes and boxes of classified missions they'd been on to figure out why Team Four had been targeted. Only after two attempts on the lives of the remaining four men on the hit list did they find out who wanted them dead and why. Since then, both the senator and hit-man had met with their own untimely demises. During all the chaos, Devon and Kristen met and fell in love.

Devon pinched his fiancée's ass hard, and she jumped and squealed, almost dropping the raw hamburger in her

HIS ANGEL

hands. "Who says we can't? And don't roll your eyes at a roomful of Doms, Pet."

The others all chuckled, knowing the sweet submissive wanted to glare at them and say something snarky before she thought better of it. Her ass would be spanked red if she did. "Fine, but come on, guys. This is the first date I've heard of her go on since she moved down here. You should be happy she's doing something fun, especially with the anniversary of her parents' deaths coming up. I'm sure she'll introduce you to the guy if there's a second or third date."

Ian had stayed with Jenn for three months in Virginia following the murders so she could finish up her high school education. She'd moved to Tampa and into Ian's apartment before moving again into a dorm room at the University of Tampa, where she was now enrolled. It'd taken her a while to deal with the loss of her parents, which everyone understood. But between counseling, her new school and friends, and her beloved uncles, Jenn was coming out of her shell and returning to the bubbly, outgoing woman they all knew and loved. The men mumbled their reluctant assents and changed the subject.

"Hey, Boss-man." Brody handed Ian a bottle of Bud Light. "It seems you're shit-out-of-luck with my new neighbor."

Ian's eyes narrowed and grew cold. "What're you talking about?"

Brody shrugged his broad shoulders. "Some guy's been hanging out with Angie all day, and they seem kinda chummy. His car was in her driveway all through last night. A little scruffy-looking, which I wouldn't think was her type, but it's obvious they know each other pretty well. *Too* well to be a relative."

7

Ian had met Brody's next-door neighbor, Angelina Beckett, once while helping his buddy move into his new house. She was a pretty woman, about thirty-three years old, with a killer body that made Ian's cock react like a snappy salute to an Admiral—fast and stiff. She'd starred in several of his dreams over the last two months with her long blond hair down to her shoulder blades, soft green eyes, lush breasts, and an ass he would love to get his hands on. More than once, he'd gotten off in the shower imagining her on her knees in front of him, giving him the blow job of a lifetime. Since their introduction, he'd only had a few glimpses of her, but his teammate must have noticed his interest in her.

Without saying another word, he uncapped his beer and took a swig before heading out to the patio with Beau on his heels. While the dog ran straight to the grass and began to sniff everything in sight, Ian sat at the outdoor table facing Ms. Beckett's backyard. She was also sitting at her patio table with her back toward him, although her chair was turned slightly so she was facing her guest. The strands of her long hair were twined in a braid that lay down the center of her back atop her teal blue shirt. He preferred her hair down and wished he had the right to walk over there and undo the confined tresses. Shifting his gaze to the strange man who sat at a ninety-degree angle next to her, Ian studied him.

Brody was right. The man was a little on the disheveled side, with a scraggly beard, mustache, and shoulder-length hair. But otherwise, he appeared clean, wearing a black T-shirt, blue jeans, and white sneakers. He seemed to be around the same age as her. What pissed Ian off, though, was how the guy had Angie's bare feet in his lap, massaging them as the two spoke. He watched as Angie's boyfriend's eyes flashed to his, then back again to hers. Ian wasn't fooled. In that split second, the stranger had noticed, evaluated, and determined Ian wasn't an immediate threat. It was obvious the man had training. His honed physique and body language screamed former military to Ian, yet he could almost disguise it. In fact, if Ian hadn't been just like him, he may have underestimated the man.

As the rest of Ian's team filtered out to the patio and took seats around the table, the man's gaze flashed over to them before settling again on Angie. Ian watched as she stood with the grace of a prima ballerina, her long legs and heart-shaped ass encased in faded capri jeans making his mouth water. When she turned toward her back door, he heard her say to her boyfriend, "Give me a few minutes to freshen up, and we'll grab something to eat. I hope you're in the mood for Mexican."

The moment she disappeared into the house, without hesitation, her boyfriend turned his attention to the six men beyond the chain-link property fence. Standing, he approached them like a lion interested in intruders entering his domain. He was about six-one, two hundred and ten lean pounds, with brown hair and eyes. Several tattoos were peeking out from under the arms of his short-sleeved T-shirt. He was also smart enough to stop two feet from the chest-high divider when he noticed Beau run over and place his big body between his humans and the stranger. Ian took it as a good sign that the dog, while in protective mode, wasn't growling a warning.

Warily, Brody stood and walked over to the fence to greet the man. "Hi, I'm Brody Evans, Angie's new neighbor."

Crossing his arms over his muscular chest, the other man nodded at Brody before intensely gazing at Ian and

Devon. "I'm aware of who you are, Evans. I was wondering if I could meet with you and your employers, the Sawyer brothers over there, sometime tomorrow morning at the Trident Security offices."

Ian's eyes narrowed as his stunned teammates looked back and forth between him and the stranger, who knew quite a few things about them, while they knew nothing about him, including his name. None of them were happy with the fact either. Staying in his seat, he leaned forward, put his beer bottle down, and pinned the bearded man with a warning look. "Who are you?"

He glanced over his shoulder before continuing, and Ian wondered why he didn't want Angie to hear the confrontation. "My name's James Athos, and I'll explain the rest tomorrow, but for now, let's just say we have a mutual friend, and I need your help."

Ian raised one eyebrow, his icy stare never wavering. "Friend? And who would this friend be?"

"A man named Carter."

If any of them were further surprised at the guy's revelation of knowing their longtime friend, associate, and U.S. government spy, T. Carter, they didn't show it. Carter was so deep into the world of black ops that Ian's team had no idea who the man actually worked for. He seemed to have very high connections in every alphabet agency in Washington D.C.—FBI, CIA, NSA, et cetera—as well as in the Pentagon, 1600 Pennsylvania Avenue, and several foreign countries. He was also the man who'd killed the hitman targeting the team several months ago and most likely the senator who'd hired the guy, although none of them would ever know for sure.

Ian's eyes flashed to the backdoor beyond Athos before

HIS ANGEL

returning to the man's face. "Tell me one thing . . . is she in danger?"

Athos shook his head. "No, and I'd like to keep it that way. I also don't want her to know anything about our conversation. Angie means the world to me, and I'll do whatever I can to protect her. What time can I meet you?"

Ian did a mental check of tomorrow's schedule. "Oh-eight-hundred?"

As Athos nodded his agreement, the woman in question chose that moment to come back outside and lock the door behind her. Now wearing white canvas slip-on shoes and carrying a small white purse, she strolled over to where her boyfriend stood. With automatic reflexes, the men relaxed their tense expressions, giving her no indication anything was wrong. When she stopped next to Athos, she looked at Brody, then the rest of the men with a friendly smile on her pretty face. "Hi, Brody. Hi, guys. I see you've met Jimmy."

Ian felt a jealous punch to his gut as the other man put his arm around her shoulders and kissed her on her temple tenderly. "I introduced myself, babe. I'm glad your new neighbor seems like a nice guy. I was worried you would get someone like the last asshole who couldn't seem to keep his hands to himself. That was until I had a little conversation with him and threatened to tell his wife after I beat the crap out of him." There was a not-so-subtle warning in there to the other men.

Angie rolled her eyes and smacked the guy in the stomach with her hand. "I told you I had it under control. And you didn't threaten to beat him. If I recall, you threatened to cut off George's manhood and shove it down his throat, followed by his fingers. Now come on, I'm starving. Take me to dinner."

"Your wish is my command, babe."

11

She looked back over the fence and gave the men a cute little girlie wave. "Have a nice night, everyone." As they turned toward the path leading to her driveway, Ian could have sworn she looked straight at him with a flash of heat in her eyes. But it was gone so fast he must have been mistaken. Whether it was real or imagined didn't matter to his dick which twitched inside his khakis at the sight of her retreating buttocks. Fuck, how he wanted to take a bite out of those ass cheeks.

"What the fuck?" Boomer asked. "Who the hell is he?"

Ian was still staring at where the two of them had disappeared around the side of her house. "I don't know, but you can be sure I'll find out. You know how much I hate surprises."

No one said anything more about the mystery man as Kristen came outside with a plate of hamburgers and chicken cutlets ready for Brody to grill. A few minutes later, the conversation returned to the usual banter that always occurred when they were together. However, Ian was no longer in a relaxed and talkative mood.

CHAPTER TWO

Angie sat across from her best friend, Jimmy, as they ate at a new Mexican restaurant she'd been dying to try. They continued to catch up with each other, and she wished his visit didn't have to be so short. While they'd both been raised in upstate New York, after high school graduation, she'd attended college in New York while he had gone into the Marines.

Six years later, he'd been recruited by the DEA and had to change his last name for safety reasons. He now worked in their Atlanta office. At least she didn't have to worry about his job as much as she used to since he was no longer working deep undercover assignments. Those had kept them from seeing or talking over the phone to each other for months at a time. Now he worked with a team who backed up the undercover guys, but he still had his beard and long hair, which she hated but knew was necessary. He was a good-looking guy when his facial hair was trimmed close, but without it, the man was an absolute hunk and had been since she first met him their freshman year of high school.

They'd tried dating once in their sophomore year, but it didn't last long because both of them were afraid to ruin the strong friendship which had developed between them. However, he took her to their senior prom after she broke up with the guy she'd been seeing a month earlier. Now the two friends tended to bust chops about each other's dates yet remained protective of each other. That was why she hadn't been surprised when Jimmy had made the veiled threat to Brody and his friends . . . talk about hunks.

While her best friend excused himself to use the restroom, Angie's mind drifted back to her new neighbor and his friends . . . to be more specific, one friend . . . Ian Sawyer. With his black hair, blue eyes, handsome face, and sculpted body, which made her panties wet, the man could be a movie star if he wanted to. Brody had told her Ian was retired from the Navy and owned the security consulting company Brody and the others worked for.

Lately, she'd considered having them upgrade her burglar alarm system. Jimmy always bugged her about how easy it was to bypass the one which had come with the home she'd purchased three years ago. She doubted the company's owner would do it himself, but she often fantasized about him coming over and installing a new alarm.

In her daydreams, he had on the tight faded jeans and snug, royal-blue T-shirt he'd been wearing the first day she met him while he was helping his friend move in. The color of his shirt had made his eyes stand out to the point she was certain she could drown in them. And, holy crap, his deep voice had sent shivers up and down her spine before settling between her legs. When Brody introduced her to his teammates, she thought Ian had held her hand a moment longer than the others, but it was probably wishful thinking on her part.

"And I was thinking of dying my hair purple and getting a heart tattoo that says 'bite-me' on my forehead."

Angie shook the wayward thoughts from her brain and stared at Jimmy, who was laughing at her shocked expression. "Huh? What're you talking about?"

"I was wondering where you were. I sat back down and asked you a question, but you were on another planet. I wanted to see how long I could talk gibberish before you noticed."

She threw a piece of tortilla chip at him. "Jerk. What was the question?"

Tossing the wayward chip in his mouth, he chewed and swallowed before answering her. "How's work going? Any new clients?"

Angie was a graphic designer who worked from home. She had several corporate clients who sent her a large amount of work, as well as many individual clients needing one-time-only or occasional projects. "I do have a new client, and I'm so excited about them. I've been contracted to be one of the designers of romance novel covers for a publishing company called Red Rose Books."

"Really? That's awesome, Ang. How'd you hook up with them?"

Grabbing her smartphone, she brought up a photo and showed it to him. "This was one I did for a former advertising client who's now writing romance books. She thought of me when she was self-publishing her first book and asked if I would design the cover for her. Someone from Red Rose saw it and thought it was edgy and something they'd be interested in, so they tracked me down. It's a great contract with a decent payout for each one I do. I'll do about one or two a week, so I can still concentrate on my other customers."

Jimmy smiled at her. He was always her biggest supporter when it came to her art. "Great. Mr. Abraham would be proud you've come this far."

Mr. Clark Abraham had been her high school art teacher and the first one to recognize the artistic talent even Angie hadn't known she had. He'd introduced her to the many different art mediums and encouraged her to try them all until she found what fit her best. In addition to graphite pencil drawings and computerized graphic arts, she also dabbled in oil painting and had sold several pieces at a local art gallery over the years.

Thinking of the gray-haired man who'd become her friend and mentor was always bittersweet. He'd suffered a heart attack in his empty classroom during lunch period one afternoon the year after she graduated, and by the time someone found him, it'd been too late.

"Yeah, I know he would have." Lowering her voice a few octaves, she imitated the old man, "Reds, Angie, why are you so obsessed with the reds? Throw some blue and green in there, maybe a little yellow. Surprise me sometimes, will ya!"

They laughed as they finished their meal and talked about everything under the sun. Angie would miss her friend when he returned to Atlanta tomorrow morning, but for now, she'd make the most of their time together.

Ian threw the pen down when he realized he'd been chewing on it and glanced at the small brass anchor clock on the right side of his desk. His brother had an identical one, and both had been gifts from their mother when they

HIS ANGEL

finally had desks to put them on. He heaved a sigh in frustration because it was only oh-seven-thirty. He had another half hour before Angie's boyfriend showed up and started answering the many questions Ian had for him.

Before he left Brody's last night, he'd told the geek to find out everything he could about James Athos and call him as soon as he had it. In the meantime, Ian left a message with Carter to contact him ASAP. Although knowing his friend, it could be a while before the call was returned. Ian didn't have a direct line to get a hold of the guy—no one did—and had to leave a voice mail at the number he'd memorized years ago. Carter would check his messages only when it was safe for him to do so, which meant it could be hours or days before he got a chance, depending on what he was working on.

The quiet in the empty office he usually enjoyed was getting to him this morning. Standing, he headed outside for some fresh air, with Beau following on his heels. He'd tossed and turned all night with thoughts of Angie doing erotic things to him, alternating with speculation of what her boyfriend wanted with Trident Security. Brody had called him a little before midnight with an update, brief as it was. He got a copy of the thirty-three-year-old's Georgia driver's license and found out he had some minor drug and assault arrests on file with no jail time served. All of which could be part of an undercover persona, as Ian had a feeling it was. Interestingly, prior to nine years ago, James Athos didn't exist, and Ian wondered how well Angie knew her boyfriend.

Pushing on the office entrance door, he stepped outside, inhaled deeply, and glanced around. From the outside, the complex looked like what it had formerly been—an abandoned warehouse facility on the outskirts of Tampa. Over three years earlier, when he first saw the property, Ian knew it would be the perfect compound for Trident Security. The company he co-owned with his brother specialized in personal security, investigations, and the more-than-occasional black op for Uncle Sam. An import-export company once used the complex until the authorities discovered the main product being processed through there had been cocaine. After the business shut down, Ian purchased the ten-acre lot of land at a government auction for a fraction of its estimated value.

The property contained four identical two-story warehouses lined in a row and was pretty much isolated from everyday traffic, sitting a good mile away from the main thoroughfare. With a mini forest of trees between the buildings and the highway, it was afforded a great deal of privacy.

After extensive renovations, the smallest and last of the warehouses on the property had become the living quarters for both Sawyer brothers. Ian's three thousand square foot three-bedroom 'apartment' was on the first floor, while stairs led up to Devon and Kristen's place, which had an identical floor plan. The remaining six thousand square feet of the warehouse behind the two apartments was being used as storage, but that would change when they added two new apartments. One would belong to Ian's goddaughter, and the other was for Nick, the youngest of the Sawyer clan and current Navy SEAL based in California. It would be his for when he visited and eventually retired from the military.

Glancing over at the main gate, Ian waved hello to the morning guard while Beau sniffed along the compound's fence line. When a person entered the compound through a manned security gate, the first warehouse they came to was home to The Covenant, a club that catered to those who enjoyed some kink in their lives. This was another reason why the property had been ideal for them.

A few years earlier, their cousin, Mitch, approached the brothers with the idea around the same time they were trying to get Trident Security off the ground. The exclusive club they all belonged to before then had closed down after the owner was indicted for tax evasion. The closing had left the members searching for a new place where they could practice their individual sexual fetishes without them becoming public knowledge. Since Ian and Devon were focused on Trident, Mitch, with his MBA, was the obvious choice to manage the club. However, sometimes his cousin deferred to Ian on a few issues since he was the more experienced Dom.

To get from the first warehouse to the remaining three in the compound, visitors had to pass through another security gate which was unmanned. To get through that one, a person had to be either buzzed in or scan their handprint on the sophisticated identification system. The first of those buildings, which Ian was now standing in front of, was separated into two areas, with the main offices of Trident security at the front. At the back end was a large vehicle garage along with the equipment, weapon, and ammunition vaults.

The next structure contained an indoor shooting range, a gym and training room, and a panic-security room in case of an emergency. Some might call the Sawyer brothers paranoid, but one never knew when one's enemies might come calling, so it was always better to be prepared. In fact, several months ago, the team had almost been picked off by a sniper who'd set up in a tree just past the security system's line of detection. As a result, Ian and Devon were working on acquiring several undeveloped properties surrounding theirs so they could extend their lines of defense outward.

Ian picked up the hard rubber ball Beau had dropped at his feet and played fetch for about ten minutes until Devon strolled over to greet him, a cup of coffee in his hand. "Morning. Brody find out anything?"

He filled his brother in as he threw Beau's ball again before turning around and walking back inside to his office. Stopping along the way in their break room, he grabbed his third cup of coffee of the morning and a blueberry muffin from a Tupperware container. The leftover muffins from yesterday were courtesy of Mrs. Kemple, their office manager, since the inception of Trident Security. She'd resigned and moved to Miami to help her daughter with newborn triplets last summer after training a new manager.

Unfortunately, her replacement, Paula Leighton, had become too nosy for her own good and was fired three weeks ago after Brody found her one morning looking through files in the team's war-room. It was one of the few places which she knew damn well she wasn't supposed to have access to. He'd run over to the club to help Mitch with a computer glitch and left his office door open, thinking he would be right back. After he was gone longer than expected, Paula's curiosity must have gotten the best of her because when Brody returned, she was standing in his war-room with her nose in one of his files.

Ian had fired her that day. Marco had been the most relieved about the woman's termination since she'd seemed to have her eye on him for a relationship that went beyond co-workers, and the man had not been interested at all.

HIS ANGEL

Mrs. Kemple had come back for a short time to train Colleen McKinley, a submissive from the club. When Ian had been talking to Colleen's Dom, Master Reggie Helm, a few hours after firing Paula, the Dom mentioned his sub wasn't happy with her current job and was looking for a change. Ian brought her in for an interview the next day and hired her on the spot.

The only problem they faced with Colleen so far was getting her to call them all by their first names and not Master or Sir while at the office. It also took the guys a little getting used to seeing her in something other than the lingerie her Dom liked her to wear at the club. Her clothes tended to be quite conservative and professional looking at work. At least they didn't have to hide from Colleen the fact that Trident Security was run by, and employed, a group of Dominants, as they had with Paula. Mrs. Kemple had known about the club since it opened and never batted an eye over it.

Five minutes before eight, Ian's phone rang. It was the guard at the front gate advising him he was buzzing one James Athos through the second gate. Brody, who'd come in a few minutes ago, stood and went to the front door to escort the man in while Ian and Devon remained in the conference room. Ian would've preferred to have this meeting after he spoke with Carter, but the spy hadn't gotten back to him yet.

Brody strode back in with Athos right behind him, and both men took seats at the table. Ian wasn't in the mood to offer Athos coffee or anything else, and apparently, neither was his brother, who also remained silent.

"I'm sure you investigated me last night and are frustrated with what you found and, more importantly, what you didn't find. Did Carter return your call yet? Because I know that's the first thing you did after I left." Athos leaned back in his chair and rested one ankle on the opposite knee as if he didn't have a care in the world, but Ian knew it wasn't the case. The man had something on his mind and was worried about it.

Ian tapped his hand on the table. "No, he didn't. Now, instead of me asking you the hundred and one questions I have, why don't you start from the beginning and tell us what you want."

"As I'm sure you've figured out, Athos isn't my last name. There are only two people in this world who can conclusively connect me to the man I was nine years ago. One is Angie, and the other is my handler at the DEA in Atlanta."

Ian raised his eyebrow but said nothing. Neither did Devon nor Brody, but the geek jumped onto his laptop, presumably getting the number to the Atlanta office.

"I was recruited from the Marines after a six-year stint, four of which were spent in Special Forces. I was given a new identity, and my military record was expunged. Spent my first three years undercover with a biker gang out in Arizona and New Mexico. They were running a lucrative cocaine business from over the border. It took me a while to work my way up the ladder, but after a long investigation, we were able to shut down the pipeline. But as you know, you shut down one of those fuckers, three more pop up. From there, I worked my way around the States until I got tired of living under rocks with the scum of the earth. My handler, who was also my recruiter, pulled me in, and I've been working with a support team out of the Atlanta office for the past two years. Again, it was under a new identity— as far as anyone at the DEA knows, my last name is Austin. One of the advantages of coming in is I can see and talk to

HIS ANGEL

Angie almost anytime I want to, but I still keep my connection to her a secret from my co-workers."

Ian held up his hand to interrupt. Athos's statement from yesterday was still eating away at his gut. *Angie means the world to me* . . "Who is she to you?"

The man's hard face softened. "I told you yesterday, she's my world—she is and always will be. We met our freshman year of high school and clicked right away. She's been my best friend ever since. If it weren't for her, I would've fallen apart years ago after my mother and baby sister were murdered by a drug dealer whom I didn't know my sister got herself mixed up with. It was while I was still in the Marines and overseas. I would've hunted the bastard down and killed him myself if the cops hadn't already done it before I could get home.

"Angie was my rock, my savior, and she's the only family I have now, and I'm all she has. Her folks were older when they had her, and both of them died several months apart of natural causes in their late fifties. She had a much older brother who was killed in a car accident when she was nine, and I think that's what eventually killed her folks because neither one of them ever got over it. Anyway, we've always been there for each other over the years, and it would destroy me if anything ever happened to her because of me."

"You went into the DEA as a way to avenge your sister and mother's deaths." Ian didn't ask it as a question, and Athos didn't deny it. "So, where do we fit in?"

"Before Angie closed on her house three years ago, I did what I always do when it comes to her and ran a check on all her neighbors." He shrugged. Even though some of the inquiries he'd made were technically illegal, he didn't seem ashamed to admit it in front of men who most likely would've done the exact same thing. "When she mentioned Evans moved in next door, I checked him out too. I saw his connection to Trident Security and remembered Carter mentioning the name one night a few years ago. He'd said if I ever need help with anything in Tampa or the rest of Florida, I should contact Trident, and you guys would get it done. Just to make sure things hadn't changed, I contacted him again, and he told me he trusted you guys with his life. I've known the man for over seven years, he's saved my sorry ass twice, and so it was a good enough endorsement for me."

His voice became hard again and filled with venom. Ian could see the barely contained rage in his eyes. "Two weeks ago, an undercover agent, Aaron Reinhardt, working in New Orleans, was tortured and killed. We have no idea how he was made and if they broke him or not. I saw the crime scene photos and wouldn't be surprised if the poor guy did crack—most agents would've.

"The worst part was his parents and brother were found dead with him. Their bodies were discovered before anyone ever reported them missing, dumped next to a garbage bin behind a strip mall near their family home in Illinois. Small consolation, his family wasn't tortured, but each was shot once in the back of the head. Like most undercover agents, Aaron's next of kin was only available to his handler. We both have the same handler, Artie Giles, and both trusted him with the information—I still do. Whoever found out about his family, it didn't come from Artie.

"Aaron was a friend of mine." It was obvious Athos had respected the dead man. "I worked with him on and off for years. He was one of the good guys, and this was supposed to be his last undercover because he'd gotten to the point where he wanted to meet a nice girl and settle down. When we found out what happened, I told Artie I wanted the job. I maintained and updated my cover, which I cultivated over the years, in case I ever needed it again. I'm heading to New Orleans after I leave here today to start working my way under. I told Angie last night after dinner, and right now, she's really pissed at me, although I can't blame her. I'd sworn to her I was done with undercover work, but this is something I need to do. I can't let the bastards win."

He leaned forward and set his elbows on the conference table. "So, this is where you all come in. I need you to keep an eye on her for me without her knowing it. If she finds out, she'll be pissed off enough to fight any attempts to protect her and end up getting herself hurt or killed. She's smart but stubborn at times, and I'm worried if my cover gets blown, someone could come after her to get to me. Like I said, though, it's highly unlikely because Artie is the only one who can make the connection between the two of us. His files are kept in a safe at his home office, and the name Athos and my birth surname don't appear anywhere in my file, nor does Angie's name. There's only her cell phone listed along with the passphrase he has to say to verify it's him who's calling her. They're also on two separate papers, so if someone gets into his safe somehow, the two don't appear related. Neither of them has ever met nor spoken on the phone. If anyone claiming to be from the DEA contacts her without that phrase, she has instructions on how to disappear without a trace until I can catch up with her. No one else in the agency knows she exists in my life."

"As far as you know. Nothing is ever one hundred percent hidden," Ian said wryly.

"True." The agent nodded his head in reluctant agreement. "But I've been as careful as possible over the years.

Hell, I've spent a small fortune on burner phones because I destroyed each one after I called her. I still do, even though I'm no longer under. I don't want something or someone from one of my past gigs to come back and bite me on the ass."

Athos was about to say something more, but Ian's cell phone rang. He glanced at the screen and then at Angie's friend before hitting the speaker button to connect the call. A deep voice rumbled over the line. "Ian, you rang? Sorry I couldn't get back to you sooner. What's up?"

He leaned forward so he could be heard without raising his voice. "No problem, Carter. It seems I have an acquaintance of yours sitting in my office with Devon and Brody."

The sounds of traffic in the background came through the speaker. "Really? Who?"

Ian arched his eyebrow at the DEA agent, indicating he should announce himself.

"Hey, man, it's Athos."

There was a two-second pause. "Confirm."

"Tinkerbell gives good head."

While the other three men smirked and shook their heads at the inane passphrase, Carter barked out a laugh. "Long time no hear, dude. How's it hangin'? Have you shaved the bush yet?"

An amused snort escaped Athos. "A little low lately, and no, I haven't."

"Ian, all is good. I trust this scruffy-faced jackass as much as I trust you, and you know that's a lot. He loves his alphabet soup at oh-four-hundred, and whatever he says is on the level."

Alphabet soup was a reference to the multiple abbreviated government agencies in the US, and "at oh-four-hundred" signified the fourth letter of the alphabet, which was "D." It was as close to saying "DEA" as the spy would get over the phone. As Athos said earlier, Carter's endorsement was all Ian needed.

"Do you need anything else? I've only got a minute." In a reflexive reaction, Ian shook his head and said "no" simultaneously. "All right, cool. A-man, you take care of yourself. If you need anything, ring me up. It's been a long time since you, and I raised hell together. Devil Dog, tell your pretty fiancée I'll be in Tampa in a few weeks, and I'm looking forward to being re-introduced to the little librarian."

While Brody and Ian gave him curious looks, Devon chuckled. There was a story there they weren't privy to, but they had a good idea what it might be. Master Carter was known to take the third spot in an occasional ménage when visiting The Covenant. "I'll tell her, and I'm sure she'll be looking forward to it too. Hey, how'd you know we got engaged? You haven't been here in months."

"The almighty Carter knows all. I gotta go. Catch ya all later."

The connection dropped, and Ian looked at Devon and Brody, who both nodded their silent approval, and then at Athos. "Give us the details."

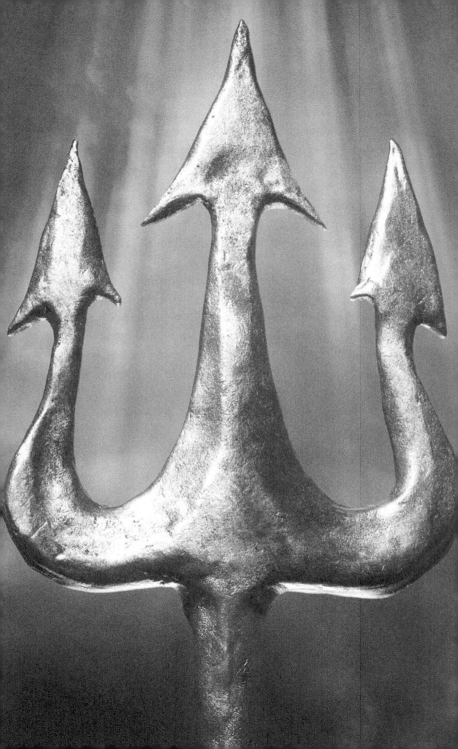

CHAPTER THREE

Angie paced back and forth across her living room, wondering what the hell she was doing. One of her friends insisted on hooking her up with a blind date, which she swore she'd never do again after the last disastrous one. However, here she was, all dressed up, with nothing to do but wait another fifteen minutes before she left for the restaurant where she planned to meet Melvin Fromm, an accountant.

Really? Melvin? When her friend had told Angie about him, she'd called him Mel, not Melvin, which is how he'd introduced himself when he first called her. It was all Angie could do not to imagine him showing up with a pocket protector and glasses held together with a piece of tape. She would kill Mandy if this didn't work out—not that she expected it would. Which brought her back to her original question—what the hell was she doing?

It'd been over three weeks since Jimmy dropped the bomb that he was going back undercover for one more case, and she was still pissed at him. She had no idea why, after two years, he decided to go back and, as always, he couldn't give her details because it was classified. At least, that's what he always told her. But she figured it was more of a cross between he couldn't give her any details, and he didn't want to worry her with them. Either way, she was in the dark and would be apprehensive until he contacted her again. And from experience, she knew it could be a week or six months from now.

Damn him.

She'd always understood why he'd gone to work undercover for the DEA. It was his way of getting some sort of revenge for the deaths of his family. Mrs. Andrews had been a very nice, single mother whose husband walked out on her two months after their daughter, Ruthie, was born to hook up with another woman with no kids. The only time she had ever gotten child support from her ex was when the court finally garnered his paycheck when Ruthie was three. That had lasted two months before he moved out of state and disappeared for good. As a result, the woman worked hard at two jobs for the next eighteen years to support Jimmy and his younger sister. Some mothers may have grown to resent their kids in a similar situation, but Dorothy Andrews' children were her world, and she let them know she loved them every chance she got. She'd also loved Angie as much as her son's best friend had loved her back.

Little Ruthie had been a sweet girl who'd gotten mixed up with the wrong crowd in high school. It ultimately led to her and her mother being shot to death over what the police described as a case of mistaken identity. One of her girlfriends swiped some drugs from a dealer they both knew, and the dealer blamed the missing drugs on Ruthie. It wasn't until after the police killed the suspect that the

HIS ANGEL

other girl came forward and admitted her role in the incident. The same girl died of an overdose two years later.

Jimmy Andrews, now Jimmy Athos, was determined to rid the world of as many drug dealers as possible. Angie wished it wasn't at the expense of his life, though. Not only was he in danger of being killed on the job, but she also worried about him in other ways.

He rarely dated, as far as she knew, and when he did, the dates never resulted in any relationship which lasted past the two- or three-week mark. She was afraid he would never find someone to love and grow old with, not that she'd found her soulmate yet, either.

Sometimes she wished they'd tried a romantic relationship, but the fear of losing everything had always stopped them. For some reason, Angie had been positive that's what would've happened, so instead, they were more like brother and sister. A shrink might say they were using each other to replace the siblings they'd both lost, but neither of them had ever felt that way, having discussed the subject a few times over the years. Ultimately, she wanted him to be happy with no regrets when he looked back on his life while on his deathbed. However, she didn't think it was possible for him, at least not at this point in his life.

Sighing, Angie looked at the time on her cable box again and was about to grab her purse when her cell phone rang. Glancing at the screen, she saw Melvin was calling her ten minutes before their date. She groaned, knowing what the man would say with the last-minute call. Connecting the call, she walked to her back door and stepped out on the lanai because she had a feeling she was going to need some fresh air.

* * *

Ian took two steps across Brody's living room toward

the sliding glass door which led out to the patio and stopped. What the fuck was he doing? He was only supposed to swing by and pick up a file his employee had to leave at his house after getting a frantic call from a corporate client very early that morning. The geek had hopped into his truck and headed straight to Orlando after alerting Ian to the problem. One of the company's computer geeks had figured out a way to embezzle $800,000 from a corporate account. They needed Brody's help to figure out how the guy did it and how to prevent it from happening again. So, Egghead was now near Disney World for at least another day or two, and Ian was standing in the guy's living room. And he was trying to talk himself out of going out the back door to see if Angie was in her own backyard.

After Athos had told them what he wanted them to do, they got to work doing what they could to keep his best friend safe. They'd gotten lucky when she agreed to have her security system upgraded. Brody brought up the subject as subtly as possible while talking to her over their shared fence, and the woman took the bait. The next day, her new neighbor and Boomer installed their best system while telling her it was a normal setup for normal people who led normal lives and were probably not in any danger. Athos told them to spare no expense and gave them a credit card number to cover any cost differences from a basic unit. He had to let her pay something for the new installation. Otherwise, she'd be suspicious.

The teammates installed the whole system in one day. Then while Brody took Angie around the house and showed her all the neat features of it, Boomer took the time to install the last few things they didn't want her to know about. He'd placed a few strategic audio bugs and remote cameras, then installed a tracking device on her phone, wallet, and car. He'd also managed to get a few of them inside several of her shoes, which he'd found in her closet. Looking at how worn the soles were, he was able to pick the ones she seemed to wear the most. The flat discs were very small, and he tried to put them where she or anyone else wouldn't notice them. If she did find one, chances were slim she would know what it was.

Brody had also gotten friendlier with his new neighbor, not too close, or Ian would've killed him, but enough so he found ways to check on her before and after work. Two days ago, he even invited her to join him for dinner on his patio and threw a couple of steaks on the grill for them. They wanted her comfortable enough with the geek in case anything ever went wrong. Athos had given them his handler's number and a backup passphrase Angie was aware of if they had to bypass the DEA altogether.

If Brody knew that Ian had been watching the live footage of Angie walking around her house for the past three weeks, he would have laughed at what a stalker his boss was being. The feed was being recorded on equipment in Trident's war-room for security purposes, in case they needed to review it for any reason. But Ian hadn't been able to help himself from bringing up the feeds on his computer a few times a day just to see her. None of the cameras were in her bathroom, and the cameras in her bedroom only faced the windows and door, thus giving her a small amount of privacy so he didn't consider himself a stalker. He was a voyeur—what the difference was, he wasn't sure, but if someone asked, he was confident he could think of something.

With the file he needed in his hand, he was about to turn around and leave when movement outside one of the windows caught his eye, and he realized it was Angie on her patio. Sighing and calling himself ten kinds of an idiot, he continued toward the sliding glass door, opened it, and stepped outside. He took one look toward her backyard and almost swallowed his tongue.

"Fuck," he muttered to himself. She stood with her head down, dressed in a navy, wrap-around cotton dress that stopped an inch above her knees. The V-neck, while conservative, showed some of her ample cleavage, which made him want to beg to see more. Her legs looked amazing, and a pair of navy and white polka-dot heels brought her height up three inches to about five-foot-eleven. He could imagine where the top of her head would come if she stood next to his six-foot-three frame. Her blonde hair was down the way he liked it, and he longed to run his fingers through the gentle waves which gave the strands some volume. Her makeup was subtle, and her jewelry was understated. All combined, it was one tempting little package making his mouth water.

It took him a moment to notice she was on her cell phone, and he heard her say, "No, really. It's all right. These things happen." She paused to listen to whoever was on the other end of the call. "Yes. That's fine. Call me if you want to reschedule, and I'll think about it. Bye."

Ian realized she hadn't known he was there until her pretty, green eyes met his and widened a bit before she gave him a shy smile and a little wave. "Hi, Ian."

He was surprised she remembered his name since, as far as he knew, she'd only heard it the first time they'd met, and he craved for her to repeat it. He'd never thought hearing his name verbalized could be a turn-on, but that was before he heard it fall from her plump, red lips.

"Hey, Angie." He took a few steps toward the fence and was pleased when she did the same. "You look very nice

HIS ANGEL

tonight. Going somewhere?" He figured from her conversation that her plans had been canceled, but he was curious as to what they had been in the first place.

She shrugged, although she didn't look too disappointed her plans had changed. "I was supposed to go on a date, but he canceled at the last minute."

"Must have been a blind date."

Giving him a curious look, Angie tilted her head. "It was, but how did you know?"

His blue eyes grew darker as his gaze covered her from head to toe and back up again. "Because if he knew how exquisite you look right now, he never would've canceled. He'd be thinking of how to end the night with you in his bed."

A blush stained her cheeks, and after a moment, she tore her eyes away from his, gesturing with her head toward her backdoor. "Well, his loss, I guess. I'll just go change into a pair of sweats, pig out on a container of Ben & Jerry's, and find some old movie to watch."

"Or, you could let me take you out to dinner." What the hell had made him say that? Oh, yeah, the little head in his pants did. Glancing down, he was happy to see his khakis were loose enough to cover his semi-hard-on. He was also dressed nice enough, with his black polo shirt and loafers, to take her to dinner—if she said yes.

She was still blushing, and the pinkness was not only on her cheeks but on her upper chest as well. He wondered if it was the same color as her nipples, and the thought made his dick twitch.

"You don't have to do that. I'm sure you have other plans," she told him.

"One thing you should know about me, Angie, I never say things I don't mean, and I don't do anything I don't want to do. I just order one of my employees to do it for me." She smiled as he'd intended. "I'd like to take you to dinner if you'd let me." He tried to keep the desire he knew was in his eyes to a minimum. If she knew how much he wanted to strip her naked, tie her to his bed, and do nasty, erotic things to every inch of her body, she'd run from the yard, screaming.

Her expression was more eager than shy, and he liked the combination. "Well, since I'm already dressed, and I think I'm running a little low on the Ben & Jerry's . . . yes, I'd like to go out to dinner with you. But this isn't a date." At his raised eyebrow, she added, "I mean, it's not like this was planned, so we'll go Dutch."

Shaking his head, he smiled at her. "Uh-uh. I asked you out to dinner, and it's my treat. I'm not expecting anything in return, Angie, just the pleasure of your company for the evening. And maybe a goodnight kiss if you decide you had a good time."

Now why did he tack on that last sentence? He was about to give himself a mental ass-kicking when she beamed at him. "We'll see." She turned toward her door as his heart beat a little faster. "Let me grab my purse, and I'll meet you out front."

Five minutes later, Angie was sitting in the passenger seat of Ian's Ford Expedition, wondering how she ended up there. Did he ask her to dinner out of pity for her having been stood up at the last minute? Or did he truly want to spend some time with her? When he'd said she looked exquisite, her girly parts had stood up and taken notice.

Could he really be interested in her? And what about his comment about a goodnight kiss? Was he planning on kissing her later? Would she let him? The way her body had tingled when he'd taken her hand and helped her into the high seat of the SUV, she knew if asked to kiss her right now, she would let him.

She thought about what little she knew about him from talking to Brody. Of course, when she'd asked her neighbor a bunch of questions the other night over their steak dinner, she'd made them sound as if she were curious about the whole team and not one member in particular.

She knew Ian was single, never married, and thirty-eight years old. He had a nineteen-year-old goddaughter, Jennifer, who lived with him when she wasn't at college at the nearby University of Tampa. Ian had taken the girl in after her parents were murdered a year ago in a brutal home invasion in Virginia. His brother and business partner was Devon, who was engaged to a woman named Kristen. Angie had gotten a glimpse of the other woman in passing when they'd visited Brody, but she hadn't been introduced to her yet.

The other men were all single as well. They'd served together on the Navy's SEAL Team Four, which she'd been impressed to learn. She'd heard what SEALs had to endure physically and mentally to achieve the well-respected position. Ian had held the highest rank in the group as Lieutenant, but only for the two years before he retired. There had been a three-year period when all six had been together before they started retiring, one or two at a time.

Ian and Devon had started up Trident Security and hired their former teammates as trusted employees as soon as each one left the Navy. Trident performed numerous security jobs for their clients, including bodyguard work, home and business security systems, investigations, corporate security, and recovery of kidnap victims or stolen merchandise. The company also did the occasional job for the government, which Brody said he couldn't elaborate on. They contracted several agents from another agency who supplied manpower to companies like theirs, and they were talking about hiring six more people to create a second team.

Angie suddenly realized Ian had parked the car after their brief ride and was shutting the engine off. She looked through the windshield and saw the quiet steakhouse they'd agreed upon. Without saying a word, Ian exited the car, closed his door, and walked around to open hers while she waited. Somehow, she knew he would do that, and she liked the gesture. It'd been a while since someone other than Jimmy had opened a door for her.

As they walked across the parking lot, Ian took her hand and hooked it under his elbow. He skillfully avoided puddles left over from the late afternoon shower which had passed through the area and held the restaurant door open for her. She felt he wasn't doing all those things to impress her, but he did them naturally for any woman he was out with. The thought made her feel like this evening was between routine and special to him, but she hoped it was leaning toward the latter.

After they were seated and ordered their drinks, Ian rested his forearms on the table instead of picking up his menu and studied her for a moment. "So, tell me about this blind date you were going on, so I can get this jealousy I'm feeling out of my system."

She laughed, figuring he was kidding, but played along. "Well, there's not much to tell. My friend hooked me up with Melvin Fromm, a thirty-five-year-old CPA with rude manners since he canceled on me ten minutes before I was supposed to meet him. And the best excuse he could think of was 'something came up.'"

The corners of Ian's mouth twitched twice before he could no longer hide his grin and a quiet snort. "Melvin, huh?" She nodded with her own amused smile. "Okay, I don't think I have to worry about him sweeping you off your feet any time soon, so I'll tamp my jealousy back down. I'll just be grateful the idiot canceled on you because it gave me the opportunity to spend the evening with an incredibly beautiful woman."

Oh, Lord, why couldn't she stop blushing around this man? It wasn't as if she'd never had a good-looking guy compliment her and flirt with her before. She dated often, but for some reason, Ian took it to a whole new level for her. Their drinks were delivered, a draft beer for him and a cosmopolitan for her, and they fell into an easy conversation about normal, everyday subjects. It wasn't until their waitress checked on them for a third time, did they pick up their menus to order something.

"So," Ian said after the waitress left to place their orders, "tell me what you do as a graphic designer because I've never met one before. Wait . . . first tell me how you became one. Is it something you always wanted to do?"

Angie took a sip of her drink and then shook her head. "I never realized I had any artistic ability, beyond doodling, until my sophomore year in high school when I had to take a mandatory art class. My teacher, Mr. Abraham, was the first person to see I had talent and pushed and inspired me to learn more about every artistic medium out there. He became my mentor, took me to art shows and museums, and helped me cultivate my own style. I ended up with pencil drawings, oil painting, and computer graphics as my main interests, although I dabble in some watercolors and sculpting when inspiration hits.

"I earned a partial scholarship to the School of Visual Arts in New York and got my Master of Fine Arts. I spent the next six years working for a large graphic design company in New York City before I couldn't take the bitter winters anymore. The last straw was when a taxi hit a slush puddle near me and covered me from head to toe in cold, nasty water while I was on my way to work." Ian gave her a sympathetic laugh at the image of her looking like an enraged, drowned rat.

"Anyway, I'd visited a few friends who live in Tampa before and knew I liked it. So, I packed up, moved south five years ago, and never looked back. I'd been doing some side work for a few internet clients while still in New York, so I branched out and built my own business from there. I design websites, printed brochures, graphics for magazines, books, and company logos—basically whatever a client wants."

She took out her cell phone and flipped to the e-book cover she'd shown Jimmy a few weeks earlier. "Here's a book cover I designed for a client last month, and it ended up getting me a new contract with a publishing company."

He took the phone from her and studied the picture. It was a photo of a man's bare muscular back and shoulders stopping just above his neck and down to his black leather-covered ass. A bullwhip was between his two hands and stretched taut across his back from shoulder to hip. Female hands came from around his front, clutching both of his butt cheeks, and were the only visible parts of her body. Her long fingernails were painted a deep red which almost looked like blood. From how the woman's hands were situated, anyone looking at the picture would know her face was in the guy's crotch, and it made one wonder if she was giving him a blowjob yet or not. The book's title *Lydia's Desire,* and the author's name were done in the same red as the woman's nails.

Ian looked up at Angie and smiled. "A guy's ass and naked back aren't my thing, but I know a lot of women who would be drooling over this cover. It's erotic-looking with the whip."

"Well, it's an erotic romance with BDSM, so I had to spice it up. It's actually a good book."

Handing her phone back to her, he raised one eyebrow. "You read stories with BDSM?"

Kristen had once explained to him and Devon that, in literature, erotica and erotic romance were two different genres. If you took the sexual content out of an erotica book, the rest of the story couldn't stand alone. Erotic romance contains more than just sex, such as the meet-cute, relationship development, character growth, and suspense, among other things. If the sex scenes were removed, a story would still be told.

Putting her phone back in her purse, she shrugged her shoulders, a little embarrassed she'd admitted that. "There's so much of it out there nowadays. It's hard to avoid, even if you aren't into it. You can't always tell by the title and cover of a book, but some of it is fun to read and fantasize about."

* * *

Ian took a casual sip of his beer. She'd answered his question loud and clear, even if her response was a bit vague. He knew she was submissive by her mannerism, but being a submissive and knowing you were one and wanted to participate in the lifestyle were two different things. Not just apples and oranges, it was more like mice and elephants—they were two different species, and one could crush the other if not careful.

He intentionally lowered his voice to his Dominant tone. "Does the BDSM lifestyle interest you?"

Her blush returned, and her gaze shifted to the table. His heart rate picked up, and his cock began to harden. Whether she admitted it to him verbally or not, the subject interested her, and he wondered if she'd experimented with sex before. At thirty-three, he doubted she was a virgin, but what had her past sexual encounters consisted of? Had they been pure vanilla, or had she let any of her lovers tie her up, spank her, or flog her? Had any of them pushed her limits, fucked her heart-shaped ass? Given her orgasms which took forever to come down from? Had anyone ever fucked those moist, red lips of hers and come down her throat?

Part of him wanted her to tell him she practiced the life-style, but he didn't want to think of any man doing any of those things to her. He wanted to be the one to introduce her to his world of kink. Thinking she would appreciate it, he decided to let her off the hook . . . for now.

He cleared his throat to let her know he was changing the subject. "My soon-to-be-sister-in-law's cousin . . . huh, how's that for a roundabout way for saying I know a guy . . . who's the assistant curator for the Tampa Museum of Art. They're opening a new exhibit tomorrow night at some big gala for their staff and benefactors. Since my brother and I recently made a donation, we received invites. I was going to go stag, stay for a half hour, and then beat it, but now I have a better idea. Would you please put me out of my misery by attending it with me so I don't have to talk to a whole bunch of stuffy, boring people? Kristen and her cousin Will would kill me if I bail, so I have to make an appearance."

HIS ANGEL

Her face became animated with excitement. "Is that the exhibit that's on loan from the Louvre?" When he nodded, she gushed, "Oh my God, I would love to go. I planned to take a whole day off next week to see it."

"Well, you can see it tomorrow night, as long as you don't mind me not knowing a bloody thing about art. I can look at something and say 'yes, I like it,' or 'no, I hate it,' but that's about it."

Her smile was flirtatious and infectious. "I'd be happy to teach you a bit about what I know."

"Only if you let me teach you a bit about something I know some time." Ian was going to hell. He knew it the moment the word "deal" came out of her pretty red lips, and he couldn't help but think, what a way to go.

The waitress brought their meals, and Ian waited until she walked away again after ensuring they didn't need anything else. "The gala starts at seven, so I'll pick you up about twenty of, since we'll be dealing with Friday night traffic. Oh, and it's black-tie."

Angie picked up her knife and fork and cut into her chicken cordon bleu. "I have the perfect dress, then. A friend of mine got married at the Guggenheim last year, and it was black-tie also. I only wore the dress once, and I always hoped for a chance to wear it again because I love it."

"Well, in that case, I can't wait to see you in it." And hopefully, he thought, peel it off you at the night's end.

43

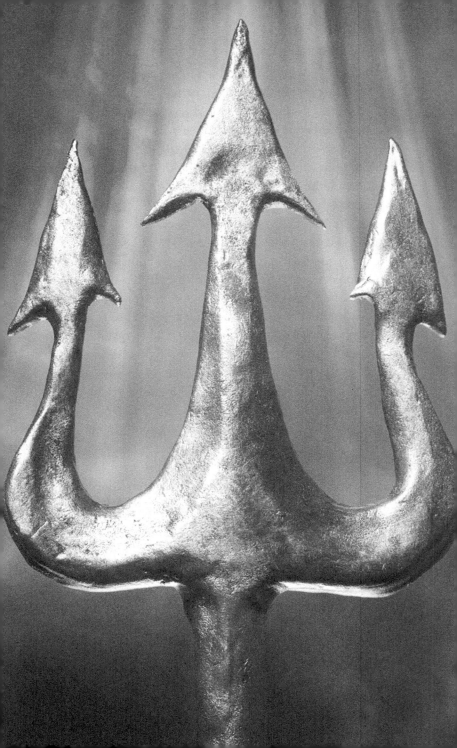

CHAPTER FOUR

After Ian took Angie's wrap and gave it to the coat check, he added the claim stub to the valet one inside his coat pocket. He placed a possessive hand on the skin of her lower back above the edge of her dress and steered her in the right direction. He let the warmth of his hand sink into her body and was thrilled to feel a shiver go through her.

As he led her toward the wing where the exhibit and gala were taking place, he stopped at a tuxedoed waiter holding a tray of champagne. Taking one glass, he handed it to Angie before acquiring one for himself, never removing his other hand from her back. They began walking again, and as they approached the entrance to the north wing, he heard a male voice call his name. Scanning the people around him, he spotted Will striding toward them.

The man extended his hand, forcing Ian to remove the one on Angie's back before returning it to its original spot after greeting his friend. Will looked curiously at Angie, and Ian introduced them. "Will, this is my date and Egghead's new neighbor, Angelina Beckett. Angie, this is Will Anders."

The two shook hands as Will gave Angie a quick head-to-toe inspection. "I always knew you had good taste, Boss-man. Angie, it's a pleasure to meet you, love. Too bad I don't swing your way because you are absolutely gorgeous. I do have some lez friends who would be interested, though. Just say the word."

If Ian didn't know Will was gay and joking with her, he might have ripped the guy's throat out. As it was, he was leaning toward removing the man's tongue from his mouth.

Angie grinned at Will, obviously charmed and not at all embarrassed by what the man had implied. "It's nice to meet you too, and thanks for the offer, but dating women isn't my thing." She changed the subject with ease. "Ian tells me you're the assistant curator here. I envy you."

"Angie's an artist," Ian explained. "Although I haven't seen her work yet, except for a digital piece, I'm hoping she'll show it to me someday."

He watched the other man's face light up even more. "Really, love? What's your medium?"

"Mostly oils and graphite," Angie replied, "but I some-times fool around with clay and watercolors. I've sold a few paintings over the years through venues that feature amateur artists like me, but if it weren't for my graphic design business, I would definitely be a starving artist."

A man with a rosebud pinned to the lapel of his black tuxedo rushed up and informed Will he was needed at the front door. Before he hurried away, Will said, "I would love to see your work, and if you ever want a personal tour of the museum, let me know. Ian—my cousin, Dev, Roxy, and Kayla are waiting for you near the bar to your left when you walk into the great room. They didn't want to start looking around without you. I'll see you both in a bit. Ciao."

While the assistant curator took off in one direction, Ian guided Angie toward the exhibit's main room and immediately spotted the foursome. Since he wasn't sure if she remembered his brother's name, he introduced her again to Devon and then to his fiancée, Kristen, followed by Dr. Roxanne and Kayla London, who were good friends of Kristen and Will's. They were also new members of The Covenant, which, of course, he didn't add.

The three women looked radiant in their evening wear, and his brother had donned his Hugo Boss tuxedo for the occasion. Kristen was wearing a blue dress with a high waist, and her brunette hair was up, similar to Angie's. Her jewelry included the matching blue sapphire and diamond submissive collar and engagement ring, which Dev had a jeweler design for her.

Roxy's thick auburn hair flowed down past her shoulders in soft waves, and she had forgone her usual Domme black for a beautiful red evening gown. The dress had more than one man in the room lusting for the sexy siren, but Roxy only had eyes for her submissive wife. A blue-eyed blonde, Kayla was the complete opposite of her spouse, with her shorter hourglass frame decked out in a dark gray gown with cap sleeves.

After everyone greeted them, Angie's eyebrows furrowed in thought. "Kristen Anders. Why do I know that name?"

Before the woman could say anything, Kayla piped up first. "Kristen doesn't like to brag, so I'll do it for her. She's a popular author of romance novels. Maybe you've read one of them."

Ian wasn't prepared for the response that statement got from Angie. She gasped, her eyes going wide in surprise. "Oh my gosh!"

Kayla grinned and elbowed Kristen's arm. "See, I keep telling you you're famous."

"No, yes, no, I mean, yes," Angie stuttered before laughing and holding her hand like a crossing guard stopping traffic. She took a deep breath before attempting to speak again. "Okay, let me start all over. I swear, I'm not normally a blithering idiot, and I do have social skills." The others chuckled with amused expressions. "Yes, I've read all your books, but it's not why I recognize your name. I just got a contract yesterday from Red Rose Books to design the cover of your new one."

It was Kristen's turn to be flabbergasted. "Oh, my God! What're the odds of that happening? My editor told me they were giving *Leather and Lace* to someone new because the woman in Seattle, who did *Satin and Sin*, was taking a hiatus due to health problems. This is so cool. Talk about a small world."

"I'm so excited to design it now. We'll have to chat later, so I can get your input before I start playing around with ideas." Ian could only imagine what Angie would come up with after seeing the other book cover she'd done.

"Great! I haven't had much input in my covers since I signed on with Red Rose. Now they narrow it down to three similar covers, and my editor and I chose one."

As the two women continued talking about the publishing business, with Roxy and Kayla giving occasional input, Ian and Devon both took a half step to the side. They looked at each other while rolling their eyes. As much as they were proud of Kristen's success and popularity, chic-lit was not their thing.

What Ian had latched onto, though, was when Angie said she'd read all Kristen's books. He assumed they included the last one, *Satin and Sin*, a book that had surprised Devon when the couple first met since it was a best-selling erotica romance involving a BDSM club. The follow-up, *Leather and Lace*, which the women were now discussing, was a story about one of the previous book's sub-characters, Master Xavier.

Ian studied Angie as his brain spun. It was the second time she'd admitted she read erotica, and the thoughts flying through his mind might shock her. But then again, maybe not.

* * *

They spent an hour or so roaming through the crowded north wing of the museum, looking at the exhibits and talking about a gamut of subjects, including art, literature, and local news. Angie grew more comfortable with Ian, his family, and friends as the evening progressed. Will had popped over to visit a few times before rushing off to avert another crisis, and numerous people greeted the group while further introductions were made.

She found it interesting how every time Ian introduced her to one of the many women drooling over him, he barely glanced at them before his gaze returned to her. And when it was a man being introduced, Ian would tuck her closer into his side in what appeared to be a possessive gesture. She liked his responses and hoped she wasn't misreading them and his interest in her. She also liked how his hand was in contact with a part of her body—her back, neck, hand, or arm—as much as possible. The rough calluses on his palm and fingers felt seductive against her soft skin.

As they walked from painting to painting, she found he understood art more than he admitted to her and probably to himself. He listened to her, not with half an ear as some of her past boyfriends or dates had, and held his own as they discussed what they did or did not like about each piece.

When a new round of champagne flutes, along with tonic water and lime for Devon, arrived via another sharp-dressed waiter, Angie glanced around and spotted a ladies' room a short distance away. When she excused herself from the group, Kristen said she would join her.

Devon groaned. "What is with women that they must go to the restrooms together?"

Everyone laughed when his fiancée deadpanned, "It's in the women's rule book of socialization, sweetheart. Why don't you look it up sometime?"

Growling softly, he grabbed Kristen around the waist and whispered something into her ear, which made her blush and bite her bottom lip. Angie could have sworn she heard the woman mumble, "Yes, Sir," before joining her on the walk across the room while the other four members of their group stayed and chuckled behind them.

The elegant ladies' room was almost empty, and after quick stops at the toilets, followed by the sinks, Kristen met Angie at the mirrored vanity near a sitting area. After two other women exited the facilities, they found themselves alone. Angie reapplied her lipstick and eyed the other woman's dress and shoes. She'd been admiring the blue empire-waist creation and silver Manolo Blahnik heels all evening and told her so.

Kristen grinned with freshly painted lips. "Thanks. I had the shoes, but Will and Kayla took me shopping the other day for the dress. I'm fine with picking out everyday clothes, but I get flustered if I have to play dress-up. I can never tell if I look drab, slutty, or sexy."

HIS ANGEL

"My vote is drab and slutty, you bitch."

Angie gasped at the sudden insult as Kristen whirled around with rage in her eyes and faced the woman who'd said it. Neither one of them had noticed her come in.

Crossing her arms over her chest, Angie's new friend stood taller as she stared at the skinny redhead in a white strapless gown. "Seriously, Heather? Who let your skanky ass in here? You wouldn't know art if it slapped you. Oh, wait a minute, it looks like you already took an oil painting to the face, or is that your makeup? I can't quite tell."

If Angie hadn't been so shocked, she would've laughed at Kristen's retort because it was a good one considering the building they were in.

"Honestly, you cow, I have no idea what Master Devon sees in your fat ass." The redhead's hatred-filled gaze zeroed in on Angie next. "And let me guess—you're Master Ian's new fuck. Don't get too comfortable, whore. Everyone knows he goes through subs like a pig goes through slop."

What? Wait a minute . . . Master Ian? New fuck? Whore? Subs? Pig?

Shock and pure anger at this stranger who came in, hurling insults at them, took over Angie's mind and body. She stepped forward to confront the nasty woman when a hand on her forearm stopped her. Looking at Kristen, she was surprised to see a satisfied smirk on her face. But Kristen wasn't staring at Heather. Her eyes were focused on the person who'd come through the door and was now standing behind the bitch . . . Roxanne London, and *holy crap*! The good doctor looked furious and intimidating.

Heather must have realized there was someone behind her because she glanced over her shoulder, and Angie was amazed to see the redhead's face lose all color . . . at least what wasn't painted on. Roxy's pleasant demeanor from before had disappeared, and in its place was an angry, commanding, take-no-prisoners attitude. "Apparently, you don't learn, Heather. You know better than to blurt out private business in a public venue. You also know I told you last time you started harassing Kristen that I wouldn't stand for it. And now you've insulted another friend of mine who, I assume, has no idea who you are and doesn't deserve your malice. I suggest you run out and explain yourself to Scott because I'll be a minute behind you, and he and I are going to have a serious talk about your continued behavior. Now as much as I would love to see how Kristen put you flat on your face in an arm-hold the first time you two met, this is neither the time nor the place."

She stepped to the side and gave Heather a path to the restroom door. "Out. Now."

As the redhead rushed out the door, they heard her mumble under her breath, but the words were unintelligible. After the door closed behind the awful woman, the three new friends looked at each other and burst out laughing. When they finally got themselves under control, Angie opened her mouth to ask one of the many questions on the tip of her tongue. Before she could say anything, though, Roxy held up her hand and looked behind them to where the toilets and sinks were.

Kristen caught the other woman's concern and told her they were alone in the facilities. Roxy gestured to the sitting area before taking a seat on the small couch and crossing her long legs, leaving the two low-backed upholstered chairs for the other women. "In case you're wondering, I saw Heather walk in here and knew she would be her usual rude self, so I came in as backup.

HIS ANGEL

Although I'm sure you all would've had things under control."

After they joined her around a small cocktail table, Roxy looked at Angie with a mix of sympathy, concern, and understanding. "I can tell you're shocked and confused by the look on your face. I'm sure this isn't the way Ian wanted you to hear he was a Dominant, and I really think you should take most of your questions to him. Seeing how he looks at you, I think his interest in you is obvious. I don't know where you two are in your relationship, and it's none of my business about when and if he was planning on asking you to go down that road with him. He's a good man who, in the short time I've gotten to know him, I've come to respect one hundred and ten percent, and he would never force his lifestyle on anyone.

"That being said, if you want to take a moment and let the shock wear off and ask us a question or two, we'll answer them the best we can."

Angie turned toward Kristen, who nodded her agreement, then took a deep breath and said the first thing which came to mind. "Holy shit, who was that crazy bitch?"

When the other two women laughed and relaxed, she continued. "Okay, that wasn't a serious question—actually, it is, but we'll get back to it later. So, are you all into . . . it . . . I mean, the BDSM lifestyle too?"

Kristen nodded again. "Yup. I'm a newbie of only six or seven months now. I met Devon at his friend's pub and ended up asking him out on a date, not knowing he was a Dom." She let out an unladylike snort. "Hell, I didn't even know I was a sub. Anyway, if you read *Satin and Sin*, you know it involves BDSM, and when I went to the club Devon and Ian own, with their cousin, Mitch, for research . . . oops."

Angie was sure her eyes were wider than Kristen's. "Th-they own a sex club?"

Roxy leaned forward and retook command of the conversation. "Yes, and despite what some people . . . what most people might think, it's a very private, very elite club. It's where like-minded people, who enjoy a range of kink in their lives, can practice safe, sane, and consensual activities which may or may not include sex.

"Kayla and I joined The Covenant after a long application process where our lives were examined with a fine-tooth comb. This is not a place where anyone off the street can walk in and start flogging someone. And unlike Heather, most people in the lifestyle don't announce their participation, or anyone else's for that matter, when out in public. I know several other people in attendance here tonight from the clubs, but they either pretend they know me from somewhere else or not at all.

"I've been a Domme since college, and Kayla became my submissive, and then my wife, when we met a few months after I finished med school. I was the one who recognized she was a submissive and introduced her to the lifestyle I'd come to enjoy."

Trying to take everything they said in, Angie took another deep breath. "Okay, I'm not completely naïve. I've read lots of fictional books on the subject and even browsed the internet when my curiosity was piqued a few times while reading those books. And I'll admit, if I'm being honest, some things did turn me on. But I never knew anyone in the lifestyle, so I just shoved my thoughts and questions to the back of my brain and left them there. I figured there weren't real places like that, and everything I heard or read was part of a fantasy world."

The restroom door opened, startling them, and four

HIS ANGEL

chatty women walked in and headed toward the toilet stalls. Roxy stood, placed her hand on Angie's shoulder, and lowered her voice so she wouldn't be overheard. "You need to talk to Ian. As I said, he's a good man. If you are interested in exploring, he's one of the men I would recommend you do it with. If not, he'll understand, and no harm done."

"I agree," Kristen concurred while nodding her head. "He's one of the nicest guys I know, and I'm not saying that because he'll be my brother-in-law soon. Oh, and by the way, what Heather said about Ian being a pig . . . nothing I've seen or heard has ever given me the impression he's a total man-whore." She giggled. "I'm not saying he's a saint, but what man is?"

Angie grinned at Kristen and then at Roxy, feeling a little bit more at ease. "Okay, I'll talk to him, but not here."

"Good." The doctor took a few steps toward the door and glanced over her shoulder. "Can you tell my beautiful wife I'll be back in a few minutes? I need to have a conversation with a colleague of mine."

Angie looked at Kristen to clarify the statement as the other woman stormed out the door on a mission. "Heather's Mast . . . um, boyfriend . . . is a doctor on staff at the same hospital Roxy is.

"Look, I know this is a shock—it was for me too. But I've never regretted any part of my relationship with Devon. In fact, I can't imagine how I ever lived without the . . . um . . . things he does to me and with me. My ex-husband had me convinced I was a cold fish in bed. It turns out he was the problem because my sex life now is incredibly hot, and I wouldn't trade Devon for any other man. He cherishes me like I'm the most important person in the universe."

She leaned forward and dropped her voice into a

55

dramatic whisper. "And showed me what it was like to have multiple orgasms."

Kristen laughed at Angie's astonished expression and twined their arms together, tugging her new friend toward the door. "Now, let's get back to our handsome dates before they send out a search party."

CHAPTER FIVE

Ian got an uneasy feeling in his gut when he saw Angie and Kristen walk toward Devon, Kayla, and him. There must've been the usual long line in the ladies' room because they were gone an awful long time. Although they were chatting with each other as they approached, there was a pensive air about them.

"Everything okay?" he asked.

As Angie stopped by his side, Kristen sidled up to Devon and put her arm around his waist. He watched both women glance at each other before Angie seemed to find something interesting to stare at on the floor, and his concern grew. What his brother's fiancée said next made his stomach drop, and he felt the blood drain from his face. "We . . . um . . . had a run-in with Heather in the ladies' room, and I'm sorry, Ian, but she sort of ran her mouth off and said some things she shouldn't have about you and the club."

She flashed her eyes toward Angie, who was now blushing, and then back to him with an optimistic expression. "I think it's okay, but you two need to talk about a few things."

Shit! Ian dragged his hand down his face in anger and frustration. Damn, Heather was a spiteful bitch. This was not the way he wanted this to happen. He'd planned on talking his way into Angie's place tonight for a nightcap. After telling her being a Dominant was a major part of his life, he'd pray she was still interested in him and didn't kick him to the curb.

Although his ears were buzzing, he heard Kristen report how Mistress Roxanne made a brief appearance and handled things.

Upon hearing that, Kayla responded with a pout. "Damn. I hate when she goes into her Wonder Woman persona, and I'm not there to see it. She knows how much it turns me on."

Ian ignored the women's giggles and took hold of Angie's elbow, leading her toward an unoccupied corner of the great room behind a sculpture worth about seventy-five thousand dollars. When he was certain they were out of earshot, he looked at her with a pang of regret. "I'm sorry, Angel. It's not how I wanted you to learn about me and my lifestyle. I was waiting for the right opportunity to tell you."

"So, you *were* going to tell me?"

Okay, she wasn't running for the hills yet. Her face seemed filled with curiosity and something else he couldn't quite put his finger on. It didn't mean he was in the clear, but it gave him hope. "Yes, of course. I'm . . . it's a part of me I can't ignore or change. I'm not ashamed of who I am. I was going to tell you when we were alone later tonight, but now that it's out, I'll understand if you want me to take you home."

And he would. It would kill him, but if she wanted nothing to do with him after this, he'd walk away and try to scrub the memory of their kiss from his brain.

HIS ANGEL

She seemed to think things over for a moment before responding, "If you want to leave now, it's fine with me. But I'm having a good time, so I'd prefer to stay longer and finish looking at the exhibit. That is if you don't mind. It'll give me time to recover from my initial shock and think for a bit. This way, when we talk later, I'll be better prepared to ask you some questions, and boy, do I have questions." He chuckled at her wry grin. "I'll admit, Ian, I'm curious, but this came from left field, and it's something I've only read about before. That doesn't mean I'm willing to jump into things completely blindfolded ... *er*, so to speak ... but I am willing to talk later if you want."

Ian's heart soared, and his cock twitched in his pants. He still had a shot with her, and from what she said, it might not even be a long shot. He stroked his fingers along her jawline, pleased when a flash of desire appeared in her eyes. "I'd like that very much, Angel."

"Just tell me one thing."

He took a deep breath. "Anything."

"Please tell me that nasty bitch, Heather, and you never ..." She seemed unsure of what words she wanted to use, so she left the sentence hanging there, probably hoping he would fill in the blanks.

"Oh, hell no!" Ian barked. "Please give me some credit. She was a member of the club with her Master a while back but had a bad habit of harassing other submissives, and her membership was revoked as a result. She's obviously still holding a grudge. You'll have to ask Kristen about the night she got the name Ninja-girl. My future sister-in-law knows how to kick some bitchy ass."

Leading her toward their little group, Ian was thrilled to know he still had a chance with his beautiful angel.

* * *

Angie paced back and forth across her living room, trying to gather her thoughts, and Ian wasn't making it any easier for her. During the rest of the evening, he'd relaxed back into the person he'd been before Kristen told him what happened in the restroom. Now, he was sitting on her couch, having shed his tuxedo jacket and tie. One ankle was propped up against the opposite knee, and one arm was on the couch's armrest while the other was lying across the back.

Without interrupting her, he patiently observed her walk, pivot, walk, and pivot again. She didn't know what to say. She had so many thoughts running through her head it was a jumbled mess. Before leaving the museum, Kayla, Roxy, and Kristen had all given her their cell numbers in case she had any questions Ian didn't answer or was too embarrassed to ask him.

Angie wasn't ashamed to admit she was one of those women who loved sex. Most of her past boyfriends and a few temporary hook-ups, which she would qualify as being somewhere between one-night stands and actual relationships, had been enjoyable in bed. Sex had rarely been the reason for breaking up with those men. In fact, a few of them had taken control in the bedroom—not to the point of what the BDSM stories she read described, but enough that she was aroused even more than usual.

Her problem with those men had been outside the bedroom. Some became boring to her after a while, and others had only been interested in the sex, and their dates revolved around it. The longest relationship she ever had was a little over six months, and it should have been over way before then, but the guy had been sweet and kept saying he loved her. And although she liked him, she hadn't wanted to hurt him because she didn't feel the same way he did. But in the end, she had to. Her main problem was she couldn't find a man who could hold her interest in and out of the bedroom, and she refused to settle.

Coming to an abrupt halt in front of Ian, she tossed her arms out in exasperation. "Okay, I'll admit I have no idea how to start this conversation, so can you do it, please?"

Smiling a devastatingly sexy smile, he held out his hand to her. "That's what the Dom in me was waiting for. Come here, Angel, and sit next to me."

She hesitated briefly before placing her hand in his and taking a seat. He didn't release her hand, which she found comforting despite her nervousness. "Easy, sweetheart, you're shaking." She didn't realize she was until he said it. "I'm not going to throw you down and ravage you like some pirate sailing the seven seas . . . well, unless you ask me to."

She giggled and relaxed a little as he continued. "How about I tell you about how I started in the lifestyle, why I like it, and stuff like that, *hmmm*?"

When she nodded, he kissed her knuckles before resting their hands on his thigh. "Okay. I was introduced to BDSM when I was twenty-two, almost twenty-three, by one of my chiefs in the Navy. He told me he watched me one night when a bunch of us were out at this bar with some Navy groupies. Said he saw something in me which made him believe I would be interested in the lifestyle. Apparently, I acted like a Dom before I even knew what one was.

"So, one night, he and two other guys we knew took me to my first club and, shit . . . talk about a culture shock. Here I was, not a clue what I was doing there, and all these men and women from ages twenty to seventy were walking around in everything from everyday clothing to leather, lingerie, or their birthday suits. Sounds of spankings, whippings, moaning and groaning, sex, and intense orgasms came from different scenes, and I didn't know where to look first. Hell, I was embarrassed and intrigued at the same time.

"I didn't play during my first night or the next few visits either. Instead, I just walked around and observed. I talked to everyone willing to talk to me and explain what they got out of their individual kinks and what made them a Dom or a submissive. It didn't take long for me to learn a submissive has all the control in every D/s relationship."

Angie's eyes narrowed in confusion. "How's that possible? Don't they have to follow their Dom's orders?"

"Every D/s relationship—and I'm not talking about people who claim to be in the lifestyle to justify hurting someone, like a domestic abuser, or people who dabble in a little slap and tickle in the bedroom. I'm talking about a true power-exchange relationship between a Dominant and a submissive. In every relationship or one-time encounter, the submissive willingly allows his or her Dom to give them what they want and need. Submissives maintain all the control of a scene from their negotiations with a Dom to their hard and soft limits and safewords. They can end a scene anytime they want if something doesn't feel right.

"My club uses the universal color system to avoid confusion over a sub's safeword. Green is good, yellow is to slow down or clarify something, and red means stop. And I mean, everything stops, and the scene is over. The Dom immediately starts aftercare, if needed, and they talk about what went wrong, why the sub felt it necessary to stop, and how to avoid the situation in the future."

Ian paused, and she took a moment to take all it in. When she stood, she heard his breath catch, so she smiled to reassure him. Taking off her shoes, she went into the kitchen, retrieved two bottles of water from her refrigerator, and then handed him one. Both opened the bottles and took a drink.

She could feel the wheels spinning inside her head. "Okay, I think I understand what you're saying. Like I told you, I've read books based on BDSM before, so it's not a completely foreign concept. But it's hard to bring what I thought was a fantasy world into the real world."

When she sat beside him again, he retook her hand and placed it back on his thigh with his own as if needing direct contact with her. "You said you'd tell me what you get from being a Dom."

"My submissive's pleasure and trust, pure and simple." It wasn't the answer she expected, but then she didn't know what she expected. "Nothing gives me greater pleasure than knowing I've given her everything she needs to achieve her own pleasure and/or emotional release, and she trusted me to give it to her."

"Emotional release?"

Leaning forward, he placed his water bottle on a coaster on her cocktail table and sat back again. "*Mm-hm.* BDSM is not all about sex—far from it. However, that's usually an enjoyable end result of everything else. It's about getting one's individual needs met, and sometimes it means pain is involved, whether the final result is pleasure or something else.

"Let me give you an example. I met this female submissive when I first started apprenticing under a few skilled Doms. And before you ask, I never played with her since I was far too inexperienced for what she needed. Ava was a very nice but reserved woman, around thirty-five years old at the time, and her kink was to be whipped until she finally broke down crying. But there was never any sex involved in her scenes.

"One night, I got the courage to approach her, and I explained my confusion about the fact she wasn't getting pleasure from her scenes. She told me she was very young when her mother married her stepfather, a verbally cruel man. Little things always seemed to set the guy off, and if Ava cried, he'd get angrier. He'd start throwing things, breaking her toys, or tossing her clothes and possessions in the garbage. So, to save the things she loved, this little six-year-old girl shoved her emotions so far back into herself to the point she couldn't cry for any reason."

Angie gasped. "How awful. The poor girl."

"Exactly. That little girl who stopped crying turned into an adult woman who couldn't cry unless a Dom broke through her subconscious barriers to the point she could find her emotional release and let her tears fall. That's why she was in the lifestyle. It was a cleansing therapy of sorts for her." He paused. "I seem to have gotten side-tracked because I'm supposed to tell you why *I'm* in the lifestyle."

"My fault, sorry."

Ian brought her hand to his mouth for a quick kiss. "Don't apologize for asking questions, Angel. It's what tonight is all about. Anyway, I prefer to be in charge in the bedroom and sometimes out of it too. When I scene or play with a sub, I like pushing her limits, teaching her things that can make her pleasure and inner-self better than they were before. I like being responsible for my sub's pleasure and emotional or physical health and giving her what she needs, which may not always coincide with what she wants. A sub's safety and well-being are important to me. As the Dom-in-Residence, or head Dominant at the club, all the subs' safety and well-being ultimately fall under my protection.

"I know every sub's and slave's name at The Covenant, their hard limits, and what they want to get out of the lifestyle. If I see a sub not getting what they need or pushing themselves to where it could be detrimental to their physical or psychological well-being, I step in and do what I can to get them back on track.

"We have several doctors and psychologists as members who are willing to talk to any other member, whether it's a sub or a Dom, who could benefit from their expertise. Doms aren't perfect, and anyone who claims to be is a fool. We make mistakes, learn from them, and grow along with our subs."

At some point, Ian's thumb had begun rubbing over the back of her hand, and the sensations it was evoking had a direct connection to Angie's clit. She was finding it difficult to think, but one thing he said did confuse her. "You said sub or slave. Aren't they the same thing?"

He shook his head. "No, not at all. A slave tends to be in a 24/7 relationship with their Master, giving entire control of their lives over to them. From what they wear and eat to what they do each day, and of course, the sexual aspect of it. It's not for everybody, it isn't for me, and it can be quite an undertaking for some Doms. It's a lot of responsibility for them, and after a while, some find it's not what they really want. A Dom/submissive relationship is not as extreme and usually consists of control of a sub's safety and pleasure, although every relationship is unique."

"Wow. This is a lot more involved than I realized. I thought it was just about tying a woman up and spanking her."

When she paused, he let the silence drag on for a few

minutes while she digested all he'd told her, her teeth nibbling on her bottom lip. When he brought his thumb up to rescue her tender flesh, she was tempted to nibble on that instead. "I take it some parts of all this interest you since I'm still sitting here, and you haven't tossed me out on my ass yet."

Angie smiled nervously. "Yes, I'll admit, I'm intrigued but also a little scared."

"I'd be worried if you weren't. This is something new and out of your comfort zone. But, if you're willing to test your limits . . . I'd be more than happy to help you explore. If you want, we can sign an open-ended contract that outlines our D/s relationship and lists what parts of the lifestyle you're interested in and what I expect from you."

Her smile turned into a slight frown. That sounded so formal and business-like. "A contract?"

"It's not as cold as it sounds, sweetheart. Doms and submissives often sign an agreement that defines their relationship to avoid confusion or false expectations. We have general contracts available at the club, but each Dom and sub can change them to suit their needs. The negotiations they do before signing a contract force them to talk about everything so there is no guessing between them. Think back on some of your past relationships. Were there times you wondered what your boyfriend was thinking about, or you wanted something you weren't getting from him but weren't sure how to bring up the subject?"

She nodded, understanding how much communication there was between a Dom and a sub. "Yes, there were. Sometimes I'd go nuts trying to get one of them to tell me what was on their mind."

"Exactly." Ian smiled. "See, you're learning already. Is a

D/s relationship something you want to try, Angel? With me?"

Her gaze met his for the first time since she sat back down, and when she swallowed hard, his eyes fell on the movement in her throat. The pulse in her neck and her breathing picked up speed, which seemed that was all the encouragement he needed. His other hand that'd been resting on the back of the couch, wrapped around the nape of her neck before he closed the gap between them. Pausing with their lips not quite touching, he waited. When her breath hitched, he brought his mouth down on hers. A heartbeat or two later, her lips parted, and he changed the angle of his mouth to plunge his tongue inside her depths.

Heaven. Like the night before, his mouth was pure heaven combined with a touch of hell. Just enough to make her want to let him take her to the dark side of sex. His hand skimmed down her bare back, stopping at her waist before working its way back up again. Her shivers made her nipples harder than they already were, and he pulled her into his lap, never letting her mouth go. They stayed that way for a few minutes, devouring each other.

Her hands moved around his neck, and she shoved her fingers into the hair at the back of his head. When he pulled away and looked at her with lust-filled eyes, she knew her green ones revealed her own desire. They were both panting.

As much as she wanted him to retake possession of her mouth, he apparently had other things he wanted to do to her. "Let me give you a little taste of my world tonight, Angel. No pain, just pleasure. And no intercourse. I want to make you come for me. I want you to shatter under my touch. Will you let me please you?"

His whiskey-smooth tone of voice had moisture pooling

between her legs, and she didn't hesitate to answer him. "Oh, God, Ian. Yes, please."

Cupping her chin, he waited until he had her complete attention. "Say it, Angel. I want to hear you say it. I need to know you understand what you're agreeing to. And if we are going to play, I want you to call me 'Sir.'"

Angie hesitated this time. Was this really what she wanted? Her mind and body were screaming at her to tell him anything which would make him kiss her, touch her, and do anything he wanted to her.

"It's one thing to say 'yes' to me, but I need you to say the words yourself. I won't go any further until you tell me exactly what you want. I need to know we're on the same page here."

She was taking this big step, but she knew if she didn't, she would regret it for a very long time. "Yes, Sir. Please make me come. Please give me a taste, and show me what it's like to be your submissive."

He ran his thumb along her jawline, leaving a tingling in its wake. "It will be my pleasure, Angel, and all yours too. Now, I want you to go into your bedroom, undress completely, and lie on your back in the middle of the bed. You have three minutes to do that for me before I follow you." When she hesitated again, he lowered his voice and added, "The clock is ticking, sweetheart."

She jumped off his lap and hurried to her bedroom before she could change her mind. Fumbling with the catch holding her dress in place at the back of her neck, she was ready to rip it apart before it suddenly released under her trembling hands. Letting the entire garment fall from her body to the floor, she kicked it out of the way and added her thong and stockings to the pile. She climbed atop her queen-size bed and situated herself as he'd ordered, propping her head on her pillow. And then she waited.

* * *

Athos paced back and forth in the one-room studio apartment he'd rented in New Orleans. He took another gulp of water from a bottle and willed the last of the cocaine out of his system. Why anyone would freely put this junk in their body was still beyond him. The only reason it was pumping through his veins and cells at the moment was because his other choice had been a bullet in his brain. If it weren't for Angie, he would've preferred the bullet.

He'd gotten lucky and ran into a guy who knew him back when he was undercover in the Southwest. After spending the night pretending to get drunk with the asshole, he had his way in*to* the underground drug business of the city. After a few minor-league, illegal activities, he was introduced to Manny Melendez, one of the local cartel leaders and the guy probably responsible for the deaths of Aaron and his family.

The scumbag was nervous about anyone new walking into his operation. That'd been obvious. But between some recent arrests and gang-related deaths of his minions, he needed new hands willing to get a little dirty. So, Athos had a choice at their meeting—powdered crap or a hollow-point bullet up his nose.

After Melendez was satisfied with his recruit, the two of them and five other pieces of shit released a little of their temporary Superman energy brought on by the drugs. Melendez wanted to send a message to an up-and-coming gang and took it out on a few wanna-be bangers they'd found a few blocks into Melendez's territory. If Athos had to beat the crap out of someone to maintain his cover, at least the mouthy little punks deserved it.

Now, as he was coming down off his high, the few cuts and bruises he'd received in the brawl were making themselves known. But with the coke in his system, he didn't want to add anything else, whether it be OTC drugs or alcohol. He flopped down on the bed and fumbled with the TV remote until he found a ballgame to watch. Who was playing, he didn't know or care as long as there was a familiar noise in the background.

He closed his eyes and thought of Angie. He knew it was the right thing to have someone watching her, and Carter swore the men at Trident were the best. He wasn't thrilled with their extra-curricular activities in the club the Sawyer brothers owned, but as long as she didn't need to go there for any reason, it wouldn't be a problem.

Toeing off his boots, he let his mind wander, and exhaustion began to pull him under a veil of sleep. Maybe it was time to break away from the DEA. Over the years, he'd put hundreds of dealers in jail or six feet under. Maybe it was time for him to find a life outside his quest for vengeance. He could move to Tampa to be near Angie. Maybe get a job with Trident.

Maybe. Maybe. Maybe.

CHAPTER SIX

Ian counted off the one-hundred and eighty seconds in his head. In the meantime, he removed the diamond cuff links from his wrists, placed them in his jacket pocket, and rolled his sleeves up to his elbows. He took another drink from his bottled water before returning it to the coaster. His erection was aching in his pants, and he tried to ignore it. He would take care of it later on his own. When he told her there would be no intercourse tonight, he'd meant it. Tonight wasn't about his release. It was about introducing his angel to the power exchange between a Dom and a submissive.

One-seventy-eight. One-seventy-nine. One-eighty. Ready or not, Angel, here I come.

She had left the bedroom door ajar, so it only took a slight nudge to open it all the way. His breath caught, and the aching in his groin increased ten-fold. He hadn't thought she could look more beautiful than when she'd answered his knock at her front door earlier in the evening. He was wrong.

Striding to the end of her bed, he took in the sensual

sight before him. Her hair was still in its bun, or whatever the hell women called it, and her head and upper shoulders rested against two plush pillows. Ivory-colored skin covered every inch of her, and she had no tan lines, which didn't surprise him since it'd been a colder-than-usual February and March. He wondered if she would wear a one-piece or bikini bathing suit when the warmer weather returned and couldn't wait to find out. Most Doms preferred their subs to be naked under their clothing, but not Ian. He liked a woman in sexy clothing and even sexier underwear. He had a fetish for lacy bras, panties, and lingerie, finding women tended to feel more beautiful when wearing them—and naughtier.

Her modesty had kicked in while she was waiting for him. Her hands each covered a large breast, and one knee was bent, leaning over the opposite thigh so her pussy was hidden from his view. The uncertain pose turned him on more than if she was completely exposed to him, but he was dying to see all of her. Glancing above her head, he was happy to see the headboard was wrought iron with intricate scrollwork and gaps large enough for her hands to go through. It would give her something to hold on to. His gaze ran from her head to her toes and back to her anxious but heated eyes. From the light coming in through the open doorway, he watched her pupils dilate with desire. Her tongue sneaked out of her mouth, wetting her lips, now devoid of lipstick, and he groaned. His little angel was going to be the death of him before the night was over.

"You're the most beautiful woman I've ever seen." He loved how her blush deepened with his words. "But I'm going to show you how to feel that beauty. If you get scared or unsure, I want you to say the word 'yellow.' If you absolutely can't take something, say 'red.' But be warned,

HIS ANGEL

sweetheart—if you say the word red, everything stops for the night. We'll discuss your fears, then I'll go home, and we'll try something else next time. Understand?"

She silently nodded her head, and he frowned at her. Realizing her mistake, she corrected it. "Yes, I understand. 'Yellow' for scared, 'red' to stop everything."

"Good girl. When we are playing, you are to refer to me as 'Sir.' Now, we're not at the trust level where I could restrain you, so I'll have you restrain yourself. Move slowly and bring your hands above your head. Grab hold of the headboard and make sure you're comfortable because you'll keep them there for me."

He held his breath as her hands left her luscious breasts and inched upward, skimming over her collarbones and shoulders, past her head before they grasped two thin pieces of iron. He'd been right about her nipples—they were pink and aroused, making his mouth water.

Walking around the bed, he toed off his dress shoes before sitting on the mattress next to her, between her chest and hips. He placed one hand on the comforter on the opposite side of her, using it to support some of his weight, and studied her from the breasts up, touching her only with his gaze. "Tell me, Angel, when you're alone in this big bed, how do you pleasure yourself?"

She stared at him wide-eyed, biting her bottom lip again, but didn't answer. He let the Dom in him take over. He tweaked one of her nipples before releasing it, and she squeaked. "I asked you a question, and I expect an answer, or you can expect an appropriate punishment. Now, I'll make it a little easier on you since this is new. Do you use your hand to pluck these gorgeous nipples while your other hand plays with your clit and wet pussy lips? Do you finger fuck yourself to an orgasm, or do you use a vibrator or

73

dildo? There's no right or wrong answer here, but I want an honest one. And there better be a 'Sir' in there."

"I . . . I . . ." Angie cleared her suddenly dry throat and tried again. "I do all that, S-Sir. Sometimes together or sometimes without my vibrator and just my hand."

"Where do you keep your toys, sweetheart?"

What? He wanted to see her vibrators? *Oh crap.* If she told him where they were, he might see the small anal plug she sometimes used when feeling incredibly naughty. Maybe he wouldn't notice it in the darkened room. She closed her eyes, counted to three, and blurted, "In the bottom drawer of my nightstand next to you, Sir."

She watched as he sat back up and leaned over to open the drawer. He took out her favorite nine-inch silicon vibrator and held it up for her to see, his eyebrows raised in amusement. "I've never seen a florescent-green one before. Interesting."

He put the vibrator on the bed and leaned toward the drawer again after turning on the bedside lamp to see better.

Oh, mighty Zeus, please strike me dead with a lightning bolt so I don't have to die of embarrassment.

Next thing she knew, he was holding up her pink anal plug, and her mind brought up an image of him fucking her ass with it, causing her to groan and clench her thighs together.

"Well, this is an unexpected but delightful surprise." She looked at him through her lowered lashes and saw a satisfied smirk on his face. "But we'll save this for next time, even though it's on the small side. We'll have to work you up to something larger."

He chuckled as her eyes widened. *Larger?* Why did the thought terrify and excite her all at the same time? After placing the plug back into the drawer, he pulled out her bottle of K-Y lubricant and a small paperback. She groaned again when she saw the book in his hand. Sometimes, when she wanted to arouse herself faster, she'd read a short erotic story out of it and imagine she was the naughty woman getting spanked, eaten, and fucked by the hunky guy. The dirty words turned her on, and it wouldn't take long for her to come.

"*Spank Me.* Catchy title. My brother mentioned he sometimes has Kristen read him the sex parts of her books after she writes them. Says it's a real turn-on. We'll have to save that for another time, too, but I have other plans for you now."

He tossed the book back into the drawer and closed it again. She noticed her green vibrator and the K-Y were still out and wondered about those plans.

"Straighten your knee and spread your legs apart, Angel. Keep them that way. If you close them or take your hands off the headboard, I'll stop what I'm doing and let your impending orgasm fade away before I start all over. That's called orgasm deprivation, and it's quite frustrating, as you can imagine. Understand?"

She could barely get her breathy response out of her dry mouth. "Yes." Frowning, he raised his eyebrow, and she quickly added, "Sir."

"Good girl." Ian waited until she moved her legs, then nudged the inside of her knees until she spread them even wider. "Just like that. Keep them there."

She was surprised when he dropped the lube and

vibrator on the comforter between her legs and left them there before turning back to face her. She was further shocked when he didn't touch her body with his hands. Instead, he leaned forward and brushed his lips across her forehead. "Close your eyes, my sweet angel."

When she did, light kisses peppered her eyelids, nose, cheeks, ears, and jaw. He avoided her mouth and explored her face before moving downward. Her neck, shoulders, and collarbones were next, and she was breathing heavier by that point. Every kiss seemed to send bolts of electricity through her body to her throbbing core, boosting her arousal further. Each time his lips touched her skin, she felt the tip of his tongue dart out for a brief taste before moving on to the next spot.

Her body was covered in goosebumps, and she was more turned on than she'd ever been in her entire life, and he hadn't even gotten to her breasts or pussy yet. Lord help her when he did because she was sure she'd go off like a ton of fireworks. She was desperate to close her legs to try to create a little friction and give herself some relief, but his warning of what would happen if she did blared in her head. There was no way she wanted him to stop and start all over.

Ian trailed his mouth further down her delicious body, bypassing her nipples but giving the upper and lower swells of her breasts little licks and nibbles. He shifted onto his hands and knees and crawled between her legs while he explored her abdomen, still only using his mouth and tongue. As he inhaled deeply, the scent of her body lotion mixed with the aroma of her arousal, and the combination made him light-headed and harder, which he hadn't thought was possible.

He felt the shivers that coursed through her body when he kissed and licked the creases of her hips. Again, he bypassed where he knew she wanted him the most and tasted her from her hip down to her left foot. After nibbling each toe, he licked her arch, causing her foot and leg to twitch. When she giggled and moaned simultaneously, he moved to her other foot and did the same. He loved how she was ticklish there, but she still managed to keep her legs wide for him.

She was a natural submissive, eager to please him, and didn't even realize it. On his way back up her right leg, he stared at her pussy, letting it draw him nearer with an invisible string. She was almost bare but kept a small trim patch of blonde hair on her mound above her clit, proving the hair on her head was its natural color. He liked his women waxed or shaven since it increased their sensitivity and pleasure.

As he kissed and suckled on the inside of her knee, he watched her ass cheeks and vagina clench simultaneously. Her hips levitated off the bed, and juices flowed from her folds, soaking her even more. She was drenched for him, and he forced himself not to dive in for a taste. He wanted her to the point she was begging him to feast on her.

Crawling back up her body, he latched onto one nipple, sucking it hard into his mouth before laving it with short swipes of his tongue. He began to alternate between sucking, licking, and grazing his teeth on the hard nub, encouraged by her hedonistic moans and cries, increased breathing, and mumbled words of surrender.

When her hips bucked off the bed again, seeking fulfillment in her core, he moved over to her other breast and gave it the same treatment. Her reactions amplified, becoming almost frantic, yet she still held her ordered position.

Releasing her breast from his mouth with a pop, he looked up at her face. "Tell me what you want, Angel. What part of your body do you want me to eat next?"

She was rocking her head back and forth, her hips bucking as she pleaded with him. "Please, Sir! Eat my pussy, please! Make me come! I need to come!"

Ian moved back down between her legs, shoved his hands under her ass, and lifted her to his waiting mouth. "Then come for me, sweetheart." He ate her like a man starved—licking and sucking on her labia before spearing his tongue into her slit as deep as it could go. She shattered around him, screaming her release to the heavens above, but he didn't let up, drawing her orgasm out as long as possible.

When she finally started floating back to Earth, he slowed his ministrations while ensuring he drank every drop of her sweet cream. She was panting but somehow managed to speak a few words. "Oh, oh, my God, th-that was incredible. Holy crap!"

Smirking at her, he stayed right where he was and reached for her vibrator and the bottle of lube. "But I'm not finished yet, my little angel. As a matter of fact, I'm not even halfway done with you yet. You still have a few more orgasms I want to claim as mine tonight."

Lifting her head to see him better, she stared as if he were crazy. "Wh-what? You can't be serious. There's no way I can do that again so soon."

With a devilish grin, he snickered. "Oh yes, you can, and you will."

HIS ANGEL

Not waiting for her to respond, since it wouldn't make a difference unless she said her safeword, Ian flipped the top of the bottle and poured some lubricant on his index and middle finger. When he was sure there was enough, he recapped the bottle and tossed it aside.

"Keep your legs spread, bend your knees, and place your feet flat on the bed." When she did as she was told, the new position allowed him to see the puckered rosette below her pussy. He began to rub his lubricated fingers up and down the crevice of her ass in short strokes over her little hole, loving how she moaned as the sensations assailed her.

"Relax, sweetheart. This is just like when you use that little plug on yourself." His middle finger circled her rim, then pushed in. It slid in easier than he'd expected, and it pleased him to know her use of the plug made her body willingly accept his invasion.

Slowly, he fucked her ass with one finger, twisting it as he pushed it further into the forbidden recess of her body with each pass. As she moaned and begged, her anus and vagina clenched at the same time, and the pressure almost crushed his finger.

He continued finger fucking her hole and picked up her vibrator with his other hand. Flicking the "on" button with his thumb, he grinned when her head flew forward at the sounds coming from her toy. Her eyes grew wide. "Oh, no! Ian, Sir! Please don't!"

Chuckling, he touched the quivering toy to her inner thigh and dragged it upward, drawing out the anticipation. "Six little words, and not one was a color."

She didn't use either safeword, and he knew she wouldn't because she was enjoying this way too much. Her clit had long since uncovered itself from its hood, and the moment he touched the vibrator to the hard, little bud,

Angie went off like a rocket again, screaming louder than before. She bucked wildly, and the finger in her ass almost dislodged.

He lifted the vibrator off her clit until she began to float back down before he reapplied the humming toy, sending her right back up again . . . and again . . . until she had nothing more to give him. She was half unconscious when he pulled his finger from her tight little hole. He'd never gotten the opportunity to put his second finger in, and his tongue was the only thing to penetrate her sweet pussy. He gazed at her in amazement. She was the most responsive, sensual woman he'd ever met, and he knew when he eventually got his cock inside her, she might very well kill him.

Rising from the bed, Ian entered her bathroom and turned on the light. He soaped and rinsed his hands before retrieving two washcloths from a stack in the wicker tower next to the tub. Soaking them, he added soap to one of them before wringing out the excess water from both. He returned to the bed and, with a gentle hand, cleaned her up.

When he was done, he lifted her into his arms to work the comforter and sheet down to the bottom of the bed. Once she was back on one side of the bed with the covers pulled up to her waist, he closed the bedroom door to block out the lights that were still on in her living room. Rounding the other side of her bed, he climbed in next to her, still fully dressed. If he took his clothes off, he wouldn't be able to stop himself from taking her.

He pulled her close into his embrace, and as she drifted off to sleep, he heard her mumble, "Thank you, Sir."

HIS ANGEL

At eight o'clock the following day, Angie woke up alone and completely rested. She knew Ian hadn't left before four a.m. because that was the last time she'd roused in his arms before cuddling closer and falling asleep again. Stretching, she looked around and noticed a piece of paper on her nightstand. Unfolding the note, she read the words on it and smiled.

Hope you slept well. I'd like to see you today for lunch. Will call around ten. Wear something sexy. I left out the underwear I want you to put on.
-Ian.

He'd gone through her underwear drawer? While it should have sounded stalker-ish, it didn't. Instead, it turned her on, and she scanned the room again, spotting her sheer, white lace bra and thong set he'd left on top of her dresser. It was one of her favorites with its pink trim and tiny bows. The cut of the bra gave the girls a lift up and in, with one bow nestling between them. The other one was at the "y" junction of the thong and would sit at the top of her ass.

She was excited he wanted to see her again so soon and hopped into the shower with a cheeky grin on her face. While the water warmed up, she removed all the bobby pins still in her now ruined up-do. Her body still tingled from all the attention it'd received from Ian's hands, mouth, and tongue.

Never in her life had she had multiple orgasms, and, honestly, she'd thought they were a myth. But he had proven her wrong over and over. It wasn't until halfway

81

through her shower routine that she realized that although she had come several times, he hadn't. In fact, he'd kept his clothes on the entire night. The thought stunned her. None of her ex-lovers had ever gotten her off without doing the same.

A few minutes later, she finished her shower, dried off, and wrapped her wet hair in a towel before applying her favorite body lotion. She returned to her bedroom and retrieved the bra and thong Ian had left out for her. As she put them on, she could almost feel his hands and fingers caressing her. She wondered which other sets of her undergarments he'd touched and if she would feel the same sensations when she wore them.

Now in her underwear, she went to her closet to find something sexy to wear, per his instructions. She settled on a tight gray mini-skirt and a snug short-sleeve sweater. The deep V-neck was low enough to be sexy yet not too revealing to be considered slutty. Before she went out, she would finish the outfit with her knee-high, black leather boots—the ones with the three-inch heels. For now, though, she laid the clothes on her bed. Throwing on her short silk robe, which she always felt sensual in, she headed to the kitchen for a cup of coffee and granola cereal for breakfast.

Five minutes after ten, her cell phone rang from across the room. Hoping it was Ian, she hit the save icon on her laptop so she didn't lose what she'd been working on and dove for the phone.

"H-hello. Crap!" She fumbled the phone, and it fell to the floor. "Wait! Hold on!" Snatching it up again, she looked quickly to ensure she hadn't dropped the call and saw it was still connected. "Hello?"

HIS ANGEL

His low chuckle came over the line, and it aroused her instantly. "Hi, Angel. Everything okay?"

Giggling, she plopped down on the couch. "It is now. Sorry about that. I dropped the phone."

"I figured as much. Did you sleep well?"

Holy cow. How did he make a simple question sound so loaded with sex? "I did. You tuckered me out, and I slept later than usual."

"Glad I could be of service." He paused, and then his voice became deeper, silkier. "What are you wearing right now?"

A delicious shiver went through her body. "What you left out for me and my robe."

"Take your robe off."

Looking around her living room, she realized the vertical blinds on her sliding glass door were drawn open as usual. Not that anyone was in her backyard to see her, but Brody had gotten into the habit of popping over during the day to say hi. "Um, just a second. Let me go into my bedroom."

"No," he growled into the phone. "That's not what I told you to do, Angel. Where are you? And don't say your bedroom."

Really? Is he serious?

"Answer the question, Angel. You don't want me to ask again because your bottom will pay for it later."

Holy shit! "Um, I'm in my living room, but the blinds are open on my doors and windows. What if Brody comes over to say hi?" He was the only person who knocked on her back door.

Several miles away, Ian knew that wouldn't happen since his employee was right down the hall in the war-room,

83

remotely finishing some work from Orlando. But he wasn't about to fill Angie in on the fact. He had a feeling she would like the idea of possibly getting caught while being wicked and wild. "That's not my concern. If he does, he'll get an eyeful and probably jack off. Now, do as you're told and take off your robe. Let it slide down your incredible body until it pools at your feet. Let me know when you're standing there in your underwear."

His voice was pure velvet, and Angie let it wrap around her as the silky material slid off her shoulders and dropped to the ground. She was certain he could hear her increased breathing. Her heart was pounding as well, in anticipation of his next command. "Okay, it's off. I'm in my panties and bra."

"Good girl. Now go into your kitchen and open your freezer." Frowning in confusion, Angie did as she was told and opened the door. *Oh, no!* He had to be kidding her! Sitting front and center so she couldn't miss them were her florescent green vibrator and the bottle of K-Y.

As soon as he heard her gasp, Ian snickered. "Your toy and lube should be nicely chilled by now. Put the phone on speaker and set it down." When she did, he gave her further instructions. "Take out your jolly green giant and put the batteries back in. They're sitting on the counter."

She groaned at his pun. "Really, Ian? The 'jolly green giant' is a name for my peas and carrots, not my vibrator." Her hand shook a little as she grabbed the adult toy, and her anxiety went up a few notches, as well as her excitement, when she felt the freezing plastic. She knew exactly what he was going to make her do with it.

"I'll call it whatever I want, sweetheart, and since we're playing, you should be calling me 'Sir.' Are the batteries in it yet?"

"Yes, Sir."

HIS ANGEL

In his office, Ian got up and locked his door before grabbing a hand towel from the room's attached half-bath. He sat again at his desk and released his throbbing erection. The fist-fuck he'd given himself this morning, followed by a cold shower, had done nothing to relieve the aching in his groin.

He opened the bottom drawer of his desk and, toward the back, found a tube of lubricant he hadn't used in a long while. He wished he could have seen her face when she first saw her vibrator in the icebox. Before calling her, he told Brody to let her hidden kitchen cameras and audio bugs go dark for a while. He would love to watch the scene which was about to take place, but it would be a breach of trust without her knowledge. At least he would hear her over the phone. "Grab the K-Y and hop up on the kitchen island, Angel. You're going to fuck yourself with that ice-cold cock and make me come in my hand while I listen to you."

Holy shit! It'd been a long time since Angie had indulged in phone sex with a man, but this was already hotter than anything she'd ever experienced. She moved the phone to the island and set the lube and vibrator beside it. Using her hands and arms, she jumped up and twisted, gasping as the cold granite registered on her bare ass cheeks. "O-okay, I'm on the island. What next?"

Her heart was pounding, and her pussy was quivering.

"Take off your thong, but leave the sexy bra on. Put some lube on your pussy lips and get them all nice and wet."

"I think I'm wet enough." She ripped her thong down her legs and threw it on the floor. "I don't need the K-Y, Sir."

His voice became stricter. "I didn't ask your opinion, Angel. When I tell you to do something, you do it without questioning me unless it jeopardizes your safety or frightens you. Do you understand?"

She grabbed the cold bottle and immediately realized why he wanted her to use it. The chilled liquid on her hot sex was going to be torture. "Yes, Sir."

"Good girl. Now talk to me, nice and dirty, while you finger fuck yourself."

That she could do. She always enjoyed dirty talk during sex. "I have the cold lube on my fingers—a lot of it. I'm spreading my legs wide, and my bare pussy is open for you to see. I'm drenched. Have been since I first heard your voice on the phone." Angie gasped as she touched her nether lips, the chilled lube sending shivers and goose-bumps throughout her body. "Oh, God! It's s-so cold, but it's heating up fast. I'm spreading it all over. One finger is going into my slit, ooohhhhhh, now two. I'm rubbing my clit with my other hand and fucking myself with my fingers. You're kneeling in front of me, staring at my pussy. Oh, Sir, it feels so good. I'm soaked, and I wish you were here to lick my juices up with your tongue. Oh yes, eat me and fuck me with your fingers, Sir . . . Faster."

"Slow down, Angel." Ian's groan sounded tortured. "You're killing me here. I've got my fist around my cock. It's so fucking hard, and all for you. Get the vibrator, sweetheart. Turn it on and touch it to your nipples through your lacy bra, but keep finger fucking yourself. Whatever you do, don't come until I tell you to, sweetheart. You won't like the spanking you'll get."

Whimpering at the appealing thought of him smacking her bare ass with his hand, she grabbed the cold, plastic toy and flipped the switch on the end of it. "Okay, it's on and . . . oh crap! It's so cold, and my nipples are so hard. Oh, lick them, Sir. Please, suck them into your mouth and heat

HIS ANGEL

them again. Oh fuck, I can feel it going from my tits to my pussy."

"Baby, you're so fucking hot. I wish I were there to see you. I don't think I'd be able to watch you more than a minute, though, before I rammed my cock into your hot pussy and fucked you until neither one of us could walk. Put the vibrator on your clit, Angel, and keep those fucking fingers moving in and out."

"I'm still pumping them. I'm so tight and wet, and you feel so good. I'm about to . . . *ooohhhhhh*! Shit! Oh, it's so fucking cold, making my clit throb harder. Please, Sir, touch my clit again . . . *Aaahhhh*! Oh, fuck yeah . . . Oh please, Sir, let me fuck myself with your hard cock. Let me put your shaft deep into my pussy."

"Shit, baby, do it. Put that frozen cock in your hot little pussy and fuck it hard." Back in his office, Ian's breathing was keeping pace with Angie's panting. He was going to explode the moment he let her come. How long had it been since he had phone sex with a woman? And had it ever been this good? He doubted it.

Angie shrieked. "*Aaahhh*, fuuuucccckkk!!! Oh sh-shit, it's still ice cold, but my tight, hot walls are melting it fast. Oh, fuck me, Sir! Hard and fast."

Ian's hand tightened around his cock and sped up. He grunted and groaned as the sounds of her fucking herself for him rushed over the phone. "Yeah, baby. Damn, I can feel your hot, wet sex around my dick. It feels so fucking good. Rub your clit. Get there, Angel, get ready to come."

"I'm ready, Sir. Please hurry!"

"Come now!"

On opposite ends of the phone lines, the sounds of ecstasy reached each other's ears as they both exploded, squirting their individual come together as wave after wave of intense gratification hit them. Angie screamed her release, but Ian didn't want his secretary or anyone else to overhear him masturbating in his office. It was hard to keep his cries of completion to mere growls and murmurs, but somehow, he succeeded. For the first time since he saw her dressed for her blind date two nights ago, his dick was finally sated and flaccid, and he still hadn't gotten inside her . . . yet.

CHAPTER SEVEN

At twelve noon, Angie pulled her Toyota Camry up to the security shack at the gate leading into the fenced-in compound. Thank goodness Ian had told her the complex had four blue metal warehouses. Otherwise, she would have thought she made a wrong turn somewhere, although she'd only made one turn off the main highway. The compound was in the middle of nowhere, but he'd said both his businesses and home were on the property. She wondered where his home was because she didn't see any houses.

The guard at the gate approached her car, and she rolled down the driver's window. "Hi, my name is Angie, and I'm here to see Ian. He said you would know I was coming."

The burly, mustached man with a gun on his hip tipped his navy blue baseball cap at her and smiled. "Good afternoon, Ms. Beckett. I'm Murray, and Ian did indeed tell me you were coming, but I still need to see some ID."

She grabbed her purse. "Oh, right, I'm sorry, he told me

that. And you're going to take my picture for future reference?"

"Yes, ma'am. You won't need your ID again, but until the other guards get to know you, they'll scan your registration sticker and bring up your photo on the computer before letting you in. Due to the nature of Ian's businesses, security and privacy are a high priority here."

He took her license and ran it through a hand-held scanner. When the machine beeped, he returned the card to her and scanned the vehicle registration sticker on her windshield. "Thank you, ma'am. Almost done. Let me grab the camera."

A few moments later, her picture taken, the gate slid open, and Angie drove through it. It closed behind her as she parked next to the first building, as Ian had told her to do. Another gate and fence separated the warehouse from three others, but that gate was unmanned.

As she climbed out of her Toyota Camry, she saw Ian bounding down a flight of outside stairs with a large, black Labrador mix heeling tight at his left leg. Smiling as he reached her, his hands cupped her face, and his mouth came down hard on hers. His kiss was insistent, and the moment her lips parted, his tongue plunged inside—licking, tasting, consuming.

As quickly as the kiss started, though, it ended when he pulled his lips away and groaned, touching his forehead to hers. "That phone sex was one of the hottest experiences of my life, Angel. If I don't stop kissing you, I'll bend you over the hood of your car and fuck you like crazy, and I won't care if Murray or anyone else is watching."

Angie couldn't help the shudder that went through her nor the moan that escaped her mouth. Ian lifted his head and stared at her momentarily before his face lit up with a

HIS ANGEL

seductively evil expression. "You like the sound of that, don't you? It seems my little angel is a bit of an exhibitionist."

She blushed and tried to look away, but his hands still held her jaw, and he wouldn't let her. "I think we'll have to explore that theory, but in the meantime, come with me, and I'll show you the club. As I told you on the phone, we have strict rules which apply to everyone from the owners down. No play occurs between a member and a guest anywhere in the club until a full background check and health exam are completed. And if Devon, Mitch, and I skimp on rules, then members will start asking for favors, and it will just cause problems. So unfortunately . . . this will be a no-touch tour when we get inside because if I *do* touch you, I'm going to throw the rule book out the window."

She laughed despite the fact she felt the same way. Turning her attention to the dog sitting anxiously at their feet, she admired its patience. He appeared to be waiting for the okay to jump on her and lick her to death. "Who's this sweet boy? I saw him at Brody's one day, right? What breed is he?"

Extending her hand, she tried to allow the pup to sniff her, but instead, he looked up at Ian. His stubby little tail wriggled madly, but he remained sitting beside his owner.

Ian looked at his charge with pride. "This is Beau. I found him as a pup. All we know is he's a lab-pit mix. When he's not being a goofball or a pest with his rubber ball, he's a trained guard dog and tracker. Beau, this is Angie. *In Ordnung.*"

Given permission, Beau stuck his nose in her hand and sniffed with gusto. Angie's confusion was evident. "*In Ordnung*? What does that mean?"

SAMANTHA COLE

"It means 'okay' in German. He only knows a few words of English. Most military, police, and security dogs are trained in German because it's not a common language in the states."

Angie leaned down to pet the dog's head and scratch his soft, velvety ears. She laughed when he did a canine version of a happy dance. "I've heard that before or read it somewhere. That way, unless the bad guys know German, they can't give the dog commands."

"Exactly." Taking her other hand, Ian pointed toward the fence between the buildings, and Beau's head swiveled in the same direction. "*Geh rein.*"

The dog bounded for the fence, his big tongue hanging out the side of his mouth, and Angie saw a swinging doggie door had been cut into a portion of the chain link. A small black box was above it, under a transparent plastic hood. As Beau approached it, the light on the device turned from red to green and back to red again after the dog passed through the door to the other side. He ran toward the next building and disappeared through another doggie door.

Tugging Angie's hand, Ian led her toward the stairs he'd descended earlier. "He has a microchip under his skin that unlocks the dog doors for him. That's the headquarters for Trident, and he'll find someone in there to bug for a game of fetch."

Ian placed his palm on a scanner next to the door, and she heard a click as the door unlocked. Looking around for a sign, she didn't see one. "This is the club?"

It couldn't be. The building was blue metal and tan concrete, a basic run-of-the-mill warehouse.

He let her enter first, and she gasped at the interior, causing him to chuckle. "Yup, this is my club, although you can't tell from the exterior."

92

HIS ANGEL

The enclosed area she'd stepped into was similar to the small lobby of a five-star hotel with a reception desk and sitting area consisting of a couch, chairs, tables, and lamps. Adding in the gray carpeting, dark red walls, stylish furniture, artwork, and accessories, the first word that came to her mind was opulent. A set of antique carved wooden doors with wrought iron pulls blended with the décor, and she assumed they opened into the rest of the club.

A painting on one wall caught her eye, and she stepped forward to look closer. The scene was erotic yet beautiful and elegant, with two naked women at the feet of what appeared to be an equally nude, bearded Greek god. Handfuls of the women's hair were wrapped around his palms and wrists as he pulled their heads back, demanding their surrender. And, *holy crap,* the god was hung like a horse!

Tearing her eyes away from the huge erection, she looked at the artist's signature and was surprised she recognized it. "I know her. I mean, I don't know her personally, but she's local, and I've seen her paintings in some galleries around Tampa. She's very good."

She hadn't realized Ian was standing so close behind her until she felt his warm breath on her ear, and she almost jumped at the low rumble of his voice. "Yes, she is. We have several more pieces of her work inside. She's a club member but a bit eccentric and doesn't stop in often. It seems when she does make an appearance, she's looking for creative inspiration more than kink."

Angie snorted and giggled. "I can see if your style is erotica, then coming to a kinky sex club for inspiration makes sense."

Stepping away, he laughed along with her as he crossed the room to the reception desk. He picked up a stack of

93

papers and handed them to her sans two. "Put these in your purse and read them over later. It includes the rules and protocols of the club and a submissive limit list. Learn the rules and protocols. Appropriate punishment is administered for infractions. The first rule for you to learn is, when we're in the club, you will address me and any other Dom as Master or Mistress and their name if you know it. But if you don't, use Sir or Ma'am.

"The second rule is rude comments are frowned upon and will usually result in a form of discipline for a sub. Innocent teasing from other Doms is normal, but if a Dom is rude to you, let me know, and I'll take care of it. But I doubt it will happen.

"When you're here, you will wear a simple collar I'll give you later. It shows other Doms you are spoken for, and they must speak to me before interacting with you beyond pleasantries. It also means no one is allowed to touch you or discipline you without my consent, and since it's something I rarely give, you won't have to worry. Other submissives will ask my permission to speak with you if we are standing together. If I give them my consent, you may also speak to them unless I tell you otherwise. I know this is a lot to take in at once, but most of this is in the protocols I gave you. Understood?"

Holy shit. This was way more than she expected, but it didn't dissuade her. The more she learned, the more she wanted to experience it. "Yes, Sir. I understand so far."

"There's a submissive limit list in there, which I want you to complete later and return to me. Check off which activities you enjoy, which ones you want to try, and which are hard limits you don't want to try. The starred activities at the end are extreme ones not permitted in the club." He paused. "Now, if learning to play in BDSM with me is what

HIS ANGEL

you truly want, then there are a few more requirements we need to go over so we can scene in the club."

If last night and this morning were indications of the "play" he was referring to, then she was all for it. "Yes, Sir, that's what I want."

Obviously pleased with her answer and her easy use of the word 'Sir,' he continued. "You'll need to have a complete physical, including blood work, with your gynecologist or one of our staff doctors and have them complete the form on the back of the rules. Are you on birth control?"

She nodded, not the least bit embarrassed about the important question. "Yes, I get the shot every three months because I find it easier than the pill. I also had my annual physical with my GYN a few weeks ago, so having her fill out the form won't be a problem."

"Good. Members need to have a physical every six months to maintain play privileges. Condoms are mandatory here at the club, but I always use them. My health clearance is on file here if you want to see it." She shook her head. "Okay, the next thing is, every potential member and guest has to go through a background check to ensure they're not a threat to the safety and privacy of others. Is that going to be a problem for you?"

Angie bit her lip, and her eyes widened in alarm, causing Ian's smile to disappear. "Um, well, let's see, you already know about my addiction to Ben & Jerry's, but there is one incident I was involved in that might be a problem."

She couldn't hold back her grin, and it became apparent she was teasing him. He let out a breath and shook his finger at her. "And what would that be, my little brat?"

"When my friend and I were twelve, we got kicked out of Girl Scout camp for sneaking over to the Boy Scout camp

95

to spy on them while they were changing out of their bathing suits."

He threw his head back and let out a hearty laugh. "Oh, you naughty little trollop."

She tried to look innocent but didn't think she was convincing him. "What? We were curious after we heard two older girls talking about what boys' wee-wees looked like. They were thirteen and more experienced than us. Unfortunately, we were caught before we could see anything good. When I got home at the end of the week, my mom took me for my first GYN appointment, and my dad grounded me for a month."

"I get the feeling it wasn't the first or last time you were grounded." He laughed again and shook his head when she shot him a saucy grin. "You're absolutely adorable. I bet you kept your parents on their toes."

He gave her one of the two papers he was still holding and handed her a pen. "Okay, these are the last things we need to go over. The first is a privacy contract stating that no cameras or recording equipment are allowed in the club. Cell phones must be placed on vibrate and carried in a pocket or purse. If anyone gets a call or text, they're not allowed to take out their phones unless they're here in the lobby or outside, and that includes the locker rooms.

"You cannot repeat to anyone who or what you see here in the club. Privacy and anonymity in BDSM are valued and expected. If you run into someone from the club in public, either pretend you know them from somewhere else or don't acknowledge them at all. It's not considered rude to pretend you don't know them, and you shouldn't be offended if they do the same. Read this over and sign at the bottom. It's a binding contract with legal consequences if it's violated."

HIS ANGEL

Angie read over the paper, which was pretty much what he'd told her. Turning around, she leaned over the coffee table in the seating area for something hard to write on while she signed it and heard Ian groan. Looking over her shoulder, she saw he was staring at her ass. Knowing the hem of her skirt was a scant inch away from showing what she was hiding underneath, she gave a seductive wiggle of her hips, making him growl this time. He gave her a quick and stinging slap to her ass, making her yelp and him chuckle.

"You're killing me, Angel. Keep it up, and I'll be spanking your sweet ass sooner than you'd expect. I love bratty submissives as much as I love disciplining them." An idea seemed to come to him, and she gave him a wary look as he grabbed his phone, sending out a quick text before putting it back into the pocket of his cargo pants.

"What was that about?"

Grinning, he shook his head. "Nothing for you to be worried about . . . yet." He took the pen and contract she handed back to him, placing them on the reception desk. "One of the submissives who works the desk will file this later. This last page is a general contract. We'll go through it and sign it later. For now, let's get on with the tour, shall we?"

He opened one of the double doors and gestured for her to precede him. Angie's jaw dropped in astonishment two steps over the threshold. The currently empty club was gorgeous, and the décor from the lobby extended into the great space before them. The huge 'U' shaped upper floor they were on overlooked the floor below. There was a curved, dark wood bar along the base of the 'U,' or horseshoe, and at the other end, there was a small store and offices. Down the sides of the balcony were numerous sitting areas against the walls and pub-style tables and chairs at the brass railing so people could observe what was happening on the first floor. Across from the bar was an elegant grand staircase leading downward. In the center, hanging from the ceiling above the first floor, were three large wrought iron chandeliers matching the wall sconces. "Wow, Ian, this is beautiful. It's something out of an old French castle or something. I don't know what I expected, but this wasn't it."

"Thanks, I'm glad you like it." He was clearly proud of the place. "A lot of hard work went into making The Covenant the premier place to practice BDSM in the Tampa Bay area. Devon and I toured a few elite U.S. and European clubs with Mitch before deciding on the final plans. We found and consulted with designers who had experience in the lifestyle before we settled on this look. New members and guests tend to have the same reaction you did. The door next to the bar over there leads to staircases into the locker rooms below, and there are entrances downstairs too. Some people come straight from work or some other place, and this way, they can change into their club wear here. Come on, let me show you the pit."

"The pit?'" she asked curiously.

He chuckled. "It's what we call downstairs."

"I would think you'd call it a dungeon."

Looking at his watch, he picked up his pace and led her down the grand staircase. She was wondering what the hurry was.

"It was called the dungeon in the beginning, but members who like to watch from up above dubbed it the 'pit' not long after we opened, and the name stuck."

They reached the bottom of the stairs, and he watched

HIS ANGEL

her face as she took in the large playing area with a mixture of awe, curiosity, and even a touch of eagerness.

All along the walls were individual scene stations, each blocked off with red velvet ropes and brass stands normally used at a theater. Because of the square footage, they'd been able to put ten large roped-off areas on each side under the straightaways of the upstairs horseshoe. The locker rooms were located under the stairs and bar.

Down two separate hallways on the far end of the pit, under the store, offices, and storage areas, were twelve suites and theme rooms for private play. Inside the downstairs 'U' were numerous sitting areas. Some of them had couches, wing-back chairs, and chaise lounges, while others consisted of small tables with matching chairs where conversations and/or sexual play could take place. All the furniture was either leather or wood, which was easy to clean.

But the pièce de résistance of the club was the large St. Andrew's cross atop a small two-foot-high stage in the center of the pit. The seven-foot-tall medieval torture device was covered in black leather and had wrist and ankle restraints at the ends. And it was where Ian was leading her to now. "We use this for demos and commitment or collaring ceremonies like the one Kristen and Devon had a few months back. Step up on the stage, sweetheart."

His voice dropped to that whiskey-laced tone she was starting to recognize as his Dom voice, and her eyes widened. She only hesitated briefly before taking the two steps up and saw his gaze trail up and down her body. "I love the knee-high leather boots. Those you can keep on. As for the sweater and skirt . . . undress to your bra and panties, Angel."

"I-I thought we couldn't play?" She was nervous and

99

excited at the same time, and the statement came out as a question. Ian's mouth turned into the evil grin he liked to give her—the one which made her body shudder and her pussy lips quiver with anticipation.

He crossed his arms over his chest and spread his legs shoulder-width apart. "Just because we won't be playing or touching doesn't mean I don't get to see the pretty lingerie you have on. I've been fantasizing about it all day. Now, either undress or say your safeword."

Angie gulped, but she grabbed the bottom of her sweater, pulled it over her head, and tossed it to the floor next to her. Her nipples tightened under the sheer lace of her bra at his heated stare, and she felt a gush of her juices flood from her pussy, soaking her little thong. Her eyes latched on to his as she reached behind her, releasing the catch at the top of her skirt and pulling down the zipper, feeling each tooth release from its mate. When the garment fell to her feet in a puddle, she stepped to the side and kicked it over to join her top on the stage floor.

"You're beautiful, sweetheart. Exquisite. Turn around slowly for me, all the way . . . holy fuck! I should fall to my knees to thank the Lord above for bestowing such beauty on your backside, Angel. I want to bite down on that little pink bow and rip those off you with my teeth."

His words made her heart beat faster. She wasn't used to a man being so vocal about her body. When she completed the rotation, he pointed the cross behind her. "Step back against the cross. Lift your arms and grab hold of the wrist restraints, then stay like that."

She'd just taken hold of the second Velcro cuff when they both heard the upstairs double doors open and the sounds of men's voices. Angie was about to bring her hands down to cover herself or dive for her clothes when he stopped her. "Uh-uh, Angel. Unless you want to use your safeword, stay the way you were. I've decided to push your limits a little more today. The team and I need to have a meeting, and afterward, I'll show you the rest of the compound. Of course, I'll let you get dressed again before we go outside."

Turning his head, he raised his voice so the others could hear him. "Stay upstairs for a count of thirty."

The voices went quiet, and he looked at her again. "You have twenty of those seconds to use your safeword. If you do, you can get dressed and sit on the couch over there for a few minutes until we're done. I won't be mad or disappointed at all. If you don't use your safeword, then my men and I will have our meeting while you give us something beautiful to look at. No one will touch you or say anything that will make you uncomfortable. They'll admire your lovely body like I'm doing."

As Ian checked his watch, Angie's mind raced. She'd never been undressed in front of more than one man before. While the thought made her nervous, it aroused her even more. She swallowed and made her decision known. "I'll stay where I am, Sir."

He smiled, and her heart squeezed, knowing she pleased him.

"Damn, she makes a pretty ornament. We should have all our meetings this way."

Angie gasped, and her cheeks burned red, but she stayed where she was and didn't utter a word. She hadn't realized how fast thirty seconds would be. The five other members of his team, including her next-door neighbor, had come down the stairs and approached the two of them. She wasn't sure who had commented since they were all staring at her—not lewdly, but appreciatively—and it made her feel beautiful, sexy, and downright naughty. There she was, in her underwear, looking like a dancer in a strip joint, and she wasn't embarrassed.

Crap! She was an exhibitionist. How come she never knew that?

She saw Jake break away first, smiling and shaking his head, before sitting in a winged-back chair. The rest all grinned or winked at her before sitting down until Ian was the only one still standing before her. "You please me, Angel, very much." She glowed under his praise. "I'd like you to keep your arms up for now, but when it gets uncomfortable, just let me know. Understand?"

When she nodded, he shook his head with a frown. *Oh yeah!* "Yes, Sir. I understand."

"Good girl. This will take about fifteen or twenty minutes, but I suspect you'll tire before we finish. Don't worry about interrupting since you're already a delicious distraction."

He turned and took the last seat facing her. The men could see her easily from how they were all situated, except for Jake, whose back was to her. She thought it odd he wasn't looking at her like the others were, but it didn't bother her. In fact, she was getting wetter by the second and clenched her thighs together.

Devon had started whatever meeting they were having, but her eyes remained on Ian's face. When he saw her squirm, he pointed at her feet and indicated with his hands that he wanted her to spread her legs wide.

Shit. The thong gave her limited coverage in her crotch, and they'd all be able to see most of her glistening pussy. She closed her eyes and took a deep breath before spreading her legs and then looking at Ian again to see his approving nod. She stood there in her underwear while the men had

HIS ANGEL

their meeting, all but ignoring her except for the occasional glance, grin, or wink.

* * *

Devon opened a file in his hand. "We've narrowed the new team of six down to fourteen candidates. Eleven men and three women, all highly recommended by their superiors or, in some cases, their subordinates or protected assets. Four are with the FBI with military backgrounds. Seven are recently retired or are about to be from various Special Forces, one of whom was a P.O.W. for a week in Afghanistan. Two are from SWAT teams—one in L.A. and the other from Chicago.

The last one is from the Secret Service and has experience with high-level targets. He was the one who personally, and single-handedly, I might add, prevented the kidnapping of the House Speaker's young daughter on a family vacation to Jamaica last year. I'm sure everyone remembers the incident."

Three low-level and over-zealous members of Al Qaeda tried to take the twelve-year-old girl from the hotel her family was staying at. Two other Secret Service agents were shot to death, and if it wasn't for Special Agent Cain Foster, the child might have been beheaded at some point for a videotaped jihad.

Ian took over, his gaze flicking to her every few moments to ensure she was okay. "We'd like to try and get at least one of the three women on the team if we can, but not at the expense of passing over a better-qualified asset. Having a woman on-call for an op, if needed, keeps us from tracking one down through our contractors. We are considering hiring one of the women for reasons other than the Omega team, which is what the second team will be called."

Boomer snorted. "As long as they know they're not the Alpha team, which is what I just decided our team will be called." The group of men chuckled at the pun since they were all alpha-male Doms at the club and had never needed a team name for themselves.

"What's the extra position?" Jake asked.

Devon grinned like a guy with a new toy. "Chopper pilot."

"Holy shit, we're getting a helicopter?" It was Boomer's turn to sound like a kid in a toy store . . . or a Dom in a sex toy store because he looked like he was ready to blow a load, and it wasn't because there was a woman in sexy lingerie standing less than ten feet away from him.

Ian nodded. "Yup, I've got a line on one, and I'm hoping we can work out a deal by the end of the month. As you know, we purchased the ten acres north of the compound last month, and that's where the helipad will be built. Polo, I know you have plenty of flight time, and we'll use you as backup, but I don't want an empty spot on the team if you have to stay behind with the bird on an op."

Marco nodded his head. "Fine with me. I'll take it up and do some training with the new pilot in case I need to take over in an emergency."

"Good idea." Ian paused when he glanced over at Angie. "Excuse me a second," he said to his team as he stood and approached the stage. "Are your arms tired, Angel?"

* * *

Her arms were uncomfortable, but she did her best to keep them up. She shook her head, not wanting to disappoint him. "No, Sir, not really."

His eyes narrowed, his expression stern. "You're squirming, and I can tell you're uncomfortable by looking at your face. Would you like to try answering the question

HIS ANGEL

again, this time honestly and not with what you think I want to hear?"

Damn, she should have told him the truth the first time he asked. "Um, sorry, Sir. Yes, my arms are tired."

"The apology better be for not telling me the truth and not because you're sorry your arms got tired in that position. You lasted longer than I expected. You may bring your arms down." He walked a few feet away and returned with a wooden, straight-back chair, spun it around, and placed it on the stage so if she sat on it properly, she'd be facing the cross behind her. "Straddle the chair, Angel, and rest your hands on your thighs."

Angie didn't know what shocked her more, the position he wanted her in so they'd all have a view of her crotch through the narrow slats of the chair or the fact she obeyed him without hesitation. After she'd done as instructed, he told her to spread her knees wider.

When satisfied, he returned to his chair and continued his meeting while she sat there, her juices dripping from her slit. She didn't want to look down, but she was certain she was making a puddle on the seat under her pussy. Her walls clenched with the need for a cock to fill her. And not just any cock. Her sex wanted only one . . . Ian's. She was so high on lust that she was tempted to interrupt their meeting and beg him to fuck her right there in front of everyone, and of course, that thought inflamed her desire even further.

Less than ten minutes later, Ian got to his feet and addressed his men. "Read the candidates' files, and give Devon or me any recommendations or concerns. We'll be starting the interviews next week, and I want you each to meet as many of them as your caseloads allow. If there are no questions . . . get lost and enjoy the rest of your Sunday.

I'm taking the rest of the afternoon off to spend time with my beautiful sub."

Grins and winks were sent her way again as the men all said goodbye to her, and then she was alone with Ian. Sexually frustrated beyond anything she'd ever known, she groaned when he picked up her clothes, shook them out, and handed them to her. She'd forgotten they couldn't have sex or anything close to it while they were in the club. As she scrambled to get dressed, she hoped his house was nearby. If it weren't, she would force him to do what he said earlier and have him fuck her over the hood of her car while Murray, and anybody else who was around, watched.

CHAPTER EIGHT

"Where are we going?"

Ian led her on foot across the parking lot and through the pedestrian gate in the fence to the more significant section of the compound. As they walked past the building housing the Trident offices, Beau came running out from behind it and heeled at Ian's side without being told. "My place. We converted the last building into large apartments. Mine's on the first floor, and Devon and Kristen live on the second."

They continued across the paved lot with their canine escort. Harder than granite, Ian not-so-discreetly adjusted himself for the third time since they climbed back up the grand staircase, and Angie smirked knowingly when she caught him in the act. He was just as aroused as she was, if not more so, and he couldn't wait for them to be alone. When they reached the outside door, he placed his palm on a scanner like the one outside the club.

Opening the door for her, he let her enter before him. There was an interior door to his apartment, and next to it was a smaller dog door for Beau. Although the dog came in the same outside door they did, he didn't wait for Ian to open the second door, opting to use his own entrance. He disappeared inside as Ian stepped forward to scan his palm once again. To their left was a staircase which led to the second apartment.

When the door in front of them opened, he yanked her inside impatiently. The door slammed shut at the same time he shoved her against the wall next to it and crushed his mouth to hers. There was nothing gentle about the kiss, and he was grateful she didn't object. In fact, she was just as rough in return. Taking control, one of his hands plunged into her hair, and he made a fist. He pulled the strands only enough to sting and loved how it made her react even more frantic against him. He maneuvered her head to where he wanted it so he had better access to her mouth, which he was devouring. Her hands wrapped around his neck and held him just as possessively.

From their chests to their groins, they were fused together. Her nipples were hard, but not as hard as the erection he was grinding against her mound. They fit together like the pieces of a jigsaw puzzle. His other hand dragged down her side to her hip and under her skirt to her ass. He squeezed, and she moaned into his mouth. Bending her knee, she brought it up to his hip, wrapping her leg around his thigh, desperately trying to get closer to him even though it was physically impossible.

The door next to them popped open, and Ian ripped his lips from hers at the same time they heard a female shriek. "Oh my God, Uncle Ian! I'm so sorry. Oh, crap. Never mind, I'll go upstairs to Uncle Devon's."

"No." The word came out hoarsely, and Ian cleared his

throat. "No, don't, Baby-girl. They went out to meet Will and some friends for lunch. Just go into the kitchen and give us a minute, okay."

They were still joined at the hip, and although he knew how it looked, there was no way Ian was pulling away from her in front of his niece with the throbbing erection he had. His forehead rested on Angie's as they tried to slow down their breathing.

"It's all right, I'll go someplace else."

Glancing at the pretty young blonde as she was about to close the door again, he grabbed her arm after noticing her swollen eyes and tear-stained face. "Baby-girl? What's wrong?"

The moment he said it, he knew what the answer would be. Tomorrow night was the anniversary of her parents' murders. *Damn it.* He should have ensured she was okay today, but she'd been fine last night when he talked to her, and he'd figured she wouldn't feel the full impact until tomorrow. He'd been wrong.

"I'm so sorry, but I-I was overthinking and didn't want to be alone today. My roommate's gone until tomorrow, and I didn't want to explain what was wrong to anyone else. But I'll go find Brody or Jake."

Although he was still leaning against Angie, he pulled Jenn into the room and turned her toward the kitchen. "Go in the kitchen. Pull out the fixings for sandwiches, and we'll be there in a minute. We haven't had lunch yet."

She looked like she was going to argue, but he wouldn't let her, and the concern in his voice was evident. "That's an order, Jenn."

After she did as she was told, with Beau on her heels, he shut the door and faced Angie, who'd stood there in silence as he dealt with his niece. He cupped her jaw and softly brushed his lips over hers. He kept his voice low and said, "I'm so sorry, Angel. I wasn't expecting this to happen, but tomorrow is a bad day for her. She's my goddaughter."

"It's fine, Ian. Don't apologize. Tomorrow's the anniversary of her parents' deaths, isn't it?" She was whispering, and when his brow furrowed in confusion, she added, "Brody told me what happened and why she lived with you now."

He nodded and finally stepped away from her body. Glancing over his shoulder to ensure the coast was clear, he adjusted himself, groaning as he did. "When she's not at her dorm at U. of T., she's here." He watched as she straightened her clothes. "I'd like for you to stay and meet her, but I'll understand if you don't want to right now."

"I'd like to meet her, but wouldn't she feel better if I left?"

He ran his hands down her arms to her hands and held them, loving how her delicate fingers looked entwined with his larger, rougher ones. Her skin was so soft, he didn't want to stop touching it. "No, I think she could use the distraction. Besides, if you leave, she'll ask me twenty million questions and feel guilty, believing you left because of her. Typical teenage thinking, I know, and when she puts her mind to it, she's better than most military interrogators. She'll go much easier on you than me since she doesn't know you yet."

She laughed and looked downward at his bulging crotch. "Fine. I'll tell you what—you get your wee-wee under control, and I'll introduce myself to your niece."

His raised eyebrow made her laugh harder. He reached around and pinched her ass, and she swallowed her surprised yelp. "Brat. And stop laughing because you'll be formally introduced to my 'wee-wee' later, and I promise you that's the last time you'll call it that."

Pushing off the wall, she let her hand brush against his groin as she sashayed toward the kitchen. Sexually frustrated beyond anything he'd ever known, he dramatically thumped his head against the wall and heard her laugh at him. Grinning, he watched her walk into his kitchen and greet his goddaughter. "Hi, I'm Angie."

Angie was tucked under Ian's arm on the couch four hours later, while Jenn was curled up in her favorite extra-wide chair with Beau snoring on the floor beside her. After Ian had gotten his body back down to a slow simmer, he joined them in the kitchen. Jenn had already made her own sandwich and been putting the final touches on his usual choice as Angie was finishing her creation. They'd also hauled out some coleslaw and Jenn's beloved sour cream and onion potato chips.

The two women had taken to each other instantly. It didn't take long to convince Jenn there was no need to apologize for her interruption, and Angie soon had his niece talking about school and her job as a waitress at Jake's brother's pub. While they'd taken the sandwiches and chips into the living room and gotten comfortable, Ian grabbed three bottles of water from the fridge and followed them. Now they were watching *The Princess Bride*, which had followed *Robin Hood: Men in Tights*. Thankfully, both women were in the mood for some comedy instead of tearjerking chick flicks.

Although he was enjoying it, Ian had difficulty

accepting how comfortable the domestic scene felt. It was a rare occasion if he brought a woman back to his place, and this was the first woman in a very long time he'd introduced to his goddaughter. He'd dated numerous women since his engagement had ended ten years ago. Some of the relationships even lasted for a few months, but every time a woman pushed him for more, he broke it off. He didn't go into a relationship intending to end it at a certain point. However, it's what always eventually happened. As long as the woman kept things light and uncomplicated, Ian was fine, but he refused to let a woman get too close to him again. Despite his best efforts to move on, it always came down to one thing—he didn't want to go through what he'd experienced when Kaliope broke his heart.

There had been a time when he'd believed in soulmates and thought he'd found his. He'd never been the most romantic man in the world. He didn't spout poetry or think to bring a woman flowers just because he felt like it. She'd known how he was from the beginning of their relationship, but Kaliope thought she could change him.

He'd tried to show her he loved her in his unique way—he made sure her car was always in tip-top shape so it wouldn't break down on her; he shared the household chores with her, making sure he did the heavier stuff and never let her take out the dirty garbage; he praised and supported her in everything she did whether it was a success or failure. She'd been a local newscaster in Virginia while he was stationed nearby and fantasized about landing an anchor position on a national news program. Unfortunately, so did every other TV reporter in the United States. The competition could be harsh, and even though Ian had been proud of her no matter what she did, it hadn't been enough for her. If he tried to comfort her after an

HIS ANGEL

audition with a broader network fell through, she'd get mad, yelling he was only patronizing her. The worst had been when she'd told him he was holding her back from her dreams. He had cherished Kaliope, but in the end, it hadn't been good enough for her. Now Ian kept his relationships simple, refusing to have his heart ripped out again.

When the end credits began to scroll up the sixty-inch flat-screen TV, Jenn gathered the crumb-filled plates left over from their earlier meal. "I'm going to my room to work on my term paper. Don't worry about me for dinner. I'll nuke something later." She leaned down and kissed his cheek. "Thanks for everything, Uncle Ian. You, too, Angie, and it was so nice to meet you. Again, I'm really sorry I interrupted your afternoon."

They both smiled at her, telling her it was fine and she had to stop apologizing for needing company. After she and Beau left them alone, Ian grabbed the last of their lunch residue and an empty bowl of popcorn, carrying it all into the kitchen. Angie glanced around the apartment again, if she could call it an apartment since it looked more like a vast penthouse suite in an upscale hotel. The living room had couches and chairs, seating for at least ten people, and a massive entertainment center. Behind the couch was another conversation area with a four-seat wood and mirrored bar. A dart board hung between the bar and corner of the room, with a section of cork protecting the wall from misthrows. The attached dining area contained an eight-seat formal table, chairs, and a china hutch with two extra chairs that could be used when the leaf was in use. An eat-in gourmet kitchen was on the other side of the dining area, complete with stainless steel appliances. It was a party hostess's dream.

Earlier in the afternoon, Angie had removed her boots

and tried to get comfortable on the couch next to Ian without her crotch showing under her short skirt. Noticing she was uneasy, Jenn had offered her a pair of yoga pants and a University of Tampa T-shirt to change into. Grateful, Angie had accepted the offer and used the master bedroom suite to make the quick change. There were also two additional bedrooms–the furthest away from Ian's room was Jenn's–and a guest bath off the hallway. The two smaller bedrooms were larger than Angie's living room.

The only odd thing about the apartment was the horizontal windows in every room were elevated about eight feet up the ten-foot walls, allowing plenty of light in without anyone being able to see in from outside. She figured it was a security feature due to his line of work. Except for the young woman's pink and purple chic bedroom, the rest of the house was beautifully decorated in earth tones. Ian had explained his mother had taken over after the apartments became livable and hired an interior decorator for both her sons. Otherwise, they would have looked like typical bachelor pads with mismatched furniture and nothing on the walls but the dart board. As it was, he had to convince the decorator to include it in the décor.

As she stared at an older photo on one of the end tables, Ian returned from the kitchen. The picture was of him and his brothers about twenty years ago. He was in the center with two slightly younger boys on either side of him, and he was holding another boy, around the age of six, up by the armpits. "This is you, the oldest, but which one of these two is Devon? Are they twins?"

He pointed to the teenager on his left. "This one's Dev. The little guy in front is our brother Nick, and this is John, and no, Devon's eleven months older, but many people had trouble telling them apart."

"Do Nick and John live in Florida too?"

Taking her hand, he tugged her up from the couch and pulled her close. "Nick is twenty-five now and in the Navy in San Diego." A sad expression took over his face. "And John died when he was seventeen."

Feeling awful for his loss, she realized they had more in common than she initially thought. "I'm sorry. I lost my brother when he was seventeen, too, and I was nine. He was killed in a car crash with three of his friends."

Ian cupped her cheek, his thumb caressing her jawline. "I'm sorry for your loss. Unbeknownst to us, John had become an alcoholic and got drunk one day after cutting school. He died after he passed out and threw up. Aspirated. My dad found him."

He swallowed at the memory, then cleared his throat. "It was hard on all of us, but Devon took it really bad. He tortured himself over some misplaced guilt that he could've stopped John from spiraling down. The problem was the kid hid his addiction well, and none of us knew about it. And we're a close-knit family. Anyway, Dev thought he should've been able to see the problem and take control of the situation. The fact that he didn't became an issue for him. His hurt and anger were starting to get the best of him, so after we ended up on the same SEAL team, I introduced him to the lifestyle to help him deal with it. Taking control of other aspects of his life allowed Dev to better deal with John's death."

Bringing her hands from around his waist and to his chest, she explored his physique as she spoke. "Is that why Devon doesn't drink alcohol? I only saw him have tonic water last night."

Had the gala only been last night? It seemed like so much had happened between Ian and her since then.

"Yeah." He pulled her hips into his, rubbing his erection against her. "But I really don't want to talk about Devon or anyone else but you right now. We have some unfinished business to take care of, little one."

Feeling wicked, she licked her lips, slow and seductive, and he groaned at the sight as she walked her fingers up his chest. "What about Jenn?"

Bending forward, he nuzzled her neck. "She'll be busy with her term paper, and my bedroom is far enough away she won't hear a thing as long as we keep our voices and your screams down to a whisper."

"Sorry," she mumbled as she blushed.

He took her hand and led her down the hallway past Jenn's closed door. "Don't be. I love how vocal you are. I just don't want my niece to know it, and I'm sure she doesn't either. And don't worry because she always uses her headphones and listens to her iPod while doing schoolwork."

After closing and locking his bedroom door behind them, he pulled her back into his embrace and kissed her. It didn't start as explosive as their earlier one, but it wasn't long until they returned to that level. They spent several minutes consuming each other before Ian eased back and released her. He walked over to a small sitting area next to a gas fireplace on the far side of his bed and sat on a blue and green, striped upholstered chair. He picked up a remote, and soft jazz music filled the air. "Strip for me, Angel. Nice and slow. Tease me. Do you remember what your safeword is?"

Damn, he made her hotter than lava when he spoke to her in that deep, commanding voice. "My safeword is red, Sir."

She loved to dance, and swinging her hips to the music came naturally as she gave Ian the best strip tease and lap

HIS ANGEL

dance of his life. It didn't take long for her to shed her tee and yoga pants, but then she slowed down. Trailing her hands up and down her body sensually, she played with her breasts and clit through the fabric of her underwear until Ian had to undo his pants to get some much-needed room for his straining erection. She was shocked and thrilled to see he'd gone commando, and she moaned, knowing his hard shaft had been one zip away from her touch most of the day. The dark purple head was weeping, and she looked forward to tasting him, but not yet. She wasn't done teasing him.

Turning around, she bent over and reached back to spread her ass cheeks, smiling and wriggling her hips when he growled. "Fuck, Angel. Someday soon, I will take your sweet ass and fuck it hard and fast. And I promise you, you'll love every minute of it."

Her pussy quivered at the thought of him fucking her there, a place where no other man had been. Standing back up, she remained facing away from him as she reached back and unhooked her bra. Holding the front in place, she lowered the straps, inch by inch, until her arms were free. She threw the lacy piece over her head in his direction. When she saw he caught it, she shimmed her hips and lowered her thong, drawing out the process as long as possible. She then stepped out of them, turned around, and tossed them at him too. When he snatched the garment this time, he brought it to his face, inhaling deeply.

His blue eyes flared and darkened with heated desire. "Damn, sweetheart. I wish I could bottle your scent and carry it with me everywhere. Run your fingers through your pussy and taste yourself. I want you to taste what I do when I eat you."

Holy crap! She'd never tasted herself before, but even

though she blushed, the demand didn't turn her off. In fact, she felt her reaction to it gush from between her legs as if her body was giving her plenty to sample. Leisurely, she ran her flattened hand down her abdomen while her fingers stretched downward, leading the way. They brushed over her clit and into her saturated folds. After gathering her moisture, she brought her fingers to her mouth and licked each finger one by one, moaning at the spiciness when it hit her tongue.

Ian crooked a finger at her. "Come here, baby, and do it again. It's my turn for a taste."

She sashayed several steps forward and stopped with her legs straddling his knees. Repeating the process of collecting her cream, she brought her hand up and held it a few inches from his mouth, making him reach for her. Grabbing her wrist, he parted his lips, took two of her fingers, and sucked them clean before moving to the next two and, at last, her thumb, which he nibbled on. The sounds of his slurping and satisfied humming made her want to put other things in his mouth, mainly her tits and clit.

"On your knees, Angel. I want you to suck me."

Oh, thank fuck! She loved giving head and was dying to taste the pre-cum seeping from his tip. She knelt before him and crawled forward between his knees when he spread them apart. He still had his cargo pants and shirt on, and this time, she felt wicked that he was dressed and she was naked.

When she reached for his cock, he stopped her. "Your mouth only, sweetheart. Hands behind your back, like when you were a kid, bobbing for apples."

Smirking, she licked her lips and did as she was told.

Using his thumb and forefinger, he positioned his dick to point at the ceiling. He grabbed a handful of her hair and guided her mouth toward the tip. She swiped her tongue across the head and tasted him. He was delicious, and she did it again before he slowly impaled her mouth with his shaft. Shifting his hips forward so she could take more of him in, he set the slow pace he wanted her to use as her head bobbed up and down. He eased the grip of his hand in her hair, then pushed away the loose strands that had fallen around her face and tucked them behind her ears so he could see her mouth better.

Reaching down, he played with her nipples as she worked him in and out of her mouth. He pinched, pulled, and rolled her stiff little peaks, and when she purred, she knew he felt it down the length of his cock and into his balls. Using her tongue, she licked him like an ice cream cone on every upstroke, teasing the v-shaped notch on the underside of his cock, and it was his turn to hum with satisfaction.

Ian's eyes rolled back into his head. "Fuck, Angel. The only thing better than how this feels is how you look, taking my cock between your plump, red lips. Suck me, baby, as hard as you . . . *aaahhhh*, fuck! Shit! Do it again."

He began to breathe heavily, his hips jerking upwards, and she took him so far back into her mouth that he hit her throat. *Fuck!* She either had no gag reflex or had exceptional control.

Her throat closed around him when she swallowed, and he saw stars while moaning in ecstasy. He would have to stop her soon because he wanted to be in her pussy when he came inside her body for the first time, but it felt too good to stop her yet. "Holy shit, baby. I want to thank then kill the bastard who taught you how to give a blow job 'cause you're so fucking good at it. But I don't want to imagine you doing this to anyone else but me."

He couldn't take it anymore. Grabbing her hair again, he pulled her off him, but she managed to take one last swipe of his head with her tongue, the little brat. Giving her a hand, he helped her stand.

As she licked her swollen lips, he said, "Climb up on my bed and get on your hands and knees so I can take you from behind. You were teasing me with your hot little ass earlier in the lobby, and now I'm going to spank it before I fuck you. There are consequences for teasing a Dom when you haven't been told to do so."

Angie all but dove onto the bed. She needed him inside her and wasn't ashamed to admit she longed for the roughness he offered her. She'd always wanted to be spanked, but the one boyfriend who'd agreed to do it hadn't been too into it, and the experience left her wanting much more than she had gotten. Two of her other boyfriends had looked at her as if she were crazy when she told them what she wanted, so she stopped asking for it. But she had a feeling Ian would give her not only what she wanted but what she craved.

After she was in position, she looked over her shoulder at him. Standing beside the bed, he stared at her ass while removing his clothes. "Eyes forward."

She snapped her head around and heard him open a nightstand drawer, then the sound of a condom wrapper being opened. The bed dipped as he climbed up behind her, and she was startled when he began caressing and squeezing the globes of her ass instead of spanking her right away. "Beautiful, Angel. You've got the prettiest ass

HIS ANGEL

I've ever seen. And it'll look even prettier when I turn it a nice shade of pink."

She wasn't prepared for the first smack, and even though he hadn't hit her too hard, she still let out a yelp and instinctively tried to move forward. Ian grabbed her hips and held her in place. "Going somewhere, sweetheart?"

Damn him. He sounded amused, and she rolled her eyes, grateful he couldn't see her face. "No, Sir. I just didn't expect it."

"Well, now you will. Remember, Jenn is down the hall, so no yelling."

She was glad he reminded her about his niece because Angie had forgotten about the younger woman. It must've been why he'd raised the music volume a little before joining her on the bed because it would muffle the sound of his hand hitting her bare flesh. His other hand lifted and smacked her other cheek. That was a little harder than the first, but she stayed in position and bit back her squeal.

By the time he gave her the third, fourth, and fifth spanks, her ass was starting to feel like it was on fire. He hadn't struck the same spot twice, dispersing them across her cheeks and upper thighs. And instead of trying to get away, she was bowing her back and pushing her hips higher, giving him better access. Was it wrong to enjoy the pain to the point she was soaking wet and ready to beg him to fuck her?

He stopped after the eighth one and held his hand atop the flesh he'd just smacked, keeping the heat in, and she moaned. "Are you okay, Angel? Give me a color—green, yellow, or red?"

"Green . . . Sir." Her breathing had increased after the

third or fourth spank, and now she was outright panting. "Oh, God . . . so green."

"Really?" She could hear the smile in his voice. "Why don't I feel for myself, *hmm?*" Before she could respond, his hand slid down between her legs. "*Mmmm.* So nice and wet. But no coming without permission."

He removed his exploring fingers, and she heard him clean them with his mouth. She felt him move closer to her and rub the head of his cock through her drenched folds before shoving it deep into her pussy in one swift motion, groaning as he did so.

Holy crap, he's so big! She felt so full as he held himself inside her, waiting for her body to adjust to his size. She had to hold back the urge to beg him to move and prayed he wouldn't make her wait too long before giving her permission to come because she was on the edge of the precipice.

He dragged his shaft back out as her greedy pussy clenched, attempting to keep him in. He stopped with the head just inside her, and she pushed her hips back, trying to get him to go deep again. His hand smacked her right butt cheek, and she gasped. "You don't set the pace, sweetheart. I do. And right now, I'm savoring the feel of you around me, so stay still."

"Y-Yes, Sir. S-Sorry, but you feel so good."

* * *

Ian eased back inside her until he was buried to the hilt and repeated the cycle, complete with a hard spank on her ass, several more times. "Damn, Angel. You feel incredible. So hot and tight. I don't think I'm going to last very long."

It might end up being quicker than he wanted, but he'd make sure it was good for her before he found his own release. The drag of her walls against his cock felt so good— it was sinful. Grabbing her hips, he couldn't help speeding up, setting an almost frantic rhythm as he pounded into her from behind. The sounds of flesh slapping on flesh filled the room as his hips bounced off her luscious backside.

"Oh God, I'm going to come. Please, Ian!" Although her words were pleading whispers, he could still hear her desperation.

"Not yet, Angel. Almost." After a few more thrusts, when he felt the tingling in his spine shoot into his balls, he knew he had to send her over. Reaching around her hip, he located her clit and pinched it. "Now!"

That one word and pinch were all she needed as she shattered around him. Her cries of release were muffled as she yelled into the comforter and milked the seed from his body. She tightened around him, and he saw black spots before his eyes. He kept pumping his hips, trying to extend their orgasms for as long as possible until her entire body finally sagged to the bed. He fell forward onto his fore-arms with one on either side of her head. With his chest to her back, he managed to keep some of his weight off her. They were both gasping for air, their bodies covered in sweat, and as much as it killed him to do so, Ian eased out of her.

When he was sure he could stand without collapsing, he caressed her back and ass as he crawled off the bed. "Stay there, sweetheart. I'll be right back."

He smiled at her mumbled reply as she straightened her knees and laid flat on her stomach. Discarding his condom in the bathroom, he reached into the shower and turned on the water to let it warm up. He moved back to the bedside and looked down at her satiated body, not surprised when he started getting hard again at the sight of her. He couldn't get enough of his little angel. After grabbing another condom, he wrapped his hands around her ankles and hauled her toward him. When she grumbled a weak protest, he smacked her pink ass and got her attention.

Flipping over, she glared at him. "What was that for?"

He gave her an evil grin. "The Dom in me felt like it."

"Well, tell the Dom in you to have a little sympathy for the half-unconscious. You wore me out."

Chuckling, he picked her up in his arms, carrying her into the bathroom and straight into his extra-large walk-in shower. "I hope I didn't wear you out too much because I'm ready for more."

Her expression was one of shock as she eyed his groin after he let go of her legs, allowing her to stand. Grinning, he walked her backward under the spray of hot water coming from both sides of the shower and above. She reached down and made a fist around his still-growing erection. "I think I might have some energy left since you're obviously up for it."

He let her slowly pump his shaft as he tossed the condom on a shelf, grabbed a bottle of body soap, and squirted some into his hand. Lathering it up, he started with her neck and shoulders and cleaned every inch of her body, spending extra attention to her breasts, ass, and crotch. When he was done, he allowed her to do the same to him, letting her explore, to her obvious delight. She admired his two tattoos—the tribal band around his left upper arm and the American flag and anchor above his right shoulder blade.

Her hands traced his various scars, asking how he'd gotten each one. He couldn't recall how he got some of them, but there were three he received in combat, which he would never forget. The three-inch scar on his left upper arm and another five-inch one on his abdomen were knife wounds that had caused minor damage. But a gunshot wound pucker on his left chest above his heart was a constant reminder of how dangerous some of his Navy tours had been. The doctors had told him if he'd been hit a little lower, he would've left Iraq in a body bag.

He hadn't been wearing his bullet-proof vest as he left the mess hall when an Iraqi policeman, who'd been allowed on their base for training, decided to switch his allegiance. While two marines had been killed, he and another SEAL had been wounded in the three-second attack before the traitor was taken out by Marco, who'd been a few steps behind Ian. Luckily, one of his ribs stopped the low-caliber bullet, and after only two days in the hospital, he could return to the States until cleared for duty again. His Purple Heart was stored with the rest of his medals in a valet box on his dresser.

After he told her about the scars he could remember getting, she kissed each one, and her tender actions touched him. But he soon shook those thoughts from his brain, not wanting to let her close to his heart where he was most vulnerable because he was never letting history repeat itself. He grabbed her hips and spun her around to face a built-in tiled bench before reaching for the condom he'd tossed earlier. "Bend over, sweetheart, and put your hands on the bench. You can come whenever you need to this time."

Ian sheathed himself, then squirted a little more soap into his hands. Running his fingers down the crack of her ass, he worked his slick fingers into her back hole. First one, followed by two. He soon had her moaning and writhing as he thrust them in and out, scissoring them to stretch her further. As much as he wanted to take her there, she wasn't ready for the size of him. He'd have to pick up a set of progressive anal plugs to prepare her properly. For now, though, he'd use his fingers. As he continued to fuck her ass, he lined his latex-covered cock up with her core and plunged into her. She came instantly, but he had more control this time and set a steady pace, determined to get one or two more orgasms from her.

Angie's legs shook as one orgasm ebbed and another built behind it like waves in the ocean. Was it possible to die from too much incredible sex? She hoped not because she wanted to experience as much of it as she could before she died. Ian was a skilled lover who could make her body sing in ways it never had before. He shifted his hips and, with the new angle, found her hidden G-spot and sent her over the edge again. The combination of his cock and fingers taking her simultaneously made her come hard, and if it weren't for him holding her around the waist with his free hand, she would've sank to the tiled floor. The third time she exploded, she took him with her, and he grunted his release.

Several hours later, Angie awoke to Ian's mouth and tongue between her legs. The man was insatiable, and apparently, so was she, as she came twice before he took her pussy again. He reluctantly agreed to let her go home after she told him she didn't want to spend the whole night with his niece sleeping down the hallway. After making her promise to text him when she got home safe, he allowed her to get dressed in the clothes and flip-flops Jenn had loaned her. In the meantime, he threw on a pair of sweatpants and a tee. She grabbed her other clothes, and he walked her to her car, still parked by the club, with Beau as

HIS ANGEL

an escort. The lot was empty since the club had closed about an hour earlier, and the guard had secured the exterior gate after everyone had left before heading home. Before Angie got into her car, Ian kissed her with a vow to call her in the afternoon and then walked over to open the gate for her. She drove home with a very satisfied smile and delicious aches throughout her body.

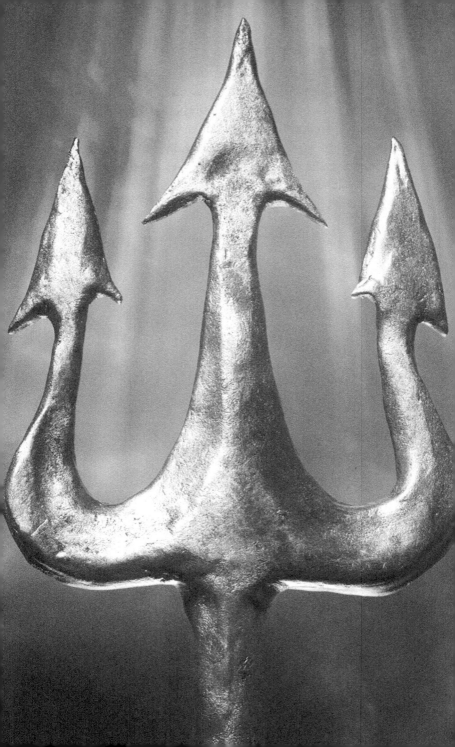

CHAPTER NINE

Angie stood naked in her bathroom as she aimed the hairdryer at her wet locks. It was Friday evening, and Ian was taking her to his club tonight. They'd seen each other twice during the week, but Trident meetings, interviews, and cases prevented them from having more than one whole night together alone. She hadn't seen him since very early Wednesday morning. They'd had some more phone sex, which was so hot she was surprised her local cell tower didn't explode. Now, she was dying to see him again.

Monday, Ian had invited her to join everyone at Devon and Kristen's as the team got together for Jenn to help her through the first anniversary of her parent's death. Pizza, beer, and soda served as a simple dinner while they played poker and watched a video of pictures of the young woman and her parents from before she was born through her late teens. The final photos of her folks were taken during their last Christmas together. Many of the photos included some or all of the Trident team members and other former SEALs who made up Jenn's extended family.

The men and their niece had entertained Kristen and Angie with countless funny stories of the team's antics over the years. Angie left the group a little after midnight when Ian and Brody needed to have a late-night video conference with a client who'd called them with an urgent request for assistance on some matter.

She'd spent Tuesday night in Ian's arms as they finally had his apartment all to themselves. They'd also gone through the contract and discussed her limits and his expectations. She was surprised none of his requests bothered her in any way. He would control her in the bedroom and push her boundaries within her green and yellow limits. He also had control over her well-being and safety, but she felt pampered and valued instead of disliking it because he cared enough to ensure no harm came to her. While the contract was not legally binding, it took out much of the relationship's guesswork. But most of all, it stressed she had the ultimate control of their relationship through her safeword and limit list.

He'd been in Miami since Wednesday but spoke to her by phone last night and asked if she wanted to go to The Covenant with him. Waiving the club's monthly membership fee, he'd expedited her required background check. She, in turn, had her medical release completed for him, so they were free to play at the club, and she jumped at the chance to go.

She'd been shocked when Brody had stopped by earlier in the day and given her a small black shopping bag with red trim. He told her Ian had picked out two outfits from the club store and to choose one to wear to the club for her first time. Winking and grinning before he walked away, Brody informed her, "My personal favorite is the pink and white one."

HIS ANGEL

He'd left her standing there with her mouth open. When she had recovered, he was long gone, and she raced into her bedroom to see what was in the bag. The first outfit —actually, they weren't "outfits," they were lingerie sets— was a dark green silk bra with matching short shorts. But it was the pale, pink baby-doll top and thong with white trim, which she chose to wear without a second thought. The material was sheer except for two small triangles—one over each breast.

Now, as she got dressed, she realized the hem stopped right at the bottom of her butt cheeks, and if she bent over, everyone would see her bare ass even though it was already exposed through the thin material. The top's silk triangles covered the nipples of her 38Ds but left little else to the imagination. She admired herself in the mirror, and instead of feeling slutty, she felt beautiful, sexy, and very, very naughty. Technically, it showed a little more than her bikini did during the summer, but she'd never worn a bathing suit with a thong.

After she threw on a little makeup and a pair of white sandals, which Brody had recommended since, at the club, she would be barefoot, she pulled on a knee-length black cotton dress. Tank-styled, it was lightweight, and she sometimes wore it as a cover-up for her bathing suit. Grabbing a thin wrap for the cooler evening air and her overnight bag, she left her apartment and drove to the compound, excited for Ian to see her in the outfit he'd picked.

He had told her to park outside his apartment, and as she pulled up, Ian stepped out of the building, and she almost drooled at the sight of him. Damn, the man was gorgeous. Tight, black leather pants covered his long, powerful legs, and an open black leather vest showcased his sculpted chest, abdomen, and arms. Add his black leather boots, and he looked like he walked off the set of a biker movie. If the rest of the cast looked like him, she'd be front row center at the theater on opening night.

He opened her car door and extended his hand to help her out. His gaze raked possessively and seductively over her body, and that's all it took for her to become aroused. After giving her a long, leisurely kiss hello, he took her keys, purse, and overnight bag and placed them inside his apartment door before returning to her.

He removed a white and black braided band from his pocket and clasped the leather collar around her neck, telling her she was to wear it whenever they were at the club. "I also don't want you at the club unless you're with me until you become more comfortable and familiar with the protocols." He paused. "Scratch that. I don't ever want you in the club without me."

She didn't mind because she wasn't sure she wanted to go there without him. For some reason, it seemed like she would be cheating on him if she did. "Yes, Sir."

They chatted as they walked across the compound and up into the club lobby. He introduced her to Matthew, a submissive on duty at the front desk, and Tiny, the massive, bald, black bouncer at the door. Despite his intimidating size, Tiny was a very sweet man and called all the women "Miss" along with their first names, which Angie found endearing. Ian told her the man was the head of security at the club and also did the occasional bodyguard job for Trident.

After Tiny opened one of the double doors, letting them step into the club, Ian instructed her to go through the other door, which led to the locker rooms, and leave her wrap, dress, and shoes in a locker. He handed her a simple lock to use and told her to return to him at the bar, pointing to where he intended to wait for her a few feet away. She went through the door and down the closest set of stairs with a sign indicating the ladies' locker room.

In addition to the lockers, there were the bathroom and shower areas and a little lounge and vanity area. A few women were already there, and two of them politely said hello to her as they walked out the door leading to the pit. One was wearing a black vinyl catsuit while the other was dressed in only a thong with pasties on her nipples, and Angie couldn't help her gaping stare at their retreating backs. Another woman about her age smiled at her and held out her hand in greeting. "Hi, I'm Shelby. You must be new here."

Angie grinned at the woman's bubbly personality and electric-blue straight hair, matching her bra and short skirt set. She shook Shelby's hand. "Hi, I'm Angie, and yes, tonight is my first night. I've never been in a club like this, so I'm a little nervous."

Shelby's eyes widened a little, and she laughed. "A newbie-newbie? Wow, are you in for a culture shock. I remember my first time about twelve years ago, and sometimes I'm still surprised I went back a second time after some of the things I saw. Who's your Master?" At Angie's confused look, she added, "Your collar means you're someone's sub."

So nervous and excited, Angie had forgotten she had it on. Fingering the soft leather, she said, "Oh, right. I'm here with Ian . . . I mean, Master Ian."

The other submissive got a starry-eyed look on her face. "Master Ian is such a dreamboat. In fact, his brother and the other guys at Trident are too. I think it's some sort of a requirement they have over there."

Even though Angie agreed, she had a sudden pang of jealousy, wondering if Ian and Shelby had ever hooked up together. Shaking it off, she told herself she had no right to inquire about his past lovers, even though she'd asked about the bitch, Heather, the night of the gala. He hadn't asked her about her past relationships, so she assumed they were both leaving their own personal baggage behind them. The point was, he was here with her, and he'd told her earlier in the week that while they were dating, he insisted they be exclusive. Ian didn't like to share, which worked out well because neither did Angie.

"Just remember," Shelby told her, "don't be rude or snarky to a Dom or Domme, and stay out of trouble. Those are the easiest ways to get a punishment." She giggled. "Unless it's what you're in the mood for. Remember your safeword, and if you're unsure of anything, tell Master Ian immediately. The Doms aren't mindreaders, so you must speak up if there's a problem or you're scared about something. And if Master Ian isn't next to you for some reason, and there's a problem, grab any of the Dungeon Masters— they're in gold vests—or a security officer in a red shirt and bow tie."

When Shelby left her alone after saying she would see her later, Angie picked out an empty locker. She felt a little better after talking to the friendly woman, but the butterflies in her stomach were still fluttering around. Before she lost her nerve, she threw her wrap and shoes into the small metal space and lifted her dress over her head, hanging it on the hook provided. Closing the locker, she put the small three-digit lock on it, then went to a full-length mirror to ensure her hair and makeup were still okay. Satisfied, she took a deep breath and headed for the stairs again, convincing herself she was ready for anything.

Ian was right where he said he'd be, talking to Devon, Kristen, and another man Angie didn't recognize. She was happy to see Kristen again and felt less nervous when she saw the other woman in a red lace teddy and panties. The others greeted her as she approached, but her gaze was on the appreciation she saw in Ian's face. It was obvious he was delighted with her choice of lingerie for the evening. He pulled her to his side and gave her a kiss that would've knocked her socks off if she'd been wearing any. When he finally let her up for air, he introduced her to the other man beside him. "Angie, this is Master Carl. Carl, be nice to my submissive. This is her first time in a club."

The older man appeared in his fifties and was slim and a little shorter than Ian. His graying black hair, goatee, black dress shirt, and leather pants almost gave him the look of a vampire, minus the fangs, but his smile put her at ease. "Ian, I do love the Sawyer brothers' taste in women. Angie, my dear, Master Ian knows how much I enjoy teasing new subs, but since he asked me not to, I will graciously welcome you to The Covenant. But if you're ever in the mood for a whipping, please come and see me."

Angie's eyes widened in astonishment, but she relaxed again when Ian growled while Devon and Kristen laughed. "That's what you call being nice?"

Ian faced her again. "Master Carl is a sadist, Angel, in addition to being a tease. He likes to make the subs nervous, but you have nothing to worry about because underneath, he's really a big softie."

Carl scoffed. "Oh, thanks, Ian. If you give away all my secrets, I won't have any fun."

The others laughed, and Angie heard another male

voice whisper into her ear from behind, "I'm glad to see you chose the white one, darlin'."

Brody. He looked sexy in a tight, black T-shirt, snug, worn jeans, and cowboy boots. The submissives of the club must fight over him all the time. For a computer geek, he was far from nerdy looking, with his broad shoulders and chiseled torso. And for some reason, he was the only one she felt a little embarrassed about standing in front of in her current state of undress. Maybe because, aside from the day she stood in their team meeting in her underwear, he'd seen her almost every day fully clothed.

As her cheeks turned tomato-red, Brody winked, gave her a quick peck on the cheek, and then did the same to Kristen. "Hey there, Ninja-girl. You're looking as sexy as ever."

Angie was grateful Ian had ordered her a glass of wine and took a beer for himself. She knew there was a drink limit if they were planning on playing, which he'd told her they were. He was carrying her membership card for her, and it was how the bartenders and security staff kept track of everyone's alcohol consumption. Access to the pit was denied if a member had more than two drinks.

The six of them chatted for a few minutes, and Angie began to relax even more, despite Ian's possessive hand resting on her right butt cheek under her baby-doll top, squeezing her bare flesh occasionally. She looked around the bar and balcony areas, eyeing people of every shape, size, age, and ethnicity. They were also all in varying states of dress, and she found it pretty easy to figure out whether a person was a Dominant or a submissive by looking at what they were wearing. It was very odd seeing a few naked subs walking around without a care, but she imagined it was less of a distraction than being at a nudist beach where everyone would be undressed.

A waitress dressed in a short, black skirt, red bra, and black bowtie approached the group and stopped beside Brody. She waited for him to stop talking, keeping her eyes cast downward the whole time. Brody finished what he was saying to Master Carl and turned to the patient submissive. "Yes, Cassandra. What can I do for you?"

"Good evening, Master Brody." The pretty brunette kept her gaze averted from the Dom's face. "Master Marco is a DM tonight by station four and requests you go see him when you have a moment."

He smiled and, using two fingers, tilted the woman's face up so she could see him. "Thank you, sweetheart. Find me if you're interested in doing a scene when your shift is over. Okay?"

Cassandra's face lit up. "Yes, Master Brody. I will. Thank you, Sir."

The submissive walked away, smiling, and Brody excused himself before heading toward the grand staircase. Master Carl left them a minute later, and Ian looked at Angie. "Ready to go downstairs?"

She took a deep breath and nodded. She'd made it this far, so what the hell. "Yes, Sir. I am."

"Good, because so am I." He had a smile on his face, the one that always got her nervous and wet at the same time, and her heart rate increased. He took her almost empty glass and left it on the bar with his own, explaining that only bottled water was allowed in the pit so the submissives walking around barefoot didn't have to worry about broken glass.

Taking her hand, he led her to the stairs and gave her

membership card to the security guard standing at the top. The man scanned it and then Kristen's before handing them back to the two Doms. Ian escorted her down the stairs, followed by Devon and Kristen. They were about to break away from the other couple when a much younger Dom approached them and requested a moment to talk to Ian and Devon in private. Ian had mentioned earlier his cousin, Mitch, who managed the club, was home with the flu for a few days, so Ian or Devon might need to take care of a few things in his place. "Kristen, would you mind showing Angie the submissive waiting area? This will take a few minutes."

Kristen looked at her Dom for permission, and he nodded. "Yes, Sir. Come on, Angie. I'll introduce you to some of the other subs."

Before Kristen had a chance to lead her away, Ian gave Angie a quick kiss. "Stay there until I come for you. A DM is standing nearby if there are any problems, which there shouldn't be. Okay?"

"Yes, Sir."

She was glad he took the time to ensure she was comfortable leaving him because it made her feel safe. Kristen brought her to a sitting area halfway between the stairs and the stage, where several other submissives were sitting and talking. One of them was Shelby, who jumped up and hugged Kristen. Her friend explained that Shelby was one of her Beta-readers and had arranged for her to tour the club with Master Mitch. During the fateful tour the author found out her date for that night—Devon—was part owner of the place.

The two women introduced her to four other submissives, two males and two females. They all took seats on the couches, ottomans, and winged-back chairs and began to

HIS ANGEL

fill in the club's newest member on all the gossip. Suddenly, one of the male subs, also a newer member, gasped. "Who is *that* talking to Masters Devon and Ian? He's absolutely scrumptious."

Everyone looked toward the stairs to see the younger Dom had stepped away from the two men, and they now stood talking to an older Chris Hemsworth look-a-like. Even from where the subs sat, they could see his stunning blue eyes, and with his shoulder length, dark blonde hair, and chiseled face, the man was an utter hunk. If any submissive met the six-foot-four man outside a sex club, they would immediately recognize his status as a Dom. He carried himself in a commanding, mysterious manner, and Angie guessed the man was popular with the subs unless he had one of his own. Dressed in brown leather pants, boots, and a tan T-shirt, which hugged his muscular torso and arms, the man was swoon-worthy.

It was Shelby who clued everyone in after letting out a dramatic sigh. "*That* is Master Carter. He's such a dreamboat."

Angie almost chuckled because it seemed as if Shelby thought most good-looking men were "dreamboats," but Kristen's sharp inhalation caught her attention. She looked at her new friend to see the woman had her mouth open and was staring wide-eyed at the three men. "*That's* Master Carter? Holy crap!"

Shelby looked incredulous. "Haven't you met him yet, Kristen? Oh, that's right—I don't think he's been here for about six months, so I guess it makes sense."

"I've, uh, met him, sort of, but I didn't know what he looked like." Kristen's gaze stayed pinned on the men, and her answer had the other submissives eyeing her curiously.

Looking back at the male trio, Angie was about to ask

her what she was talking about when she noticed Masters Devon and Carter were smiling broadly while staring at Kristen. She thought there might be a story behind the men's gazes, but Angie wasn't sure what it was. Master Carter suddenly winked at Kristen as Master Devon crooked his finger at his fiancée in command for her to come to him. Kristen stood but seemed to remember she was watching Angie for Ian and paused. Shelby eased her concern. "I'll take care of Angie. Go before you earn a spanking, although I'll trade places with you if you want."

Shelby giggled when Kristen didn't answer her and rushed to her Dom's side, blushing furiously when Master Carter took her hand and kissed it. Angie now knew there was a story between the three and vowed to ask her friend about it if she saw her later. She was so wrapped up in what was going on with the trio that she didn't realize Ian had approached her until he stood in front of her, blocking the view of the rest of the vast room. He greeted the other subs by name as he held out his hand for her to take and helped her stand. "Come along, Angel. We'll walk around for a bit, and you can observe some of the scenes. Then maybe we can have one of our own."

Angie felt warm, wet heat between her legs as she wondered what Ian would do for her first public scene. Although they'd reviewed her limit list, he hadn't decided what would happen tonight, telling her he wanted to see her reactions first.

Ian started her tour at a spanking bench since she'd already gotten a taste of it earlier in the week. In addition to bare-handed spanking, she was able to see a flogging, a paddling, and a cropping. Moving on to other areas, they observed a male submissive shackled to the wall wearing nipple clamps, a substantial vibrating anal plug, and a cock ring. His Domme was sucking on her sub's cock yet denying the man an orgasm as punishment for an unknown infraction, and Angie almost felt sorry for the guy.

A scene involving a violet wand caught Angie's attention, and after seeing it to the end, she asked Ian if she could modify her limit list. She hadn't known what electric play entailed, and so she'd placed it in her hard-limit column, but now she wanted to try it sometime. He told her he was pleased she kept an open mind and was willing to grow with her new knowledge.

They stopped at a station that was larger than the others because it was used for bullwhip scenes, giving the Doms the room they needed for a longer whip. Currently, Master Jake was whipping a female sub while a male knelt nearby on the floor, awaiting his turn. Ian explained that Jake had mastered the bullwhip over many years and was often asked by unattached subs to perform whipping scenes with them. Other Doms would also request that Jake service their subs when they didn't have the expertise to do it themselves.

Mistress China and Master Carl were also in high demand as Whip Masters, and the three tended to alternate Thursday, Friday, and Saturday nights between them to give the others a chance to have nights off. Each session with a sub was, on average, about fifteen minutes, and with several sessions scheduled per night, swinging a bullwhip for almost two hours straight was a strain on the upper arms and back.

The naked sub strapped to the St. Andrew's cross was slipping into subspace, and Jake slowed his strikes, but the crack of the whip still could be heard over the club music.

Her back, buttocks, and upper thighs were covered in red slash marks, but none of the strikes had broken her skin. Without warning, the moaning woman's knees gave out, and Jake dropped the whip, rushing over to help her Dom release the woman from the restraints. Her Dom wrapped her in a blanket, picked her up in his arms, and carried her to a nearby chaise lounge, followed by the Whip Master.

Laying her down gently on her stomach, the man pushed her hair away from her face and said something in her ear, making her nod, although her eyes never opened. Jake monitored the exchange from beside them until he was satisfied the submissive was okay. Leaving her to her Dom's aftercare, he strode back to the station where the waiting sub was wiping down the cross with a citrus-scented cleanser so he could take his turn.

Angie watched Jake run a towel across his sweaty face and wondered why he didn't remove his soaking wet T-shirt since she was sure he would be more comfortable. He had a muscular body, and she didn't doubt he would make the subs drool if he went shirtless.

"He has some scars on his back, which he doesn't let most people see," Ian explained. "They aren't as bad as he seems to think, but he's still self-conscious about them."

She didn't realize she'd voiced her thoughts aloud. "Did he get them in combat like you did?"

Ian shook his head as another Dom and his male submissive approached to speak with him. "No, sweetheart, he got them when he was younger, and it's his tale to tell you if he chooses. Excuse me for a minute."

He pivoted and began to talk to the other two men while Angie watched Jake restrain the male submissive, who'd stripped his clothes off and stood there naked.

While the Dom started with a light flogging as a warm-

HIS ANGEL

up, Angie scanned the areas around her. Nearby, she saw a man talking to Shelby, but it was obvious the woman didn't want anything to do with him. The blue-haired sub was about to walk away from him when the man reared back and, much to Angie's horror, backhanded her across the face.

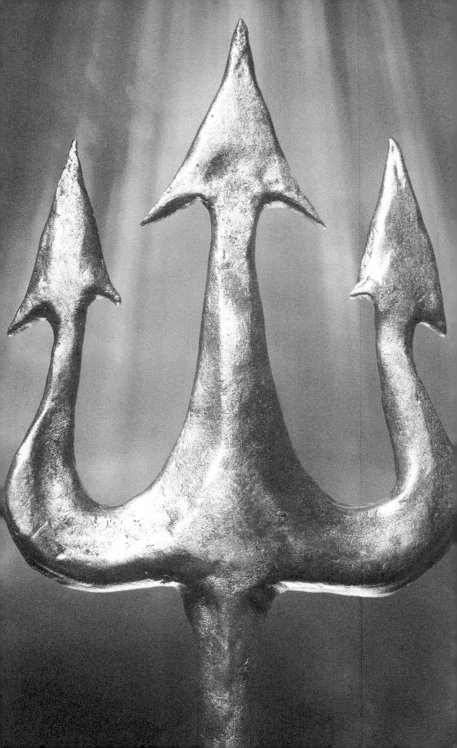

CHAPTER TEN

Ian was talking to a D/s couple when several things happened almost at once behind him. First, he heard a female cry out in pain, but it wasn't a typical cry he heard throughout the club regularly. A second later, he heard Angie scream his name and others shout. In the mere seconds it took him to turn around and locate the problem, Angie was gone from his side.

Panic seized him as he ran to where a crowd had gathered near the submissive waiting area. Pushing his way through, he took in the sight before him. Marco, in his Dungeon Master gold vest, had some guy face down on the floor, his eyes glaring with anger. One arm was yanked up the man's back in a hold he couldn't get out of, even though he was yelling and trying his best to shake the DM loose.

Angie and Mistress China knelt on the floor, comforting Shelby, who had tears coming from her shocked eyes and was holding a trembling hand to her face. From the look on Mistress China's face, the guy being detained was lucky Marco had gotten to him first. The diminutive Asian-American woman took great pleasure in giving pain to submissives, and at the moment, she looked ready to unleash her fury. Ian didn't recognize the man but spotted the yellow band on the guy's wrist, indicating he was the guest of a member, just as Master Parker pushed through the crowd.

Parker Christiansen was a longtime member whose construction company had done most of the renovations throughout the compound and was a well-liked and respected Dom. Right then, though, he looked confused and pissed as he addressed the guy Marco had pinned. "What the fuck, Dave? What the hell did you do?"

"I didn't do anything. Now get this fucking gorilla off me. I'm going to sue if he doesn't get off me." Whoever Dave was, he was the complete opposite of Parker. Whereas Parker was a confident Dom, this guy came off as a whiny jackass.

Marco growled but wouldn't let the man up. Instead, he glowered at Parker and Ian. "This asshole backhanded Shelby. I had people in my way and couldn't get here fast enough to stop him."

Ian was pissed, but Parker was beyond livid. He glanced at the crying submissive, and it appeared he would explode. His jaw clenched. "He's my brother. Let him up, Marco."

Marco stared at Parker and then at Ian. Tiny and several other security guards had pushed the crowd back to give the Doms some room. Ian stood with his arms crossed and studied Parker's face. What he saw had him nodding once to Marco, who released Dave and got to his feet after giving the guy a final shove in the back.

As Dave stood, he was stupid enough to say, "What's the big deal? Everyone slaps women around here, and I get in trouble for what y'all are doing."

HIS ANGEL

Dave brushed himself off, and Parker took a step closer to him, his voice low and barely controlled. "You okay?"

Not seeing the fury on Parker's face, the guy grinned. "Yeah, Park, I'm fine."

"Good." The Dom nodded once, then punched his brother in the face, knocking the bastard out. Without giving the prone man another glance, Parker hurried over to Shelby and crouched in front of her. "I'm so sorry, Shelby. It's my fault. I shouldn't have left him alone."

He helped her stand, but Mistress China and Angie stayed by her side for support. Parker gently pulled Shelby's hand from her cheek and growled, "I'm going to kill him," when he saw the red and swollen area, which was starting to bruise.

She grabbed his forearm, her eyes wide. "No, don't, Sir. I should have grabbed Master Marco or one of the other DMs. He was trying to negotiate with me. I saw his guest wristband and knew he wasn't allowed to play, but he wouldn't take no for an answer. When I tried to walk away, he hit me."

Parker drew the sub into his arms and held her briefly while everyone else looked on. Ian cocked his head at Tiny, who began breaking up the crowd with the other guards. The head Dom then spoke to Parker. "Let's take this to the office. What do you want us to do with him?"

Parker didn't answer Ian right away, obviously too worried about Shelby. "Go to the ladies' lounge and put some ice on your cheek. When I'm done with Ian and my asshole brother, I'll take you home."

The man's lack of using Ian's Master title in front of a sub told the Head Dom how shaken the other man was.

"You . . . you don't have to do that, I can drive myself." Shelby's face flushed, and she wouldn't look at Parker. She seemed almost shy about being in the Dom's arms, and Ian found it interesting since the pretty sub was such an outgoing person.

"I need to do this, Shelby, please. I need to make sure you're okay and get home safe. This is not negotiable." He tipped her chin up with his fingers and made her look at him. "Please."

She bit her lip but nodded her consent. Mistress China wrapped her arm around the sub's shoulder and eased her from Parker's arms. Despite being sadistic sometimes, the Domme tended to be a mother hen to the submissives. "I'll take care of her. We'll be in the lounge when you're ready."

Parker nodded his thanks to her while Ian spoke to Angie. "I'm sorry, but I have to take care of this. Please go with them and wait for me in the lounge. I'll be a few minutes."

"Yes, Sir."

He was surprised at the fierce look she threw at the still-unconscious Dave. He almost expected her to kick the guy as she followed the other two women. Marco also went with them after asking another DM to cover his station. Ian could see his teammate was upset for not being able to stop the assault before it happened. He could be a big marshmallow when it came to the submissives and was the one they tended to go to if they needed someone to talk to or some comfort.

Ian asked one of the nearby waitresses to bring an icepack to Shelby before turning to Parker, who still seemed like he wanted to commit familial homicide. The other Dom handed his keys to Tiny and asked him to not-so-gently throw his brother in the backseat of his truck so he could drive him back to the guy's motel.

He then faced Ian with an expression of regret. "Let's

HIS ANGEL

get this over with."

A few minutes later, Parker was pacing behind the closed door of Mitch's office as Ian sat against the front of the desk and watched him. "Fuck! I'm so sorry, Ian. I was only gone two minutes to take a fucking piss. I told him not to move from where we were sitting. He fucking knew he wasn't allowed to play or approach any subs.

"The only reason I brought him here is that he called me a few weeks ago and said he wanted to see the place while he was in town on business. Said he and his wife were thinking about joining a club in Boston. I knew I shouldn't have brought him here. He doesn't understand the lifestyle the way I do. I know he's cheated on his wife before, but I didn't think he was stupid enough to try something here. Fuck! I'm going to kill him."

Ian let him rant for another minute before the irate man finally took a deep breath and glanced at him. "I broke the rules. Do what you have to do." He plopped down into one of the chairs and hung his head in defeat.

Ian felt sympathy for the Dom. On top of being a nice guy, he was also one of the club's Dungeon Masters, and the last thing he wanted was for someone to be hurt because of his actions, especially a submissive. But the rules had to be enforced. "I'm sorry I have to do this, but you know you're not supposed to leave a guest alone for this exact reason. You should have asked a DM or guard to watch him for the time you needed to leave him alone."

The other man nodded but didn't say anything.

"I have to suspend your play privileges for the next twelve weeks. During that time, you'll take three DM shifts per week. I'll check the schedule and coordinate the dates and times with you tomorrow. Your guest privileges will also be suspended for two years."

Parker snorted. "Don't worry. I think this is the last time I'll bring anyone here whether they're in the lifestyle or not." He ran his hand down his face as he stood again. "I'll be back for Shelby in a few minutes. Dave's motel is about five minutes from here. I'll dump him into his room and come back. I'd call one if I thought a cab would pick up the unconscious asshole. But since Shelby's being cared for by China and Marco, I'll get rid of him first."

Ian nodded and followed him out of the office. Parker continued to the lobby at the main double doors while Ian took the door and stairs leading into the women's locker room. He found the three women and Marco sitting in the lounging area, with Shelby sitting on the Dom's lap as he cradled her, murmuring into her ear.

When she spotted Ian, she jumped up and latched onto his arm with a pleading expression. "Master Ian! Please don't discipline Master Parker. It wasn't his fault. I don't want him to get into trouble. Please don't kick him out of the club. It's all my fault. I should've walked away sooner."

Marco and Mistress China both growled at her inappropriate guilt, and Ian grabbed the near-hysterical submissive by her shoulders and guided her to sit in an empty chair. This wasn't like her—Ian had never seen the bubbly submissive upset before. "Calm down, Shelby."

His order was given in a commanding tone, instantly quieting the woman as he intended. "Master Parker knows he broke the rules, and there are consequences for what happened. None of which were your fault, and I don't want to hear those words out of your mouth again. Understand?"

"Yes, Sir. But—"

"No buts, Shelby." He didn't make a habit of discussing a member's discipline with others, but he needed to reassure the worried sub. "I didn't revoke Master Parker's

HIS ANGEL

membership, but he did receive a suspension for his irresponsible actions. He accepted full blame for what happened and agreed with the punishment. Now, he'll be back in a few minutes to take you home, so why don't you grab your things from your locker and change? Okay?"

Still crying softly, she stood and mumbled, "Yes, Sir."

Ian pulled her into his arms and hugged her. "It'll be okay, little one. I promise. I think the best thing you can do is dry your eyes, and when Master Parker comes back, give him some of your sass we all love so much and let him take care of you. I think it'll make both of you feel better, *hmm*?"

She pulled back and gave him a watery smile. "Yes, Sir. Thank you."

Marco took her arm and hugged her briefly, kissing her on the top of her blue-haired head. "Sweetheart, I'm sorry I wasn't there when you needed me."

"It's okay, Master Marco. You got there as fast as you could."

He squeezed her again and let her go to her locker before turning to Angie, sitting quietly on the couch beside Mistress China. His steel gray eyes bore into her. "And you, little subbie, have some explaining to do to your Master."

What? As Ian's expression became stern, Angie's brow furrowed in confusion. "What did you do, Angel?"

"I-I didn't do anything."

She looked back and forth between the two Doms as if unsure what Marco was referring to. Mistress China, in her black, full-length bodysuit and over-the-thigh boots, grinned and sat back to enjoy the show.

Marco shook his head and told Ian, "Your little sub tried to get to the jackass before I did. She was ready to jump on his back and start pounding on him. I almost tackled her by accident, trying to take him down."

151

Ian's eyes narrowed at her as the Domme next to her sing-songed, "Somebody's in trouble."

Ignoring the other woman, he stepped forward to his very worried-looking submissive. "Is that true, Angel?"

"I-I just reacted. I saw him hit Shelby and I . . ." Her words trail off. Ian knew the moment she figured out there was nothing she could say to get her out of the mess she found herself in. She swung her gaze to the floor. "I'm sorry, Sir."

With his hands on his hips, Ian tilted his head back and talked to the ceiling momentarily. "Lord, save me from subs who want to beat up people in my club and put themselves in danger."

Marco snorted, knowing Ian was referring to his future sister-in-law's own fight in the locker room several months earlier, which earned her the call sign "Ninja-girl" from the rest of the team. The big difference between the two incidents was Kristen had been taller and about twenty pounds heavier than Heather and another sub named Michelle and had taken self-defense classes. Parker's brother outweighed Angie by a good eighty pounds and had already hit another woman.

Ian's gaze returned to Angie's face. "You may be sorry now, but you'll be extremely sorry after I spank your pretty ass for putting yourself in danger." He ignored her surprised gasp. "We have DM's and guards for a reason in the club, Angel. We do not need little subs disregarding their own safety. You didn't know him—he's a hell of a lot bigger than you, and he could have hurt you before anyone could do anything."

"You're right, Sir." She let out a heavy sigh and nodded. "I don't know what I was thinking. I couldn't believe he'd

HIS ANGEL

hit Shelby, and my first instinct was to attack him before he struck her again."

Her agreement didn't change Ian's mind about her punishment as he eyed Marco. "Would you please find a free spanking station and ask someone to grab my bag from behind the bar?"

The other Dom nodded and said to Angie before he left the room, "I'm sorry, little one, but you earned it."

She watched him walk away with her mouth wide open, then looked up at Ian with apprehension evident on her face. "I-I'm sorry. I didn't mean . . ."

Ian's expression tempered when she paused, and he released a deep, slow breath. He squatted in front of her and took her hands in his. "I'm not angry, sweetheart. I heard you yell and turned around and didn't see you. I panicked. My stomach dropped, and I was terrified something happened to you. And because you acted with no regard for your own safety, you've earned your first public spanking." His stare never wavered as he let her process what he'd said.

Mistress China stood, and Ian had almost forgotten the other woman was in the room. She patted his shoulder and smirked. "I'm going to go and get a front-row seat. It's been a long time since I've witnessed a sub's first punishment."

He kept his eyes on Angie as the Domme left the room. He could tell she had myriad emotions running through her mind, from shock, embarrassment, and worry to anticipation, excitement, and need. The thought of a public spanking turned her on despite it being a punishment, and she wasn't sure what to make of it.

He let her think about her upcoming ass-whooping as Shelby returned to the sitting area in sweats, a tee, and high-top sneakers. She'd removed her blue wig, and her short spiked blonde hair looked like she'd run her hands through it. He got up from his crouched position and handed her the icepack as the door reopened. Parker strode into the lounge, his eyes seeking out the injured submissive. The men rarely came into the ladies' locker room, but it didn't faze anyone when they did. It wasn't as if they hadn't seen most of the women naked at one time or another.

After telling Ian he would call tomorrow to get the DM schedule, Parker tucked Shelby under one arm and escorted her out of the club. Ian knew the sub was in good hands and wondered if there might be a budding romance between the two. He wouldn't be surprised by how they'd looked at each other when Parker first walked into the room. Turning his attention to his own submissive, he took her by the hand and led her back into the pit, finding the spanking bench Marco had reserved for him. He might have enjoyed her nervousness if he still hadn't been shaking off the fear he'd felt when he'd heard her screech his name earlier. But this punishment was for his need to reinforce his rule that her safety and well-being came before anything else and be a reminder for her not to jump into a dangerous situation in the future.

The word had spread that a submissive was receiving her first-ever BDSM punishment, and Doms and subs surrounded the area around the spanking bench. It was a rite of passage for every new sub, and he knew it would set the tone for her future involvement in the lifestyle. After her spanking, he intended to reward her for pushing her own limits and accepting the consequences of her reckless actions. The crowd made her more nervous, so he spun her until she faced the bench and her back was to the still-growing throng of people. He gripped her chin and made

HIS ANGEL

sure she was focused on him. "I want you to say your safeword nice and loud so everyone hears it and knows what it is."

It wasn't necessary for the crowd's sake, but she needed to remember she had all the control despite the fact her ass was about to get a pounding.

She swallowed hard. "My . . ." She cleared her throat and tried again. "My safeword is red, Sir."

"Your punishment will be fifteen spanks with a paddle on your bare ass, Angel. Do you wish to use your safeword or accept your punishment?"

Her gaze went from his to the bench and back again several times before it finally settled on him again. She took a deep but trembling breath. "I will take my punishment, Sir."

"And what are you being punished for?"

"F-for putting myself in danger, Sir."

He smiled, and his gaze softened. "Good girl."

He retook Angie's hand and led her to the kneeling side of the bench. It looked like a modified sawhorse with padding for her knees, torso, and arms. He helped her get on it, with her knees bent and her waist lying over the center. The position angled her head down and brought her ass up, making it the prime target.

She handled having her wrists and ankles shackled very well but began hyperventilating when he brought the Velcro strap across her lower back, which would hold her in place. Her response was normal for an inexperienced sub, and Marco, who'd been standing inside the roped-off area in case he was needed, crouched down in front of her. He ran his hand over her head in an attempt to calm her. "Easy, little one. Take deep, slow breaths with me. Keep your eyes on mine."

While Ian's hands moved in a soothing caress over her back, hips, and buttocks, his teammate continued calming her down with praise and encouragement. Ian let the man do what he did best—comfort a sub. It was one of Marco's greatest pleasures about the lifestyle. He liked being needed and was damn good at it.

Angie's breathing slowed to a more normal pace, but her heart rate was still pounding, which had to be expected. When Marco asked her to repeat her safeword, she responded, "R-red, Sir."

"And what punishment will your Master give you, little one?"

She swallowed hard again, but her fear seemed to ease as her arousal grew. "Fifteen spanks with a paddle, Sir."

Marco smiled and continued to caress her head and cheek. "Good girl. Are you ready now? Do you want me to step back or stay here with you?"

Angie was clearly surprised by the man's offer, and Ian was pleased with her answer. "Please stay, Sir. I'm ready."

Also satisfied with her response, Marco knelt before her and gave Ian a nod to continue. Her Dom began to rub and squeeze her ass cheeks with more pressure. Bringing the blood to the skin's surface would make impacts easier on her. He had no intention of bruising her, but her ass would be a lovely shade of red by the time he was done. Her discomfort would be gone entirely within twenty-four hours, but she'd definitely feel and remember its cause before it was.

He eased her thong down from her hips to the middle of her thighs and left it there. It hadn't been in his way, but it would make her feel more exposed. He was thrilled to feel the fabric of the crotch drenched with her juices. As anxious as she was, she wanted this more than she feared it, even

HIS ANGEL

though she knew this would be different than the simple bare-handed spanking he'd given her the other night. That had been a play spanking, and this most certainly was not.

Stepping over to where Marco had placed his toy bag, Ian retrieved the wooden paddle he'd planned to use for her first punishment spanking. It resembled one from a ping-pong set, yet it was a little larger and not covered in rubber. The size would allow him to spread out the strikes on her buttocks instead of hitting the same spot over and over, which is what would happen if he used a larger implement. He also grabbed an anal plug, lube, and a small flogger, which he would start with. The plug would give her something else to focus on, something he usually didn't use for a discipline spanking. If this had been a pleasure spanking, he would also consider placing a vibrating bullet inside her pussy, but he didn't want her too distracted. After all, it was a punishment.

The purpose of light flogging before a spanking was to help the submissive relax a little more and release the body's endorphins. Sometimes a Dom would bypass a warm-up if the spanking was for punishment, but for Angie's first time, he wanted to make it bearable so she wouldn't fear future spankings. If everything went as he expected, by the time Ian finished meting out her discipline, she would be moments away from an intense orgasm despite her flaming backside.

He stepped over to where Marco remained in front of her and waited for her to raise her eyes to his. "I'm going to put an anal plug in you, Angel. It's a little bigger than you've used in the past, but not by much. Next, I'll start off with a light flogging. It won't be painful, more like a hard caress. After I've warmed your sweet ass up, I'll move to the punishment phase. If you need me to slow down at any point, say the word 'yellow,' and if you cannot take the paddle, say your safeword 'red.' And remember, sweetheart, as the submissive, you have the ultimate power here."

Her cheeks heated as he spoke. He knew part of her wanted to take the easy out he offered her. But another part of her wanted to satisfy the cravings and needs that had probably been churning through her body since he told her of the spanking he was about to give her. She went with the latter, showing that she trusted him with her body. "I remember, Sir. I'm ready."

Ian kissed the top of her head and then stood behind her, trailing his hand lightly down her back to her ass as he went. A strong shiver went through her body and into his, shooting straight to his groin. He placed the flogger and paddle on the bench between her knees, which were spread wide. Her bare pussy glistened, and he couldn't wait to see it dripping.

Opening the bottle, he poured lubricant into the crevice of her ass and on the plug. Her little rosette clenched and then relaxed as he rubbed the toy's tip up and down between her butt cheeks. As he pressed down on her puckered hole, it gave way to the invasion, and he heard her groan and beg for more. More than happy to give it to her, he eased the plug in and out of her, a little deeper each time, until the flared portion spread her the widest. Ian paused briefly before giving it the final push it needed and watched as her rim closed around the notch, holding it in place. His cock hardened painfully as he imagined replacing the plug with it and fucking her tight hole until neither of them could walk. *Soon.*

Grabbing the flogger, he stepped backward and took the proper stance before flicking it toward her. The first gentle strike of the soft, supple leather strands landed on her outer thigh. Although she flinched from the sudden impact, he knew it hadn't hurt. He aimed more strikes to her other outer thigh and several down her back and ass cheeks. As he watched the tension ease from her body, he sped up, giving a little more oomph to the strikes. The following two landed on her inner thighs, and he saw her strain to bring her body closer to him, not further away. She was surrendering to him and begging for more. He placed two more again on her inner thighs and then flicked his wrist, watching as the small knots at the end of each strand struck her on her pussy. Angie gasped, then moaned even louder. It was music to a Dom's ears.

He began another cycle, starting with her outer thighs and ending with a singular assault on her pussy and clit. This time, a pleading cry escaped her lips, and he stepped toward her. Caressing her ass, he leaned down to speak into her ear. "Are you okay, Angel? Give me a color."

Angie was panting, and he knew she was ready to beg for the orgasm, which was just beyond her reach. Knowing there was a crowd of people staring at her exposed buttocks and pussy was turning her on even more. "Green, Sir. I'm good."

Ian smiled and squeezed her ass cheek. "Yes, you are, Angel. Very good. I'm going to move to the paddle now. Try to stay relaxed."

* * *

Relaxed? Was he serious?

How the hell was she supposed to relax? Taking a deep breath and exhaling, Angie focused on the beat of the pulsating music, Marco's tender words and touches, Ian's caresses of her lower back, ass, and thighs, and the plug in her back hole.

By the time she heard the crack of wood against flesh

followed by the sudden sting, she'd been taken off guard. The first strike landed on her right ass cheek. Expecting one immediately behind it on her other cheek, she was surprised to feel Ian's hand rub the spot he'd hit. But as she began to ease into the caress, a strike landed on her left cheek. Again, he rubbed the spot, and despite the pain, she couldn't help but think it wasn't so bad. She was wrong.

Ian began to spank her with the paddle repeatedly, with only a momentary pause between them. Each hit landed on a different place on her cheeks and sit spots above where her thighs and ass met. And each was harder than the last. She lost count as her ass began to burn.

Oh God, how many was he giving her?

Fifteen hadn't seemed so bad when he'd said the number, but she was so lost in the mixed sensations of pain, pleasure, want, and need that it felt like he'd given her dozens of them. She was panting and straining against the straps which held her in place. Marco was still with her, observing her responses and murmuring words of reassurance.

Despite the onslaught of pain, she didn't say either of her safewords. Her ass was on fire, the heat spreading throughout her body, and all she wanted to do was beg Ian to fuck her. She hadn't known she was crying until she noticed the spanks had stopped, and Marco thumbed away the tears on her cheeks.

Ian's face appeared next to the other Dom's. "That's eleven, Angel. The last four will be the hardest, and then I'll let you come if you want. Give me a color."

"Green! Please, Sir! Don't stop! Please let me come!" She screamed the words so loudly that the members upstairs in the bar area had to have heard her over the music and distance. She was so wrapped up in her arousal and need

HIS ANGEL

that she didn't know most of the crowd chuckled appreciatively at her response. They also praised the new sub's commitment to seeing her punishment through to the end.

Ian smiled at his angel. "It'll be my pleasure, sweetheart."

* * *

Returning to his former position, he took the correct stance to paddle right atop the crack of her ass, where the end of the anal plug sat flush between her cheeks. Rearing back, he hit the same spot four times, the sound of wood against flesh resonating through the air.

Smack. Smack. Smack. Smack.

Ian dropped the paddle and thrust two fingers straight into her soaking wet pussy. That was all it took to send her screaming over the edge of release. Rubbing her clit with his thumb, he prolonged her orgasm for as long as he could until her entire body sagged with relief.

The crowd applauded the exhausted sub as Ian withdrew his hand from between her trembling legs. Her ass was bright red, and her juices coated her thighs. The two Doms worked quickly to release her restraints and rubbed each limb to ensure her blood was circulating. Marco stood, grabbed a red blanket from a nearby shelf, and handed it to Ian. "I'll take care of your stuff for you."

Ian nodded before wrapping his sub in the blanket and carrying her to an oversized leather winged-back chair. He sat with her on his lap and let her ass hang over the side of his thigh so she wasn't too uncomfortable. After she took a few sips of water from the bottle someone had handed him, she cuddled into his chest as his strong arms held her. His heart squeezed when she looked up at him through swollen, wet eyes and sighed. "Thank you, Master."

CHAPTER ELEVEN

Four days later, Angie was at home and working on the cover for a new novel from Red Rose Books. The publishers had received the final drafts for Kristen's novel, and her editor, Jillian, called Angie with high praise from her employers. They loved it and asked her to design the cover of another anticipated book from a different author. While she worked, she talked on her cell phone with her friend Mandy, who had called her all excited about a new guy she'd met.

Angie had just finished centering the title where she wanted it when her doorbell rang a little before two in the afternoon. Figuring it was her UPS man dropping off some new work for her, she clicked the save icon on her laptop and ended her call with Mandy.

Leaving her phone next to her computer, she got up to answer the door. Looking out the oblong side window, she frowned when she saw two men dressed in off-the-rack suits. One man spotted her and held up a wallet-sized folder containing a badge and an ID that read "United States Drug Enforcement Administration" in gold letters.

SAMANTHA COLE

Panic assailed her. The only reason someone from the DEA would be ringing her doorbell was if something happened to Jimmy. She punched the security code into the alarm panel and unlocked the doorknob and deadbolt before throwing open the door. "What happened? Where's Jimmy? Is he hurt?"

The shorter of the two men, who'd shown her his ID through the window, spoke in a calm but commanding voice. "Are you Ms. Angelina Beckett? May we come in to talk to you for a minute?"

"Yes, yes, please." She stepped back to allow them to walk into her home even though a warning bell sounded in her brain. Ignoring it, she shut the door before spinning around to face them. "Please tell me what happened."

The two agents walked into her living room while looking around. They seemed satisfied with what they did or did not see, and again, the shorter one spoke. "Ms. Beckett, I'm Agent Jackson, and this is Agent Holstein with the Atlanta office of the DEA." The taller man with a stern face gave her a curt nod but remained mute. "We've been instructed to take you into protective custody."

"Protective custody? Why? Who told you to do that?" The alarms in her brain were getting louder by the second.

"Agent Athos, otherwise known as Agent Austin, is worried about your safety. He thinks his cover has been blown, and as I said, he wants us to take you into protective custody and bring you to one of the DEA's safe houses."

The warnings were now screaming at her. "Is that all he said?"

Both agents' eyes narrowed in confusion. The taller one seemed to be getting impatient, but it was still the shorter one who spoke. "Isn't that enough?"

Shit! She never should have let them in the house. Now,

HIS ANGEL

she had to think of a way to get out of there in one piece. "Um, yes. I mean, I thought maybe there was a specific threat or something."

Angie jumped at the sound of a loud knock at her sliding glass door and glanced over to see who it was.

Oh, thank God.

Brody stood on her patio, curiosity and a bit of concern in his eyes as he eyed the two men in her living room and then her. He motioned for her to unlock the door, and she dashed toward it as Agent Jackson spat out, "Who the hell is that?"

She saw the man reach for his holstered gun out of the corner of her eye but was relieved when he didn't draw the weapon. Somehow, she had to warn Brody something was terribly wrong.

As she opened the slider, she responded, hoping he would catch on fast to her dilemma. "Oh, this is my boyfriend, Brody. We've only been dating for a few weeks. Brody, these men are from the DEA. This is Agent Jackson, and I'm sorry I forgot your name."

The taller man spoke for the first time. "Agent Holstein, and I'm sorry, Ms. Beckett, but we must get going. The sooner we get you to the safe house, the better."

Brody had clearly caught on because his arm went around her waist and pulled her closer to his side. Although he acted calm and convincingly confused, she felt the tension rolling off him. She prayed he was good at the bodyguard thing he did for a living. When he spoke, he thickened his Texas drawl. "DEA agents? Safe house? Darlin', what're these men all talkin' about?"

She played along, hoping they would get out of there alive. "I'm sorry, honey. I know we had plans for this weekend, but do you remember my best friend, Jimmy, who I

165

told you about?" He was still eyeing the other men but nodded, so she continued. "Well, I didn't tell you that Jimmy is with the DEA and does undercover work for them. They think his cover may be blown, and I might be a target, so they need to take me into protective custody."

"Really? Like in the movies?" Good Lord, the man could act "aw-shucks" dumb when needed. And she was positive it was an act. "Well, if y'all have to keep my baby safe . . . can I go with her?"

It was Jackson who answered while his partner glowered at the new arrival. "I'm afraid not, sir. I promise we'll take good care of her for you. She'll only be gone a few days, a week at the most, until we can ascertain she's in no danger."

Brody shrugged his shoulders as if this entire scenario was no big deal. "All right, if you think it's best. Darlin', why don't I help you throw a few clothes in a bag, and I'll say goodbye to you in private."

"We don't have time for that. Once you're safe, we can get you some clothes and anything else you need."

Plastering on a fake pleading smile, Angie jumped at the opportunity to distance them from the two agents, if that was even who they were. All she knew was Jimmy hadn't sent them, nor did his handler. "Oh, please. It'll only take a few moments to throw a few things into my duffel bag. I'd feel more comfortable with my own stuff. And I really want a minute to say goodbye to Brody. We'll be quick."

She was halfway to her bedroom door with her boyfriend-for-the-minute in tow but stopped and grabbed her cell phone and laptop from her makeshift office desk against the wall in her dining area. "I'll just throw these in with my clothes so I can work while you keep me safe."

Both men appeared beyond annoyed, but Agent Jackson

reluctantly nodded as she and Brody entered her bedroom. The instant they were over the threshold, Brody grabbed her around the waist as he closed the door behind them and said loud enough to be overheard, "Com'ere, baby-doll, and give me some sugar. I love you so much. I'm gonna miss you."

As soon as the door was shut, he quietly locked it and dragged her toward her bedroom sliding door leading out to the lanai. She kept her voice to a whisper. "I'm sorry, Brody, but I'm in big trouble. Jimmy didn't send them."

He glanced back at the alarm control panel next to the door leading to the living room, making sure he wouldn't set off the alarm when he opened the slider. His Texas twang had faded, along with the volume of his voice, although there was still a hint of the drawl. "I kind of already understood that, darlin'."

His gaze dropped to her feet, and relief came over his face when he saw she had sneakers on. "As soon as I open the door, we're going to run through the backyards away from my place. I wish we could get one of my guns, but we'd have to pass by your living room. Head for the wooded area two houses down. From there, we'll cut through to the next street over. Ready?" She nodded anxiously but remained silent. "Here goes nothing."

He silently slid the door open, and they took off across her other next-door neighbor's yard, running as fast as they could . . . well, as fast as Angie could. They were almost at the second yard when they heard the agents kick in her bedroom door, and as they neared the edge of the woods, she heard one of them yell, "Hey! Fuck!"

Brody glanced over his shoulder, but Angie kept running forward. Thankfully, the denser foliage provided them with more coverage within a short distance. He weaved them through the vegetation, and as they reached the clearing of another backyard, she heard someone crashing through the brush behind them, followed by more cursing. Even though Brody moved faster than her, she urged him on. "Hurry, I hear them."

"This way." He tugged her arm, and she almost lost her phone and laptop she was still clutching. They rounded the house and ran diagonally across the street past another dwelling into a backyard with a wooden four-foot fence separating it from the rear parking lot of a small strip mall. As they approached the fence, Brody grabbed her by the waist and just about threw her over it, vaulting the barrier himself a second later. Angie was shocked she'd landed on her feet and still had her electronics in her hands. Thank goodness she ran three miles four times a week. Otherwise, she would've passed out by now. As it was, her panic was making it hard for her to catch her breath.

Brody clasped his hand around her upper arm and took off running again. As they came around the side of the building, she stumbled, but his grip kept her from falling. When they reached the sidewalk, he turned right and kept sprinting as he hauled her past stores and businesses. She had no idea if they were still being followed and didn't dare look. On the other hand, he glanced back several times but didn't slow them down.

One block over, he pivoted and hustled them across the street into the parking lot of another strip mall. She realized he had a plan in mind, and her thoughts were confirmed when he ran to the door of a restaurant named Donovan's. Vaguely, she remembered Jenn worked here and Jake's brother owned it.

Throwing the door open, Brody dragged her inside, slowing but not stopping as he hurried her down the length

HIS ANGEL

of the bar and barked at the startled bartender. "Mike, call Ian. Tell him 'code red.' If you can't get him, call Jake or Devon. If two guys in suits come in claiming to be feds, call 9-1-1."

Mike, whoever he was, apparently knew what Brody was talking about because he threw down the rag he'd been using to wipe down the bar and snatched up the phone behind him. Brody still didn't stop moving, leading her down a hallway, past the bar's restrooms, and into a room marked "Private." He pulled her into the office, shut the door, and locked it. Finally, they came to a complete stop. Gasping for air, she was a little pissed he wasn't even breathing heavily, as if running four or five blocks on a zigzag course while someone was chasing them was an everyday occurrence.

"What . . . what if . . . they come in here?" She got the words out in between gulps of air. Her pounding heart echoed in her brain, her lungs on fire, and she didn't think she could run another step if they were found by the men chasing them.

Brody took her phone from her hand, opened the back of it, and ripped out the battery and SIM card, putting everything into the pocket of his sweatpants. He stepped over to two safes bolted to the floor underneath the paper-laden desk. Placing his middle finger on a scanner on the face of one of them, he waited three seconds, and the door clicked open. Reaching in, he pulled out a holstered Sig Sauer 9mm pistol, checked to see the magazine was filled to capacity with brass-tipped bullets, and then shut the safe's door. He clipped the re-holstered weapon to the back of his sweatpants, pulling them further down on his hips with the heavy weight of it.

Angie wasn't afraid of the weapon. In fact, she was glad

he now had one. "You've planned for situations like this, huh?"

"When we first started Trident, the team came up with a bunch of emergency plans. Never had to use one from my own place before, but I'm happy to know they work." He saw her glance nervously at the office door. "We lost them a while back, so we're safe until Ian arrives. When he does, we'll go out the back and get in his car."

He pointed at another door she assumed led to an alley or lot behind them. "Why did you come over, anyway?" It wasn't unusual for him to stop by in the morning or evening, but not in the middle of the afternoon. "I'm not complaining, mind you."

There was a single sharp knock on the door they'd come in through, and Angie jumped, but Brody held up his hand to calm her. The door didn't open, but a male voice said, "Ian's six minutes out. He'll honk twice. Seems to be all clear out front."

Brody responded with a single knock on the wooden door before turning around to face her again. "I was working late last night, so I took today off. I was heading out for a run when I saw the strange car in your driveway with government plates. I went around back to check on you, not wanting to interrupt if you didn't need me. But when I saw your face, I knew something wasn't right. By the way, you were phenomenal. You stayed calm, helped me figure out something was wrong, and acted like a pro. Have you ever thought about becoming an actress?"

She didn't answer him. Something about what he'd said made her think he wasn't being one hundred percent truthful with her, but at this point, it didn't matter. She needed his and Ian's help to get to the storage unit where her emergency vehicle, money, fake IDs, and two bags of

HIS ANGEL

clothes and other necessities were kept. After that, she could get out of town and follow the orders Jimmy had drilled into her over the years.

On the first of every month, she drove around Tampa on lesser-used roads with no set pattern. Once she was sure she wasn't being followed, she'd head to the storage unit rented under a fictitious name and check on everything. With the outside unit's door open, she'd start the old Chevy Nova's souped-up engine and let it run for a few minutes to ensure the batteries stayed charged. Then she'd turn it off again and lock the unit back up until the first of the next month when she did the whole routine again.

She drove the car every six months and took it for an oil change and a tune-up. She'd always thought the whole process was a little too much James Bond-ish, but now she was grateful she'd followed Jimmy's instructions to the letter.

"How did you know they weren't who they said they were, and your friend didn't send them?"

"They didn't know the passphrase." When he said nothing, she explained, "Jimmy set up an escape plan for me years ago in case his cover was ever blown. If he sent them, they would've said a certain passphrase that only the two of us and his handler know. They didn't say it, so neither Jimmy nor his handler sent them. Now, I have to get to my emergency stash and get out of town until he contacts me."

Brody nodded but still didn't say anything, and she wondered what he was thinking about all of this. He had to regret checking on her, but she had no idea how she would've gotten away from the men if he hadn't. Suddenly, she remembered something he said. "You said the plates on

171

the car were government plates? Does that mean they really were from the DEA?"

He nodded again. "Yeah, the plates were government-issued, but I won't know which agency and from what city until I run them through my computer. If they are real agents, then your friend has even bigger problems. He's got traitors inside his department."

Angie gasped. Her eyes widened as her body trembled. "Oh, shit, I didn't think of that. What if something happened to him? What if he can't get in touch with me?" It would kill her if anything happened to Jimmy.

Pulling her into his arms, her neighbor hugged her. "Easy, honey. One thing at a time. First, we'll get you someplace safe, and then we'll track him down."

CHAPTER TWELVE

Ian drove like a madman on cocaine. He'd raced to his car and just started the engine when Mike called him, telling him they had an emergency—Brody was in the restaurant's office with a blonde woman Mike didn't know. But Ian knew instantly who it was and thanked the stars above for his teammate. He didn't know how Egghead knew Angie was in danger, but he was thankful the geek had her in hiding.

Another call had come in less than two minutes earlier than Mike's. The screen read 'Unknown,' which was common in his business with all his contacts who preferred to remain anonymous. Throwing down the pen he'd been using to do some monthly accounting, he picked up his cell and answered it. "Sawyer."

"Daisy Duck is fucked. Get her out of there."

The line went dead, and he'd shot out of his chair, grabbed his gun, and took off running. Athos was the caller, and the stupid passphrase meant Angie was in danger. Ian's heart was pounding out of his chest as he jumped into his car. Then Mike called, and Ian almost didn't answer his phone. Thank fuck he did.

He pulled up behind Donovan's and laid on the horn twice, desperate to see his angel and ensure she was unharmed. The back door to the bar opened as he hit the lock release on the door handle next to him. Brody rushed Angie toward the SUV and almost threw her onto the rear seat before diving in after her.

"Stay down." He didn't need to say the words because his teammate knew the routine and soon had Angie lying across the entire backseat, covered with his own body. Without looking back, Ian hit the gas, getting them out of there as fast as possible.

Fifteen minutes later, Brody had filled him in about what happened, and they were almost at the private airstrip where Trident's small jet was kept. When he finally felt it was safe, he told the two they could get up, then looked into the rear-view mirror to prove to himself Angie was alive and okay.

Her confusion was evident as she whipped her head around while looking for familiar landmarks. "Where are we? I need you to take me to my emergency storage unit so I can get out of town."

Pulling into the tiny unmanned airport, he didn't answer her until after he drove into a hanger, and the rolling door came down behind them thanks to Jake, who he'd called on his way to Donovan's. Jake, in turn, contacted their pilot, a retired Air Force captain, who they had on retainer, and another associate, who'd be waiting at their destination with a vehicle for them. He threw the car in park, leaped out, opened the rear passenger door, and hauled Angie into his arms. He hadn't realized he was

HIS ANGEL

crushing her until she told him she couldn't breathe, and he reluctantly released her.

"Ian, what's going on? Why are we here? I need to get my stuff and get out of Tampa."

"I know, Angel, but your plans have changed." He didn't need to look to know Brody was getting the plane set so they could take off as soon as their pilot, Conrad Chapman, known as CC, got there and did the last-minute pre-flight checklist. Jake was outside, making sure no one sneaked up on them.

Ian was confident they weren't followed, but he had to ensure the men at her house hadn't somehow tagged her with a tracking device. He popped his trunk, retrieved a scanner, and ran it over her entire body until he was satisfied she was clean. The scanner had beeped when it had gotten to her sneaker, but a specific frequency code showed it was one of the Trident trackers Boomer had hidden in her shoes. He'd have Brody check her laptop before they left, but if she had it, her phone would be left in the vehicle.

She was baffled and began to panic. "What are you talking about? What are you doing? I have to get out of here!"

Taking a deep breath, he blurted out, "Goofy has a crush on Minnie Mouse." Shit, he felt fucking ridiculous saying that. What was with Athos and his bizarre Disney passphrases?

"What did you say?"

Her fingers covered her mouth as she stared at him in shock and stepped backward. Away from him, damn it. It was obvious she'd heard him, so he didn't bother repeating it. "Athos was afraid something might go wrong on his mission, so he asked us to watch over you and get you someplace safe if something happened."

175

The betrayal he saw in her eyes was more than he could take. "He what?" Her voice was shrill, hurting his ears, but he knew he deserved it. "You've been . . . what? Babysitting me? I don't know who I'm more pissed at, Jimmy or you. Is that why you asked me out and why you've been spending so much time with me? Did Jimmy ask you to? Oh God! Is that why Brody was so interested in my life and always checked on me? Why he wanted to be friends?"

"Yes, he was checking on you to make sure you were safe, but being your friend was Brody being Brody."

He ignored her gasp of outraged disbelief as the side door to the hanger flew open, and CC barreled past them on his way to the plane, not bothering with pleasantries. The man knew this was urgent and acted accordingly.

Ian kept his eyes on Angie's horrified ones and waited until the pilot was out of earshot again. "And no, it's not why I asked you out. I asked you because I couldn't fight my attraction to you anymore, and I *very much* wanted to get to know you better. If you believe anything, Angel, believe this. What's happened between us has been one hundred percent real."

She shook her head in suspicion and took another step back. He gritted his teeth because they didn't have time for this. "I'll explain everything on the plane, but we need to get in the air and away from the people after you."

"Why should I trust you?"

The question hit him square in the chest and almost knocked the air out of his lungs. It was hard to regain his composure, but somehow, he managed it. "Three reasons. One—Athos trusted me to take care of you. Two—I knew the passphrase, and there's only one person who could've told me that stupid thing . . . a person you trust more than anyone else in the world."

HIS ANGEL

Fuck, it killed him to say that, but it was true. They hadn't reached the point in their relationship where she trusted him one hundred percent, and he'd just taken three giant steps backward on that journey. "And three—because I care about you. You're my submissive, and it's my responsibility to keep you safe."

He reached for her arm, but she pulled away and snarled, "Don't touch me. I swear, Ian, if you touch me right now, I'll scratch your eyes out. And I'm not your submissive. Not anymore."

Fuck! As much as he wanted to prove her wrong, now was not the time. Biting his tongue, he gestured toward the jet. "Okay, fine. If you don't want me to touch you, then get on the damn plane. The longer we stay here, the greater chance whoever is after you tracks us down."

He counted to three, and she still hadn't moved beyond crossing her arms over her breasts while giving him a dirty look. Athos had been right—she was stubborn when she was angry.

He took a step forward and gave her one last warning in his deepest, firmest Dom voice. "Angel, if you don't get on the fucking plane, I'll throw you over my shoulder, carry you on, and tie you to a fucking seat. And once we're safely in the air, I'll spank your ass until my hand falls off, and you won't be able to sit for a week."

As pissed as she was, she obviously recognized the genuine threat as well as the worry in his voice. Despite the fact he'd lied to her—they had all lied to her—she had to know he would keep her safe until they could locate Jimmy. After she was reassured her best friend was okay, she would probably kick both of their asses . . . and maybe Brody's too.

She threw her hands in the air. "Fine! I'll go with you, but don't touch or talk to me unless it's absolutely necessary. And I want to know everything that's going on. No more keeping me in the dark like some shrinking violet who can't take care of herself because I won't stand for it."

Not giving him a chance to respond, she spun around, grabbed her laptop from where it sat on the backseat, and stormed over to the stairs leading to the interior cabin of the small jet. She glared at Brody, who was waiting at the bottom of the stairs when he took her computer. She didn't respond to him when he told her he needed to check it for tracking devices. Instead, she crossed her arms again, waiting as he scanned it and then nodded to Ian that all was good. The geek wouldn't turn it on until they reached the safe house, where he could scramble any signal the computer might send out, which could be used to find their location. Ian would've preferred to leave it behind, but he knew all her work was on it, so he made the small concession.

Without a word to anyone, Angie took her laptop and stomped up the stairs, disappearing into the cabin. Jake heard the plane's engines start up and approached Ian, who was still standing next to his SUV, trying to get his emotions under control. Devon and Ian had filled the rest of the team in after Athos had left the office that day.

Jake stopped in front of him. "Dev, Boomer, and Marco are headed to Angie's to see if they can find any prints or anything the agents may have left. They'll review the surveillance footage to get stills for Brody to send through his facial recognition software. Dev is also calling in reinforcements for the compound and to keep an eye on Jenn and Kristen. He'll assign someone to sit on Angie and Brody's houses. If the agents aren't stupid, they'll be able to connect Egghead to Trident without much effort. Once we know what's going on with Athos and the compound is secure, Boomer and Marco will be ready for whatever we need. Dev will stay and hold down the fort."

Ian nodded. His team knew what needed to be done, and he trusted them to do it. Brody walked over to join them and handed Angie's disassembled phone to Ian, who tossed it through the open back door of his vehicle before slamming it shut. Wisely, neither man said anything more to their boss, who was beyond pissed and terrified Angie's life was in danger. He should've never agreed to keep the protective measures from her. It was too late now, so the best he could do was guard her with his own life and try to regain her trust. He'd worry about everything else later.

Whether she wanted to admit it or not, he was still her Dom, and she was still his submissive. They had a signed contract, and he would hold her to it as long as possible. He just prayed she wouldn't decide to walk out on him because of this. He wasn't ready to let her go yet, and, God help him, he wasn't sure he ever would be.

Brody boarded the plane, with Ian following, and pulled up the stairs as Jake raised the hanger bay door. After the jet taxied out into the open, the overhead door was shut, and Brody let the stairs down again for his teammate. Less than five minutes later, they were airborne, and Ian let out a sigh of relief. His angel was safe for now, and he planned on keeping her that way.

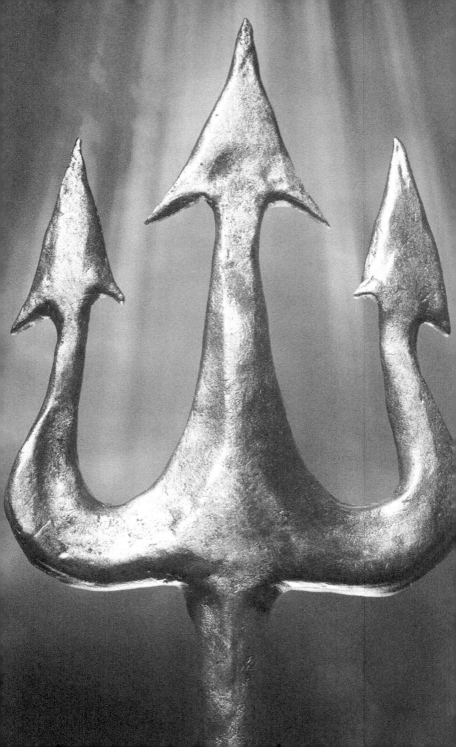

CHAPTER THIRTEEN

They'd been in the air for over a half hour, but Angie's anger was still at a near boil, and she hadn't spoken to Ian or his teammates yet. Sitting in one of the luxury seats in the first of two rows of four seats across, she'd placed her laptop on the one seat between her and the aisle in a blatant act that told the others not to attempt to sit with her. As much as she wanted answers, she didn't think she could face them just yet without wanting to throw something at one of them, especially Ian.

The three of them were behind her somewhere. She'd been so pissed when she'd boarded that the rest of the interior of the small jet was a blur to her. Now, as she stared out the window at nothing but clouds, she replayed the past few weeks over and over in her head. One of the things that stood out most in her mind was she'd been so wrapped up in her work and time with Ian that she'd barely thought about Jimmy. For the first time since they were teenagers, her thoughts of, and worry for, her best friend had taken a backseat to someone else. That'd never happened with any of the other men she'd dated over the years. And damn it to hell, the two jackasses had kept her in the dark about something which concerned her—something she should have known about from the start.

She knew over the years that Jimmy had sheltered her as best he could from the world he was determined to clean up, one scumbag drug runner at a time, but it still yanked her chain.

She peeked over when she saw someone out of the corner of her eye take a seat across the aisle from her. It was Jake, looking comfortable in jeans, a navy blue shirt, and black rubber-soled boots. Brody and Ian were wisely staying away from her for now. Out of all Ian's teammates, Jake was the one she knew the least about. He was the quietest of the six men, yet he still had that commanding presence of a dominant male. She studied his profile. His chiseled jaw, high cheekbones, and long eyelashes made her yearn for her sketch pad. She'd drawn several pencil sketches of Ian over the past few weeks and a few of Jenn and Beau, but she itched to capture the hardness and sadness she saw in Jake's face.

He glanced over, caught her staring, and gave her a small smile. "Something on your mind?"

She let out an unladylike snort. "You have no idea."

Shrugging his shoulders, he said, "Try me. I may not be as talkative as Marco is when comforting a submissive, but I'm a good listener."

"I'm not a submissive," she spat out. "Not anymore. And I don't need comfort, thank you."

His left eyebrow rose as he gave her a "yeah, right—think again" look, which irritated her because she could guess what he was about to say. "You can't turn it on and off like a switch, Angie. You can try, but you'll end up making yourself miserable. Just because you're pissed off

HIS ANGEL

doesn't mean your body stops craving what you've experienced over the past few weeks. It was a part of you that you didn't know existed, and now that you do, you'll never go back to the way you were before without regretting it."

Knowing he was right but unwilling to admit it, she turned and stared out the window again. Jake may work for Trident, but he hadn't done anything to be the recipient of her anger, and she didn't want to take it out on him. But Ian, Brody, and even Boomer were a different story, along with her pain-in-the-ass best friend. She heard Jake stand and expected him to return to where he'd been sitting before, but he picked up her laptop, set it on the seat he'd just vacated, and sat beside her.

"Talk to me. It doesn't have to be about D/s stuff or anything to do with Boss-man since he's a sore subject with you at the moment. You must have a thousand questions about what happened today, and while I don't have all the facts yet, I'll answer what I can."

Angie shifted in her seat, putting her back to the window, and studied the man. In his eyes, she saw the same compassion and understanding she'd noticed in Marco's when he stayed with her during her public spanking. The thought of that night and how she'd screamed her release for all to hear made her cheeks warm. She forced herself to think of something else, not wanting him to know where her mind went and how those thoughts still made her body tingle. "Where are we going? Let's start there."

"Fair enough. We'll land in Spartanburg, South Carolina, in a little over an hour. From there, it's about a ninety-minute drive to the safe house in Maggie Valley, North Carolina."

"Safe house? Whose?" *Did everyone have a safe house nowadays?*

Jake nodded and settled in a more comfortable position since she was asking questions. "It belongs to Ian and Devon, but it would take a long time to trace it to them since the ownership is buried under a bunch of unrelated businesses and false names. Ian and his dad found the place when he first joined the SEALs. One of the older guys told him if he had the opportunity, he should find a place where no one could track him down. With all the terrorists, drug cartels, and scum of the earth we've dealt with over the years, it's not paranoia to think we all have prices on our heads for one reason or another. But we're lucky most of them have better things to do instead of hunting down our identities and homes. And it's why Ian and Dev put so much money into the security at the compound.

"As for the safe house, we've used it several times over the years, but not always for emergencies. It's up in the mountains and a great place to get away sometimes. But we always take precautions if we go there, and our flight plan states we're going to Myrtle Beach in South Carolina. There are closer airports to Maggie Valley, but this way, it's harder for someone to track our movements."

Angie was a little stunned. She knew what the men at Trident did could be dangerous sometimes, but to have a bounty on their heads was something she only thought happened in the old Wild West or to criminals on the FBI's Most Wanted list. "How long do I have to stay there?"

"Until we hear from your friend and figure out how to end the threat against you. I don't want to scare you, but you said you wanted to be kept in the loop. I don't know if the men at your house were real agents, but we'll find out when we get to the safe house. From what we can gather,

HIS ANGEL

they were going to kidnap you and use you against Athos to get information out of him." He grimaced and added, "And probably as revenge for infiltrating the drug cartel he was undercover in."

The look he gave her said the rest—there was a strong chance neither Jimmy nor she would survive if the cartel got a hold of them. Despite her fear, a kernel of hope she hadn't known was missing began to fill her. "So, does that mean Jimmy is still alive? If they want me, that must mean they don't have him."

The tilt of Jake's head wasn't entirely reassuring. "As of a little while ago, he was alive, and we assume not captured because he contacted Ian to let us know something was wrong and told us to get you out of Tampa. Boss-man got the call right before my brother called him from the pub. If he can, Athos will be on his way to meet us in North Carolina."

"That was your brother—the guy, Mike?" She had only gotten a glimpse of the man and hadn't noticed any resemblance, but Jake nodded. "So, what happens next?"

"We wait until your friend contacts us and help him when he does. In the meantime, we'll keep you safe and try to figure out who's after you. Then we end it."

Her stomach dropped at how deadly those last four words sounded. "End it? How?"

Jake's eyes hardened and bore into hers. "We eliminate the threats and make sure they'll never come after you again."

"Y-you'd kill someone for me?" Her voice had a combination of disbelief and wonder, and she was sure the expression on her face matched it. "Why?"

"In a heartbeat, Angie. Because it's the way men like us are wired. Innocent lives are protected at all costs. It's not as if we have a death wish or anything, but if we're killed protecting or saving someone else, we'll make sure we fight to the bitter end to give them the best chance for survival. Whether you like it or not, if it comes down to saving you or myself, just remember I want a traditional Irish wake, complete with bagpipes."

Angie swallowed hard. He'd said the last part with a teasing grin, but she knew he was serious. She saw the conviction in his eyes and knew he wasn't blowing smoke by saying he'd give his life for hers. He would do it without a moment's hesitation. She realized what had her longing to draw his face earlier. Jake Donovan reminded her so much of Jimmy Andrews after he became Jimmy Athos. She wondered what had happened to Ian's friend to put the same hardness and sense of loss in the man's beautiful yet haunted green eyes.

She'd known what he meant by "eliminate" before he confirmed it, and she wasn't sure how she felt about it. The team might have to kill people to keep her safe, and she hated the fact they would have blood on their hands because of her. She wasn't naïve enough to think Ian, Jake, and the others had never killed anyone. They were former Navy SEALs in an era where terrorists from around the world were more than threatening the American way of life, as well as the lives of those same Americans. They'd been in combat, seeing and doing things most people had never imagined, but now, they wouldn't be killing anyone for all of America. Instead, they'd be killing someone for the sake of one person—her—Angelina Beckett, a graphic designer from Tampa, Florida, who wouldn't know a terrorist or drug cartel member if she tripped over him.

With that knowledge, she was done asking questions for the moment and turned back toward the window.

HIS ANGEL

After a few moments, she sensed Jake stand and move back to the area behind her, leaving her alone in her thoughts.

* * *

Ian was ready to spit nails as he watched his teammate talk to Angie. A few minutes earlier, he'd been about to storm up to the front of the plane and force her to listen to him, but Jake had stopped him. She didn't need his frustration at the moment, and it would only push her further away from him. He needed to get his emotions under control before he talked to her. So instead of doing it himself and screwing things up even more, he reluctantly allowed his friend to talk to the stubborn, pissed-off woman and soothe her ruffled feathers.

If Athos was still alive, he should be on his way to South Carolina to a pre-arranged location. When he reached it, he would contact Ian, who would then send his teammates to retrieve the agent and bring him across the state border to the safe house after ensuring they weren't followed or tracked. Once they got the low-down on who, what, where, when, and how, they would help Athos however they could while keeping Angie safe.

While Jake talked to Angie, Ian sat in the middle area of the plane, which was set up like a living room, complete with couches, recliners, and tables, all bolted to the floor. Gazing out the window at nothing, he thought about how fast the beautiful submissive had gotten under his skin, a fact he was wary about.

They had fallen into a comfortable routine since their first public scene at the club last Friday. He'd taken her back to his place after she recovered from the sub-space she'd achieved from her orgasm, and he fucked her several times until dawn, leaving them both happy and sated. Each morning, she went home, only to return to him each evening and spend the night.

They'd returned to the club on Saturday night and again on Sunday night, participating in one other public scene and a private one in the office-themed room, where she pretended to be his naughty secretary. He'd fucked her every way he could, using the desk and chair to position her how he wanted, and even sat her atop a tall filing cabinet so he could eat her sweet pussy while standing up. He loved how she embraced her naughty side and often found his mind wandering during the daytime, thinking of different scenarios for them to play out.

The club was closed on Mondays and Tuesdays, so those two nights, they'd cooked dinner in his kitchen, cuddled on the couch, and ended up pleasuring each other in various ways. The woman was as insatiable as he was and more adventurous than he'd expected. He'd given her several pieces of lingerie he'd picked out from the club store, instructing her she was to wear them and nothing else while they were alone together in his home.

Angie rocked lingerie in a way that rivaled any Victoria's Secret model. If he had his way, she wouldn't wear anything but the sexy scraps of material twenty-four hours a day. He'd even gotten into the habit of locking the dead-bolt to his front door to ensure Jenn didn't walk in on them again by accident.

He watched as Jake rose, walked back toward the sitting area, and took his earlier seat on the couch between the two recliners Ian and Brody had occupied the entire flight. Egghead was catching a brief nap since there was nothing much to do in the air, and he hadn't had time to grab one of his laptops. When they got to the safe house, he would have a smaller setup similar to the war-room back at Trident.

HIS ANGEL

From there, he would do what he did best and get them as much information about who was after Angie.

Ian glanced at Jake. "Does she still want my dick in a cock cage?"

"If I were you, I'd keep it out of her reach for a while. Your balls too." He chuckled when his boss winced and crossed his legs in an automatic response most men had at the thought of their reproductive organs being tortured. "Don't worry. I gave her some things to think about. She's worried about Athos, but I think she's also worried about you and the rest of us."

Confused, Ian tilted his head. "Me? Us? Why?"

Jake leaned forward and rested his elbows on his knees. "She may be submissive, Ian, but she's far from naïve. Angie knows there's a chance she, Athos, or any of us may end up six feet under by the time this whole thing plays out. Even though her friend is the one who brought this to her doorstep, no matter how unintentional and how much he tried to prevent it, she knows we'll do anything we have to in order to protect her. If any of us have to kill someone, which is a near one-hundred percent possibility, I think she'll have a hard time with it. And God forbid one of us is caught in the crossfire . . . she's going to feel responsible no matter what."

Taking a moment to think about things from Angie's point of view, Ian knew his teammate was right. She wasn't a part of his world where killing someone, while not ever taken lightly, was something he wouldn't hesitate to do, if needed, to protect his teammates, his family, innocent people, and the woman he loved.

Oh, fuck! He did not just think that. His stomach bottomed out, and he couldn't blame it on turbulence since there wasn't any. He couldn't be in love with Angie . . . he wouldn't let himself be. Falling in love with a woman only led to heartache, and Ian refused to go through it again.

Fuck! He dragged his hand down his face in frustration and forced the thoughts of unwanted love to the back of his mind. He'd deal with that later.

CHAPTER FOURTEEN

Angie still hadn't said anything to anyone but Jake beyond necessary "yes" or "no" answers to questions. They had landed in Spartanburg, and waiting for them was a black SUV with tinted windows and license plates, which couldn't be traced to any of them. Their pilot, CC, was instructed to grab a nearby motel room and get some rest until they figured out where they would need him to fly later on. He most likely would be heading back to Tampa to pick up and return with Marco and Boomer, but for now, Ian wanted him available in case their plans changed.

On the way to Maggie Valley, they stopped off at a Walmart to pick up some food, supplies, and clothing for Angie. While the team had spare clothes, among other things, at the safe house, she only had what she was wearing. While Brody waited in the vehicle, Jake and Ian entered the store, flanking Angie. They hit the women's section first, and at Ian's insistence, she grabbed two pairs of sweatpants, jeans, and some T-shirts.

She found another pair of sneakers more appropriate

for running than the simple Keds she had on. She quickly picked out some socks, a package of plain, white Hanes underwear, and two sports bras in the intimate aisles. She gaped and put her hands on her hips when Ian threw the six-pack of bikini briefs back on the rack and picked out several pairs of lacy thongs and boy shorts with matching bras.

While Jake ducked his head to hide his grin, Ian crossed his arms, smirked, and stared at Angie, daring her to defy him. Thankfully, she didn't argue with him in the middle of the superstore. When she spun around and stormed toward the health and beauty section for toiletries, he and Jake followed with the cart.

Although they were on the run from bad guys, Ian decided to push his angel's buttons a little more. He couldn't help it—it was the Dom in him. As she passed the sexual wellness shelves on the way to get a toothbrush in the next aisle, he picked up a box of condoms and threw it into the cart. As he expected, she snarled and snatched the box, intent on putting it back on the shelf. Before she had a chance, he took a gentle but firm hold of her wrist, plucked the package from her hand, and placed it purposely back in the cart. Then, to rattle her some more, he grabbed a second box and tossed it in with the first. Her green eyes flared with anger. She opened and closed her mouth twice before turning in an exasperated huff to continue her shopping.

After they finished up in the food aisles, they checked out, with Ian paying cash for their purchases. In his panicked rush out of his office to get to her, he'd failed to grab one of his fake identities with accompanying credit cards. While the team had backup alias IDs and credit cards at the safe house, for now, he would use cash so they couldn't be tracked through purchases.

HIS ANGEL

Less than a half hour after they entered the store, they were walking back out with a cart full of bags. Brody was waiting for them in the fire lane, and after securing Angie in the rear passenger seat, Ian and Jake quickly filled the rear storage area with their supplies. In the deli section, they'd picked out several pre-made sandwiches, then added some chips and sodas from the choices available at the registers. It wasn't the greatest meal in the world, but everyone was hungry and far from being picky at the moment. They ate in silence as Brody drove them to their final destination.

For the rest of the ride, Ian sat next to Angie in the rear seat and tried to ignore the fact she was ignoring him. He couldn't wait to get to the house so they could have a conversation that his teammates wouldn't overhear. However, he knew she wouldn't talk to him without yelling and hoped someone had left a ball gag and restraints at the house during a past weekend excursion. Ian had never brought a woman to his mountainside retreat, but some of his team members had, mainly Boomer, Brody, and Marco.

Before they'd left Tampa, the three men left their cell phones in Ian's vehicle. Ian had a throwaway phone in his trunk, along with other gear. Athos knew if Ian didn't answer his cell, he should call Devon to get the number to the throwaway. This way, they couldn't be tracked, and Athos could still contact him. Ian texted his brother when they hit Maggie Valley's town border, telling him they'd arrived safely.

A few minutes later, Brody turned up the mountain road that led to their safe house, and two miles further, he pulled into the gravel driveway. Ian looked at Angie as she gawked at the structure. He wasn't sure what she expected, but this one was top of the line as far as safe houses. It was a beautiful mountain retreat that his dad had found for him

193

over thirteen years ago. Having a billionaire real estate investor as a father came in handy sometimes.

The house had been owned by some Arab sheik who bought and sold homes worldwide as often as most people upgraded their cell phones. It was built into the mountain, so there was no backyard, but the front of the house overlooked a lake about a quarter of a mile below them. It was easily defended between the landscaping, bulletproof windows, and Brody's security set-up. Their nearest neighbor was a vacation house about two miles to the west.

If a vehicle turned up the road toward the house, an alarm would sound inside. There were also cameras and sensors in the woods surrounding the three open sides of the house. Most of the time, an alert would result from a large animal such as a deer or bear, but they'd rather get the alerts and have it be nothing instead of missing a human predator.

The house itself had eight bedrooms, each with its own bath. Six were on the second floor, with the remaining ones on the first, with a gourmet kitchen and a large living room with vaulted ceilings. A gym, game room, and hidden panic room were located in the basement.

The house also had an open den area on the second floor, overlooking the living room, and it'd been converted into the mini war-room for Brody. While it didn't have everything the geek had in his Trident office, it had what was necessary to maintain security and a sufficient computer system. A retired Navy officer, who'd been one of Ian's superiors when he first got out of basic training, lived about a half hour away and maintained the property and house for them. Devon had contacted the former lieutenant to let him know the place would be occupied and to stay away until told otherwise.

HIS ANGEL

Brody and Jake grabbed the bags from the rear of the vehicle while Ian escorted Angie to the front door and unlocked it with a scan of his palm, just like their system at the compound. He left the door open for his teammates, who were a few steps behind them, as he and Angie entered the house.

While she continued taking in her new surroundings, Jake unpacked their groceries, and Ian took the bags with Angie's supplies from Egghead. The geek headed up to the den to boot up the computers and arm the rest of the security systems, which weren't up and running on a regular basis. As Angie followed him, Ian brought her bags into his bedroom and placed them on the king-sized bed. Without a word, he left her alone and wasn't too surprised when she returned to the living room several minutes later with the bags in her hands. He raised an eyebrow at her. "Going somewhere, Angel?"

She stopped in front of where he stood while glaring at him. "Obviously, that's your bedroom with all your clothes and stuff, and I'm not staying in there. I assume in a house this size, there's an unoccupied room where I can stay."

Crossing his arms over his chest, he gave her a look that dared her to argue. "Of course, there are several unoccupied rooms, but you're not staying in any of them. You're staying in mine."

"Then where are you sleeping because it's not with me?"

This time, instead of answering her, Ian gently gripped her upper arm, led her back into his bedroom, clothes and all, and shut the door behind them. He stood in front of her escape route, so she had no choice but to listen to him. Or so he thought as she threw the bags on the bed, stormed into the attached bath, and slammed the door. He rolled his eyes when he heard the lock click. Did she honestly believe a puny lock was going to keep him out?

Instead of picking the thing, he retrieved one of those universal keys that opened most interior doors nowadays and let himself into the bathroom. He found her sitting on the closed toilet lid with her arms crossed like a pouting child. "Can't I have some privacy?"

"If you're going to act like a brat, then no. Now, are we going to have this conversation here or in the bedroom, where I'm sure you'll be more comfortable? Whether you like it or not, Angel, we will talk. It's just your decision whether I spank your ass before we do. And you better believe I won't think twice about setting your backside on fire. Now, what's it going to be?"

She'd gaped at him in disbelief when he called her a 'brat,' and then his threat of a spanking resulted in a scowl. Without saying a word, she stood and stormed back into the bedroom after he stepped aside to let her pass. Before he could say anything, she spun around and pointed her finger at him. "So, was everything a ploy to spy on me, or were you spying on me, and getting me in your bed was just a fringe benefit?"

Ian growled, and his eyes narrowed. "I was keeping you safe, not spying on you. And I never considered you a fringe benefit to a job."

As soon as the last three words were out of his mouth, he knew they'd been a mistake. A horrified expression fell over her face, and he wanted to kick his own ass.

"So, I was just a job to you? Is that how you do all your jobs, Ian, from under the bed sheets?" He recognized when a thought occurred to her and could guess what it was. "What about when you weren't around, huh? Brody wasn't home all day, so how were you keeping me safe then?" She

HIS ANGEL

watched as a guilty expression he couldn't stop came over his face, and he knew he was in deeper shit with her. "There are cameras in my house, right? Brody and Boomer put cameras in my house when they set up the security system, didn't they? Whose idea was it—yours or Jimmy's?"

She didn't wait for an answer, and her voice was getting louder with every question until she was yelling. "You fucking bastard! Was everyone at Trident enjoying the show while I showered and got dressed every day? What about the night of the gala? Did you get a porn movie out of it? Out of what you had me do in the kitchen the next day? What's the going rate for amateur porn these days, Ian?"

He couldn't take it anymore. She was borderline hysterical, thinking the absolute worst of him, and wasn't letting him get a single word in. He tried to put his hands on her shoulders and barely shifted his hips in time when she tried to knee him in the groin. Furious that she missed, Angie pounded his chest with her fists. He grabbed her wrists and forced her onto her back on the bed after pushing her bags out of the way. He didn't want to hurt her but needed her to calm down before she hurt herself, so he straddled her hips and held her arms above her head.

Squirming around and bucking her hips, trying to unseat him, tired her out pretty quick, and he relaxed a little when she slowed and then stopped fighting him altogether. Unfortunately for Ian, at this point, she started yelling at him again, calling him every name in the book and a few she must've made up on her own. For the first time, he wished he'd brought another woman up to this house before because he could use a set of restraints and a gag at the moment. Brody might have some in his room, but Ian wasn't about to bring one of his teammates into Angie's line of fire, and she was pissed off enough at

Egghead already. This was Ian's doing, and he'd take full responsibility for it.

Improvising, he unbuckled his belt with one hand and pulled the leather from the loops around his waist. With quick, practiced motions, he flipped her onto her stomach, pulled her arms behind her back, and restrained her wrists before she realized what he was doing. Still cursing him out, she bucked her hips again, trying to get him off her thighs.

"Angel," he leaned forward and growled in her ear, "all you're doing is wearing yourself out and making me harder than I already am. All your hip action makes my dick remember what it's like to be inside your sweet body while I fuck you hard and fast. Now, calm down and listen to me, or my hand and your ass will get real intimate with each other, and last Friday's paddling will seem like love taps when I'm done with you."

"You wouldn't dare!" She rotated her head to glare at him over her shoulder. Her beautiful eyes blazed with anger, and her hair was in complete disarray.

He shifted to the side to give himself access to her ass cheeks and landed one hard smack atop the right one. She screeched and tried to move away from him, but she couldn't go very far with her hands tied behind her and his right leg still over her thighs. His hand came down on her left cheek as she shrieked his name in a full-fledged fury. More followed.

Smack. Smack. Smack.

He continued until her rage finally broke, and she sobbed. Ian immediately rolled her to her side and pulled her to his chest, murmuring words of comfort. The last few hours of fear, anger, confusion, and hurt poured out of Angie with the buckets of tears she was crying.

HIS ANGEL

"It's all right, Angel. *Shhh*. It's all right. Please let me explain everything, and if you still want to stay mad at me, I'll back off. But until then, you're going to listen to me, and no matter what, you're going to do what I say when it comes to your safety. Okay?"

It was several more minutes before Angie got her emotions and tears under control again. "L-let me go."

"Not happening, sweetheart. Not until you hear me out."

She rubbed her tear-stained face against his T-shirt-covered chest. She was apparently still angry and hurt, but the fight had drained from her body, and exhaustion had taken over. "Please, Ian. I promise I'll listen to you, but no more lies. I want the truth—all of it. J-just let my hands go and give me a moment alone in the bathroom. Please."

He eased her back so he could study her face. Her eyes were red and swollen, and his chest squeezed, knowing he was the cause of her heartache. Even upset and bawling, the woman was beautiful. She blinked and looked into his eyes, and he knew she was telling him the truth about listening to him—and wasn't that fucking ironic? Reaching behind her, he undid the belt restraining her wrists as fast as he'd tied it on her. As she brought her arms back to her front, he rubbed them from her wrists to her shoulders, ensuring there was no stiffness and that her circulation was good. Before he let her sit up, he placed a single lingering kiss on her forehead and murmured, "I'm sorry, Angel."

He didn't explain further because he was sorry for more than he wanted to admit. He'd never meant to hurt her in any way, but he had, and now he had to live with the consequences, praying she would forgive him.

With a weary sigh, Angie pushed off the bed and walked into the bathroom without saying a word. This time, she didn't bother locking the door after she eased it shut. Ian turned down the covers on the bed, picked her bags up from the floor, and unpacked her new things. He folded the clothes, neatly lining everything on his dresser so she could find whatever she needed.

From the attached bath, the toilet flushed, and water began to flow into the sink before shutting off again a few minutes later. Just as he placed a winged-back chair next to the bed for their conversation, the bathroom door opened, and Angie emerged, calmer yet drained. Her hair wasn't as wild, and her tears were gone, but her eyes were still red and swollen.

She stood there, unsure what to do next, eyeing the bed and chair. When he handed her one of his T-shirts, she stared at it in confusion. Slowly spinning her around to face the bathroom door again, he gave her a slight push. "As much as I like how you sleep naked, I'd rather you wear this to bed in case we need to leave in a hurry. Jenn has a few things in the bedroom she uses, and I'll see if there's a pair of her running shorts or pajama pants for you after we talk."

Two minutes later, Angie walked out of the bathroom for the third time since they'd arrived at the house forty-five minutes earlier. She wore the T-shirt, which came down to the middle of her thighs. He wondered if she'd also removed her panties and gave himself a mental kick for even thinking about it. When her bare legs drew his gaze, he tried to ignore the twitching of his cock and gestured for her to climb into bed. She frowned and looked out the window, and he knew she was surprised to see the sun had set. It was after seven p.m., and six hours ago, her life had been normal.

After she climbed into the bed, Ian drew the covers up

HIS ANGEL

to her chest, pulled the chair closer to the head of the bed, and sat down. For the first time in years, he was unsure of himself in front of a submissive. But Angie wasn't just any submissive . . . no, she was more than that, and he had no idea what to do about it.

She watched as he dragged his hands down his face in frustration before speaking. "Let me tell you everything I know, and then you can ask questions. Okay?" He waited for a response, and when she nodded, he continued with a sigh. "Athos approached Trident after we met the night he was at your place. Apparently, he investigates all your new neighbors, which I would do if I were him."

He shrugged, unashamed. "I want to investigate any guy who Jenn goes out with, but she won't tell me their names because she knows I'll do it. Anyway, Athos told us he was going back undercover, and there was a slim chance you might be in danger if his cover was blown."

Angie's brow furrowed in confusion. "Why would it be a problem all of a sudden? He always took precautions so no one could ever connect the two of us."

So much for saving her questions until the end—he hated what he was about to tell her. "Angel, the agent he replaced was murdered along with his family after the cartel discovered he was a plant." He watched as the words took effect in her brain, and her eyes widened in horror. "It's why Athos asked us to protect you. It's also why he insisted on the security upgrades at your house. And yes, it's why we placed cameras, audio bugs, and tracking devices in your car, phone, purse, and some of your shoes."

He could see she was about to start yelling again, so he held up his hand to stop her. "Let me finish. You wanted to hear all of this, so I'm telling you everything. You can holler at me all you want when I'm done." She crossed her arms,

201

her anger still evident, but he was grateful when she remained quiet.

"No cameras were facing your bed or in your bathroom. The ones in your bedroom only faced the door to the hallway and the slider. I erased the audio from the night of the gala as soon as I got back to the compound, and the audio and video were both turned off while you and I were on the phone that morning. As long as there wasn't a reason, no one listened to or watched any of the recordings. Well, no one but me."

Her eyes narrowed, and he glanced away momentarily before taking a deep breath and forging ahead. "From the moment I met you, the day we moved Egghead into his house, I've wanted you. For some unknown reason, I was fighting my attraction to you, but every time I had a chance to go to Brody's, I took it, hoping to see you.

"The day Athos was over, I'll admit I was jealous as hell watching him massage your bare feet and seeing how familiar he was with you. I assumed you two had an intimate relationship, but Athos filled us in on everything the next morning. He told us how you met and became best friends, how you were there for each other after losing your families, and how much he tried to protect you over the years. Then he explained about his case and what he wanted us to do to keep you safe. At no time was my getting close to you part of the plan.

"Yes, Brody was keeping an eye on you and checking on you whenever he was home, but as I said before, he could have done that from a distance. Egghead is one of those guys who form friendships easily, and I'm sure you two would've become friends even without this whole mess. It's just the way he is."

Biting his bottom lip, Ian paused, trying to gather his

thoughts. "The night of your blind date, I was there to pick up a file I needed. I stood in the living room arguing with myself about going out the backdoor to see if you were there. Obviously, I lost that fight. I asked you out as a man wanting to spend time with a woman he was fascinated with and for no other reason. I found myself checking your video feeds during the day like some crazy stalker, and I'm not proud of it, but without even trying, you got under my skin. And once I tasted you, I knew it wasn't enough.

"I don't do long relationships, Angel. Not since my fiancée walked out on me ten years ago. She wanted someone more romantic, who could read her mind and anticipate her every whim. She wanted someone who would buy her flowers just because it was Wednesday or some other wacky reason. She wanted corny love songs and sky-writing proclaiming how much I loved her."

He snorted and shook his head. "And that's not me. I tried to show her I cared for her in my own way, but it wasn't enough. And I swore I would never go through that again. I would never again let a woman get close enough to me to the point where, when she left me, she took my shredded heart with her. And until I met you, it was never a problem for me." A bewildered expression fell over his face. "But you, sweetheart, *you* make me wish I never took that vow."

He closed his eyes, inhaled deeply, then slowly opened them again, afraid of what he would see in her face . . . in her eyes. Would she hate him, be disgusted with him? Would she never want to see him again, never let him kiss her again? God, he hoped not. His gaze focused on hers, and he was surprised to see sadness instead of anger. Swallowing hard, he waited for her to say something and prayed it wouldn't be "get out."

"What was her name?" Angie whispered.

Of all the things he expected her to say, that wasn't one of them. "Um, Kaliope. Kaliope Levine. She was a . . um . . a news reporter in Virginia near the Navy base."

"Was she your submissive too?"

Ian nodded, and his dropped. "Yes, she was. I met her at a club up there. We were together for almost three years."

She reached over for his hand and squeezed it before letting go again. The gesture shocked him, but not as much as her next words did. "I'm sorry for what she put you through, but I'm not her, Ian, and when this is all over, I think I'd like the chance to prove it to you. But for now, I'm still mad, hurt, and scared out of my mind—for me, you, Jimmy, and your team." She heaved a sigh. "I want to try to sleep, and maybe tomorrow I'll be more tolerant of everything you've done up to this point. I can't guarantee I won't yell some more, but I'll try to refrain from kneeing you in the balls."

Snorting, he gave her a wry grin. "My balls appreciate it, sweetheart." His face became serious again. "Look, I'm not sorry for protecting you–your safety was always a priority–but I will apologize for how we all went about it. We should have . . . I should have told you from the beginning, and I'm sorry I didn't. I stressed how trust is a large portion of BDSM, yet it should also be a major part of the rest of our relationship too. And I know I have to work at earning yours again."

He hesitated momentarily, uncertain how she would react to his next question. "Would it be all right if I sleep next to you tonight? I promise I won't push for anything more. I just want to hold you and keep you safe."

His stomach dropped, and a wave of nausea hit him when she shook her head. "Not right now, Ian." Knowing

HIS ANGEL

he deserved it, he tilted his head in understanding and stood, ready to find another bed for the night. He'd said he wouldn't push her further tonight, and he meant it. "But if you happen to come back while I'm asleep, I won't exactly have a choice, will I?"

His heart soared. Smiling, he leaned down and gave her a gentle kiss on her forehead. "No, you won't, Angel." He kissed her again. "Good night, sweetheart."

Angie buried herself under the blankets and shut her eyes as Ian turned off the lamp and left the room, closing the door behind him. Within minutes, she was asleep.

CHAPTER FIFTEEN

The sun had been up for only a few minutes when Angie awakened the following day, wrapped up in Ian's arms as he spooned her from behind. Despite his morning hard-on, his shallow breathing and heavy arm around her waist told her he was still sound asleep. She'd been so exhausted last night and fallen asleep so fast she had no idea when he'd joined her in the big, comfortable bed. She lay there for a few moments, soaking up his warmth, as everything from the prior day came rushing back to her.

Less than twenty-four hours ago, she'd been doing a job she loved, dating a guy she liked a lot, learning more about herself each day, and being truly happy for the first time in what felt like forever. Now, she was on the run from people who wanted to kidnap and use her against her best friend, who was incommunicado, while a drug cartel was after him. Her normal happy life was falling to pieces, and she didn't know how to stop it.

Although she was working past it, she was still

wrestling with the fact Ian had lied to her. Yes, the anger and hurt were still there, but so was the understanding of why he and Jimmy had done what they did. Jake had been right—men like her lover and her best friend were wired differently. They needed to feel needed and protect the people they cared about at all costs, even if she disagreed with how they went about it.

Her bladder began insisting she get up and relieve the building pressure, so she eased away from Ian and climbed out of the bed. After she finished, she took a quick shower while avoiding getting her hair wet. Instead of washing it, she put it up in an easy twist with a clip she'd picked up at the store's beauty section. She pulled on a pair of her new sweatpants and a T-shirt over one of the sports bras, thinking she might take a run later when someone could go with her.

Turning toward the bed, she examined Ian as he continued to sleep, now on his stomach with his hands under his pillow. His jaw and upper lip had the morning stubble she loved when he rubbed it against her inner thighs while going down on her. A lock of his hair had fallen onto his forehead, and she fought the urge to put it back in its place. She didn't want to wake him, knowing he probably needed the sleep. The sheet had been pushed down, exposing his muscular back and upper buttocks. Damn, the man had granite buns she wanted to take a bite out of.

If she stared at him much longer, she would jump his bones, so instead, she searched for her new toothbrush among her toiletries on his dresser. It was then she noticed he'd found a pair of cotton shorts, which she assumed were Jenn's, and left them out for her. No matter what, she had

HIS ANGEL

to admit he did show he cared in his own little ways, like making sure she was comfortable and safe and always putting her first. When they had sex, he made certain she was satisfied before he took his own pleasure. He opened doors for her and held out her chair without a second thought. At dinner at his place, he'd fill her plate before taking his own meal. Her wants and needs always seemed to come before his. And above all, he was jeopardizing his life and his team's lives because hers was in danger. She thought back to what Kristen had said in the ladies' room at the gala about how Devon made her feel cherished, and Angie realized it was precisely how Ian made her feel. So what if he wasn't a flowers and poetry kind of guy? He may not be a romantic by definition, but she would take being cherished over romance any day.

After brushing her teeth, she grabbed the art pad and sketching pencils she'd found in the craft section of Walmart. Tip-toeing out of the room, she closed the door behind her. In the kitchen, she found a Keurig coffee machine and brewed herself a single cup of the Brazilian blend she selected from the carousel next to the machine. The house was quiet except for the sounds of her coffee cup being filled.

Not wanting to cook so early and wake anybody else up, she picked out a bran muffin from the assorted box of sixteen Jake had left on the counter. She took it, along with her coffee and art supplies, outside to the front porch. It was chilly, but she wanted the fresh air, so she placed her things on a small table and returned to retrieve a blanket from the back of the living room couch. After making herself warm and comfortable in a lounge chair, which gave her a beautiful view of the lake below, she had her simple breakfast and tried not to think about the danger they were all in.

When her muffin was gone, Angie picked up the sketch pad and pulled a pencil out of the package of six. Opening the pad to the first blank page, she let her mind wander as she began to sketch. A little while later, she was startled when she heard a voice behind her. "Wow, that's me."

She looked over her shoulder. Jake stood behind her chair, rumpled in a University of Tampa T-shirt and gray sweatpants. He must've just rolled out of bed, and she hadn't heard him come out the door. He held a steaming cup of coffee in his hand as he studied the picture of his face she'd drawn from memory. She didn't need to confirm his statement since the sketch was close to what a photograph of him might look like.

"Why do I seem so sad? Is that what I look like to you?"

She nodded as he sat in a chair catty-cornered to her and crossed his sneaker-covered feet at the ankles, resting them on the bottom slats of her lounge. "Sometimes. When you think no one is watching, or your mind seems to be somewhere else, you get this sad, faraway look on your face."

"Huh," he grunted before taking a sip of his coffee, not contradicting her observations of him. "So, are you feeling better this morning? Not so stressed out and angry?" He narrowed his eyes and teased her. "You didn't murder Ian in his sleep last night or cut off his most prized possession, did you?"

Laughing, she shook her head. "No, he's breathing and still has all his man parts, but don't think I wasn't tempted a time or two."

He smiled and remained quiet as she considered his face, then made a few minor changes to the sketch she was

HIS ANGEL

still fiddling with. Without thinking, she blurted out, "Do you have a girlfriend?"

"*Ha!* Uh, no, I don't, sweetheart." His amused expression confused her until he added, "I think the more appropriate question would be 'Do I have a boyfriend?' and the answer would still be no." Her mouth gaped, and her cheeks heated, but he didn't seem fazed by her shock. "Yes, Angie, I'm gay. And yes, most people know."

"Wow." She shook her head but smiled simultaneously, not wanting him to think she believed there was anything wrong with being gay. "Um, sorry. It's just the gay guy friends I have aren't as macho and hunky as you are." She winced. "That sounded stereotypical, didn't it?"

He snorted and took another sip from his cup. "Macho and hunky, huh? Yeah, well, that's the thing about being gay–it doesn't discriminate. We come in all shapes and sizes."

She opened her mouth to ask him something but changed her mind and glanced at her sketch.

"Go ahead and ask your question, Angie. I'm not ashamed of who I am."

Glancing at him, she shrugged her right shoulder. "I didn't think you were since you came right out and told me, and you're not embarrassed about it, which you shouldn't be. I just can't help but think about how you can work with Ian and the rest of them without being attracted to any of them. I mean, you're all good-looking men."

Jake nodded in understanding and didn't give the impression her question put him off. "I'll admit I fought a lot of attractions to straight guys throughout my whole career in the Navy—hell, pretty much my whole life—but when it comes to the team, we've been together so long that they've become my brothers. I have no more attraction to any of them than I do to my own blood brother, Mike."

"When did you realize you were gay?" Her eyes widened at her unintentional bluntness. Her brain-to-mouth filter wasn't working that early in the morning. "Sorry, that's way too personal. Don't answer that."

"No, it's fine." He tilted his head and held her stare. "I like you, Angie, and I'm not like Brody, who makes friends easily wherever he goes, so I hold onto the ones I have. I like to think we've become friends in the short time I've known you."

She gave him a shy smile. "I think we've become friends too."

"Good." He raised his cup of coffee in a silent toast to their new friendship, then drank what little remained. "So, in answer to your question, I guess I've known since puberty, maybe a little earlier. Like most gay people, I struggled with it initially because it was out of the norm from how I was raised, especially since my father was a homophobic jackass."

Wincing, she asked, "How did he take it when you came out, or haven't you ever told him?"

"Oh, he found out, somehow, when I was a senior in high school. Beat the ever-living shit out of me, too, thinking it would convince me to go straight—as if I had a choice. Up to that point, he'd been living his life vicariously through me. He'd been a mediocre football player in high school, and here was his youngest son, the star quarterback on the football team, with a full ride to Rutgers. After he beat me near unconscious with his belt three months before graduation, I couldn't go to school for almost two weeks. My mother called me in sick with the flu or something and nursed me back to health. My father wouldn't let

HIS ANGEL

her take me to the hospital or even a doctor—God forbid someone found out he'd beaten his son, the faggot."

He shrugged off the fucked-up memory. "Anyway, after I recovered, I was done with him. I threw my scholarship in his face and enlisted the afternoon I graduated from high school, which also happened to be my eighteenth birthday. I would never have seen my father again if it weren't for my mom and brother. As it was, we may have said less than a dozen words to each other for the rest of his life. He died four years ago, and the only reason I ever regretted our estrangement was for how much it hurt my mother and brother."

Despite what he had said earlier about their friendship, Jake suddenly seemed shocked by how much he'd told her and stopped talking. A look of surprise came over his handsome face when she stood with tears in her eyes and pulled on his hand until he was also standing, then hugged the stuffing out of him.

With only the sounds of nature surrounding them, they held each other for a minute. Angie's heart broke for the teenager he'd been and how his father had assaulted and disowned him for something beyond Jake's control. "Is that how you got the scars on your back?" He pulled away and eyed her with confusion, probably trying to remember when she would've seen his bare back. "Ian told me it's why you didn't take your shirt off in the club the night you were Whip Master. You were soaked in sweat but kept it on."

Letting go of her completely, he nodded. "Yeah, that's why. There are several scars where the belt buckle did some permanent damage. I try not to show them to anyone if it can be avoided."

Not knowing what else to say, Angie grabbed her pad and carefully ripped Jake's sketch out before handing it to

213

him. "I hope someday I can draw you when you're truly happy and find someone you love to share your life with. You deserve it."

He gave her a wry smile and kissed her on the cheek. "I don't know if that'll ever happen, sweetheart, but if it does, I hope he's the male version of you—kick-ass and tender, all wrapped up in one beautiful package." He paused and winked at her. "And not afraid of his kinky side."

The two of them laughed. Angie was about to say something snarky when the front door opened, and Brody stuck his head out. "Athos is on the phone."

All thoughts of what she and Jake had been discussing took a backseat to her best friend's welfare. She was desperate to hear his voice and ran past Brody as he held the door open for her, then he and Jake followed her back inside. Ian was standing in the living room, talking on his cell phone. He looked like he'd just woken up, too, and as soon as he saw her, he told Athos he was putting him on speaker. Pushing a button, he held out the phone so she could hear and talk to her friend. "Jimmy? Where are you? Are you okay?"

"I'm okay, baby. I'm so sorry about this. Having you involved in this was the last thing I ever wanted. I'm on my way to meet you, and we'll talk when I get there, okay? Just do what Ian tells you to do, and stay safe."

A little more at ease after hearing his familiar, comforting voice, she looked up at Ian and said into the phone's mic, "I will. You stay safe, yourself, and get your sorry ass here as soon as possible so I can kick it from here to the moon."

A chuckle came over the line. "That's my girl. I'll see you soon."

Ian told Athos where Jake and Brody would meet him in Spartanburg, South Carolina, near the airport they'd flown into. After they were certain they weren't being followed, the three men would return to the safe house, where they would all sit down and figure out how to get Angie out of this mess. After he hung up the phone, Ian texted CC, telling the pilot to fly back to Tampa and pick up Marco, Boomer, and Tiny. He'd bring them up to Spartanburg, where another SUV would be waiting for them so they could drive to the safe house. Ian then called his brother and filled him in, ensuring all was safe and sound back at the compound.

Twenty minutes later, Jake and Brody were on their way back to South Carolina. They would reach their destination around the same time as Athos, who'd been taking the back roads since yesterday. In the meantime, Ian and Angie had about three hours to kill. She was staring out the front window at the lake when he came up behind her and wrapped his arms around her waist, pulling her rear flush against his front. He knew he wasn't out of trouble with her yet but was pleased to feel her relax into his embrace. Nuzzling his chin to her neck, he placed soft, gentle kisses on the skin covering her pulse, loving how a shiver went through her. When she tilted her head to give him better access, he nibbled and licked the tender area. She moaned and reacted by pushing her ass into his groin, which made his dick happy and hard. He smiled against her skin when she said in a husky voice, "Just so you know, I'm still mad at you."

Ian slid a hand up to play with one of her breasts while the other hand slid down and cupped her mound. "I know. But how about we try a little make-up sex, *hmm*?" The hand at her breast squeezed her lush flesh while his fingers down below rubbed her clit through her clothes. Her hips began to undulate as she reached back with both hands and grabbed hold of his ass, trying to keep him still while she teased his massive erection through his jeans. "Oh, shit, Angel. You feel so good. Let me make you forget about everything, just for a little while."

She gasped when he bit down hard on the spot where her neck and shoulder met. A swipe of his tongue followed as he soothed the sting away. He knew her body wouldn't let her deny him, even if her brain wanted to. She needed what he offered—a brief period where her mind wasn't focused on the danger they all faced. "Yeeesssss."

The single word came out as a hiss as he increased the pressure on her clit and tweaked her nipple through her thin shirt and bra. He spun her around, wrapped his arms below her hips, and lifted her so she had no choice but to hook her legs around his waist and her arms around his neck. The position put his rigid cock in contact with her mound, and she whimpered with need. She kissed him with all the passion and desperation inside her as he carried her into his bedroom, kicking the door shut behind them. After easing her down to the bed, Ian checked his phone to ensure the security system was armed and then set the device on the nightstand. His gun, holstered at the small of his back, went right next to the phone.

Pulling her up into a sitting position, he yanked off her shirt, followed by her sports bra. Her sweats and thong went next, and soon, his shirt and jeans were added to the growing pile on the floor. Kneeling next to the side of the bed, Ian put his hands under her ass and pulled her to the edge of the mattress. Placing his hand between her breasts, he urged her to lie down until she was flat on her back and then put her legs over his shoulders.

The scent of her arousal hit his nose, and his mouth watered. To hell with slow and easy. He parted her pussy lips with his thumbs and attacked her sex like a man who'd gone without for years. He licked her slit several times from bottom to top, moaning at her taste, and nibbled on both sides of her opening before stiffening his tongue and stabbing it into her. Angie's hips bounced off the bed as she screamed his name, begging for more.

Her hands dove into his hair. While one hand held his head to her core, the other pulled on the short strands, making him growl as the sexual beast inside him was unleashed. He flicked her clit with his tongue and plunged two fingers into her hot, wet pussy. Finding and rubbing the magic spot, he sent her flying, her shrill cry filling the room.

Not waiting for her to recover, Ian stood, flipped her onto her stomach and grabbed the lubricant that he'd found in Boomer's room and placed in the nightstand drawer along with the two boxes of condoms. He wouldn't need one of those this time. He'd been prepping her tight little asshole for over two weeks now, and he couldn't wait any longer to take her there. With both of their health clearances signed and completed, he wanted to fuck her ass with nothing but skin between them.

Popping open the lid of the bottle, he poured some lube down her crack while he took two fingers from his other hand and shoved them back into her still-quivering pussy. She hadn't been expecting it, and the sudden penetration sent another orgasm spiraling through her, her walls squeezing his digits together as he pumped them in and out of her channel. While she was still coming, he ran his free middle finger up the valley between her ass cheeks and coated it with the silky fluid before easing it into her back hole. She took it without a problem, and it wasn't long before he added his index finger to join the other one.

"Oh, God. Yes. Yeeesss. Yeeeeesssss. Oh, God!" Her lungs heaved, and she pushed her hips backward, trying to get him as far into her body as he could. "Please, Sir. Don't make me wait. Take me now. Fuck my ass and come inside me. Pleeeaaasseee!"

Any other time, Ian would've made her wait and drawn out the sweet torture, reminding her he was in charge and not allowing her to top from the bottom. But now he needed her as much as she needed him. While he made a scissor motion with the two fingers in her ass, stretching her more, he grabbed the bottle of lube again and poured some on his aching shaft.

After tossing the recapped bottle aside, he pulled his fingers from her puckered rosette and grabbed her hips, tugging until her feet touched the floor and her torso was bent over the bed. Using one hand to spread her cheeks, he used the other to guide the tip of his cock to where it was begging to be. Slowly, he pushed forward and watched as her body yielded to his invasion.

"*Aaahhhh.* More. Oh, fuck, Sir, give me more. It burns but feels so good. Don't stop. Oh, please don't stop."

Her pleading spurred him on, and once he was sure he wouldn't hurt her, he thrust his hips forward until he filled her, making her gasp then beg him to do it again. He growled when she tried to get him to move, holding back the desperate urge to take her like a rutting animal. "Fuck, Angel. You feel like heaven. I'm not going to last long."

He pumped his hips slowly, loving the drag of her tight rim along his length. Need whipped through him, and he couldn't refuse his body's urgent desire to mark her as his in the most primal way possible. He sped up his thrusts as they both grunted and groaned, reaching for the utmost pinnacle where they would take flight together.

A tingling started in Ian's lower spine and spread to his heavy balls, slapping against her pussy with every inward thrust. Reaching around her hip, he worked his hand between Angie's body and the bed and found her little pearl. Just before his own release ripped through him, he pinched her clit and sent her tumbling over before him. As the waves of her orgasm hit her, the muscles of her empty vagina and her stuffed ass clenched in unison, and she milked the seed from his body.

Ian wasn't sure how long he stood behind her, his cock still buried deep, while he covered her upper body with his. Most of his weight was placed on his forearms on either side of her shoulders, and he kissed her on the head. His heaving lungs sated their desperate need for oxygen, and his breathing slowed to a more normal rate. "Are you okay, Angel?"

"Mmm-hmm."

He chuckled at her exhausted response. His cock slid from her well-used hole, and they both groaned at the loss of contact. Pushing off the bed, Ian placed a hand on her buttocks until he was sure he was steady on his feet. Squeezing a fleshy globe, he told her to stay where she was while he retrieved a wet washcloth to clean her. As he finished wiping away the evidence of their wicked and wild make-up sex, his phone chimed a text, followed by an alert that a vehicle had breached the security sensor on the road leading to the safe house.

Grabbing his phone, he checked the text and saw it was from Carter, advising Ian he'd be pulling into the safe house driveway in less than five minutes.

Fuck! For once, the black-ops spy had shitty timing . . . and how the hell did he know they were here in the first place?

CHAPTER SIXTEEN

Reluctantly, Ian took a two-minute shower while Angie dozed under the covers he'd tucked around her after picking her up and putting her to bed properly. He wished he could join her in blissful slumber just to wake her in an hour or so and do everything again. Instead, he got dressed in his jeans and T-shirt again and left the bedroom barefoot, shutting the door behind him. He found Carter helping himself to a cup of coffee, a banana, and two chocolate chip muffins.

While his friend stuffed his face for a few minutes, Ian grabbed a bottle of water from the fridge and gulped down the contents. Sex with Angie always left him parched, not that he was complaining. Tossing the empty bottle in the recycling bin under the sink, he grabbed another one and sat at the kitchen island next to Carter. "Should I bother to ask how you knew we were here? And don't tell me you're here just for the food, ass-hat."

The spy showing up 'just for the food' was a long-standing flat joke between him and Ian's team and was usually brought up when they ran into each other on a mission. If the spy said that's why he was there, it meant his operation was classified and he couldn't discuss it with anyone, not even the former SEALs with government clearance, whom he considered his closest friends. For a man in his deadly business, having six friends he could count on in life-and-death situations was a lot, and he never took them for granted.

Carter grinned as he chewed the last bite of his muffins and then swallowed. He took a swig of his coffee, knowing Ian was impatient for an answer. "Nope. This time, the food is a bonus. And thanks, I was starving. As for why I'm here . . . I got a message from Athos saying he was in trouble and couldn't trust anyone in his agency. Said he was heading to Spartanburg, South Carolina, and I assumed this was his final destination. Have you heard from him yet?" Without waiting for an answer, he added, "I take it your new girlfriend is in your bedroom catching up on some much-needed sleep."

Ian rolled his eyes as the other man waggled his eyebrows, à la Groucho Marx. "You can be a real asshole sometimes. You know that, don't you?"

"Of course. It's what I do best."

With a snort, Ian shook his head at Carter's matter-of-fact statement. "Yeah, Angie's sleeping. We heard from Athos over an hour ago. Reverend and Egghead went to pick him up. Devon's holding down the fort, and CC is on his way to Tampa to bring back Boomer, Polo, and Tiny. I figured the big guy might be handy if I needed an extra body to watch over her. Once we get the full update from Athos, we'll decide what to do next."

Carter nodded, apparently satisfied there was nothing that needed his immediate attention. "Good. Since I have close to two and a half hours before they get back, I'm going to sack out for a bit."

As the other man got up and placed his empty cup in the dishwasher and his garbage in the trash, Ian told him, "Take Jenn's room. I'll give Athos the spare room my folks use." His parents didn't visit Maggie Valley often, but when they did, the primary suite on the main floor was theirs.

Without another word, Carter gave him a small salute, grabbed his military green duffel bag from where he'd left it next to the front door, and headed upstairs for a quick shower and some shut-eye.

Since his friend was now taken care of, Ian returned to his bedroom and locked the door. Stripping his shirt off once again but leaving his jeans on, he climbed into bed, pulled Angie's sleeping form into his arms, and closed his eyes.

* * *

An hour and a half later, Ian was sitting on the wide porch stairs, staring at the lake while Angie finished drying her hair after their shared shower, which took longer than necessary, as usual. He'd gotten a text a short while ago from Jake saying they would be back at the house in about forty minutes or so, and Ian was getting antsy. The faster Athos got here, the faster they could figure out how to end the threat against Angie. His cell phone alerted him to another text, and Ian checked the screen. Devon was letting him know Marco, Boomer, and Tiny were heading out to the small airport to meet CC, and they would be in the air within the hour.

The door behind him opened, and he didn't need to turn around to know it was his angel. The fresh scent of her shampoo and body soap hit him, and he felt a stirring in his groin. Damn, the woman made it hard for him to think about anything but sex when she was near him. She walked down two steps and plopped her sweet ass on the top stair beside him. "It's beautiful up here."

Ian put his arm around her, tucked her close to his body, and rested her head on his shoulder. "It certainly is. I wish I could get up here more often for pleasure instead of business. If you hadn't noticed, the compound is kind of lacking in its landscaping within the fence lines."

She giggled. "I did *kinda* notice. Will you retire up here someday?"

"Maybe," he mused with a shrug of his unoccupied shoulder. "Or maybe I'll buy a small island in the Caribbean . . . my little oasis in the middle of nowhere. Wherever I end up, there has to be water somewhere, whether it's a lake or the ocean."

They sat in silence for a few minutes before the door behind them opened again, and Carter walked out and then down the steps to the gravel below before facing the couple. He'd changed out of his cargo pants and now wore a faded pair of jeans, a clean T-shirt, and his combat boots.

Ian squeezed the woman at his side. "Angie, Carter. Carter, Angie."

The spy held out his hand to her. "He speaks so eloquently sometimes, doesn't he?"

* * *

Angie laughed and shook the man's hand. "Yes, he does, but I don't mind. It's nice to meet you."

"It's nice to meet you too, sweetheart, but I wish it were under better circumstances." Ian had told her about Carter's presence in the house and why the man was here while he'd washed her hair in the shower. "Sorry I didn't have a chance to meet you at the club the other night, but I found myself . . . occupied . . . longer than I expected. I

HIS ANGEL

would've liked to have watched your first public scene because I heard it was fantastic and had a happy ending."

Angie dipped her head and blushed while both men laughed. She didn't know why she turned so red now when being spanked and brought to an intense orgasm in front of an audience hadn't embarrassed her at all at the time. Carter gave her a wink, and she shook her head, smiling at his teasing.

She didn't have to ask what had kept him occupied at the time because Kristen had filled her in. Carter had joined the engaged couple for a repeat threesome, and Kristen hadn't been wearing a blindfold for her second introduction to the good-looking Dom. There also hadn't been any time constraints that they'd had during their first tryst, so the three of them had been in one of the private playrooms for a few hours. Her friend hadn't given her many details, but having read romances with ménages before, Angie didn't need a picture painted for her.

While she wasn't interested in experiencing a threesome for herself, she had no problem with anyone else having one. She barely survived the intense orgasms Ian gave her on a regular basis these days, and there was no way she could handle two men at once. Ian had been happy to see ménages were on her hard limit list she'd given him. He'd told her he'd been a third once, in his early days of being a Dom. And while it had been a great experience, he found he didn't like sharing his women, unlike his brother and some of their friends.

Angie got to her feet. "I was going to make myself a sandwich. Is anyone else hungry?" When both men said, "Yes, please," she looked at Carter. "I know what he wants, but what would you like to eat?"

With a broad grin, he wiggled his eyebrows, and she

laughed at his playfulness while Ian growled. "All right, since Ian's going to deck me if I say anything sexual, I'll take whatever you're making for him, but no mayo, please. I hate the stuff."

"No mayo, no problem." She ran her hand through Ian's short hair as she climbed the two steps back onto the porch, then went inside to make them lunch.

* * *

Ian growled again as Carter's blatant gaze stayed glued to Angie's ass until she disappeared into the house. "Really, asshole?"

The spy shrugged his shoulders and then sat down next to Ian. "What? Like you've said many times in the past, 'Just because I can't touch, doesn't mean I can't look.' Too bad you're not into threesomes because that is one beautiful backside, my friend, and I'd have to be six feet under not to appreciate it." He glanced sideways at the man who was still glaring at him and let out a snort. "So, she's the one, huh?"

Ian's eyes narrowed even further. Before he could respond, his phone chimed with an alert. A vehicle had activated a sensor when it turned up the road leading to the house. A second later, he received Jake's text letting him know they were coming up the hill. He glared at Carter again. "The one . . . what?"

"The one who will make you forget you ever had a bitch of a fiancée who fucked you over. It's about damn time."

"Fuck you, asshole," Ian scoffed. "You know I'm never going down that road again."

"Ha! You keep telling yourself that, dude, but from where I stand, you're not only heading down a road, but you're heading down the *right* road. And here I thought you would wallow in sorrow for the rest of your life because the woman you weren't *supposed* to spend it with walked out on you. Did you ever think the reason it happened is making your lunch right now and has a very nice ass?"

Before Ian could tell Carter to fuck off again, the team's SUV pulled into the driveway with Brody at the wheel and Jake in the front passenger seat. The vehicle parked, and when the front doors opened, so did the rear passenger door, and a clean-shaven but tired-looking Athos climbed out of the vehicle. The two men on the steps stood and approached the trio.

As Carter shook hands with the DEA agent, commenting on his de-whiskered face, Ian eyed his teammates. "How'd everything go?"

"Good," Brody told him. "No trackers, no worries."

Ian nodded at the geek, who headed toward the house. As he reached the top of the porch stairs, Angie burst out the door and ran down the steps toward the car . . . toward her best friend and jumped into his waiting arms. Ian's heart squeezed, and his fists clenched as he watched his woman hug another man as tight as she could. Grinding his teeth, he forced himself not to beat his chest and yank her out of Athos' embrace like his inner caveman wanted to do.

Next to him, Carter said in a low, amused voice that no one else could hear, "Uh-huh. Keep telling yourself she's not the one, Boss-man. Maybe someday you can convince yourself, but I doubt it."

* * *

Ten minutes later, Angie handed a plate with a heaping sandwich on rye bread to Ian and another one to Carter, then got busy making sandwiches for Jimmy and herself. Jake stood on the opposite side of the kitchen island, throwing together a similar lunch for himself and Brody. Egghead was upstairs in the den, tracking down some information they needed concerning several agents from the DEA's Atlanta office, including Agents Jackson and Holstein. Athos confirmed their identities from the surveillance photos Brody had printed out.

When they were done making the sandwiches, Jake ran Brody's lunch up to the war-room before joining Angie and the rest of them at the large dining table. Angie noticed as she sat down that Ian hadn't touched his sandwich yet. She smiled to herself when she saw he didn't pick it up until after he watched her take a bite of her own. He'd waited until he was sure she would eat as well. Since she realized he was always putting her welfare before his own, she noticed a lot more of the little things he did and loved how they made her feel. The man may not be a romantic in the traditional sense, but he was a romantic in his own way.

While they all ate, Athos filled Ian and Carter in with what he'd told the others on the way back to the house. "Things seemed fine the first two weeks. I used contacts I'd made a few years ago to work my way under. I got lucky. Met up with a guy who only knew my cover, and he vouched for me. A local cop on the take ran me for the boss, found my established arrest record, and I was in. Did some small-time runs right off the bat. They had a few run-ins with the cops and local gangs recently, so they were down a few guys. Otherwise, I don't think I would've gotten in so fast. Yesterday morning, I was doing some snooping around and overheard a big shipment was coming in next Monday through the Gulf of Mexico from Colombia's Diaz cartel—"

* * *

"Ah, shit, man," Carter interrupted, dropping his half-eaten sandwich on his plate. He glanced knowingly at Ian, who was pissed as all hell that the Diaz cartel was involved in this mess. "Emmanuel is behind all this? Damn, when you step in it, you really step in it, A-man."

Athos dragged a hand down his face in frustration. "Don't I know it. Aaron, the agent I replaced, suspected that's where the trail ended, but I don't think Diaz was behind the hit on him and his family. I think it came from lower down the food chain with inside help from the DEA." He looked at the government spy. "You know there's dirt in every agency, and mine has its fair share."

"How'd you find out you were blown?" Ian was trying to think past the cartel's involvement and his fear for Angie. His SEAL Team Four had been involved in investigating and eventually killing Emmanuel's brother, Ernesto, several years earlier. Not only was the cartel involved in drugs, but they also, at the time, had a thriving sex trade and arms trade, which Emmanuel was working hard to reestablish after his brother's death.

"Same conversation. After I overheard the details, the head honcho of New Orleans' drug trade, Manny Melendez, got a phone call from someone. The next thing I knew, he ordered the hit on me and told whoever was on the phone to find out my weaknesses. I got out of there as fast as I could and called you."

Angie sat silently between him and Ian, and he reached over and took her hand. His eyes filled with deep regret. "I'm so sorry, baby. You know I'd never do anything which would result in you getting hurt. I've always taken precautions to keep you safe."

Ian didn't know who was surprised more, him or Athos, when Angie tore her hand free from her best friend's grip and stood while glaring at him. "Really, Jimmy? If that were true, then I wouldn't have had two crooked DEA agents knocking on my door, wanting to kidnap me and probably kill me. I wouldn't be running for my life and the lives of these men," she gestured around the table, "wouldn't be in danger because they were protecting me."

Athos got up from his seat, and so did Ian, but neither man could get a word in because the woman was on a roll now, yelling and pointing her finger at her friend's nose. "I wouldn't be hiding out up here and worrying you might be dead somewhere. And don't think I forgot about you telling them to bug my house and put cameras in." She huffed and crossed her arms. "I don't even know how this whole mess will end. Am I going to be running for the rest of my life until one of those bastards catches up to me? Will I ever be able to go home again? Will I—"

"Ang, stop yelling. Calm down and sit down."

As soon as the growled orders were out of Athos' mouth, Ian knew things would get worse from the look on Angie's face. He was just glad her ire had another target this time. She snarled at her friend, her hands clenched in rage. "Don't tell me what to do, and you don't get to pull that dominant crap on me because I get more than enough from Ian."

She turned on her heel and stormed out the front door while Athos glared at Ian, who returned it to him in spades. "Is she fucking kidding me? I told you to watch over her and keep her safe, not fuck her and get her involved in your god-damned kink. And yeah, I know all about your fucking sex club, asshole, and you're not fucking taking her there."

While Ian tried to keep himself from punching the guy, the other two men stood from the table and strode toward the door after the very pissed off-woman. Jake glanced over his shoulder. "We'll go and keep an eye on Angie. Just don't kill each other until after we take care of the main objective, all right?"

HIS ANGEL

Neither man answered him because it'd been a rhetorical question. Instead, they stared each other down, and Ian was astounded when Athos broke eye contact first, sighing in frustration and running his fingers through his hair. "Fuck. Sorry. You can kick my ass later. I have no say about who she dates or what you two do. I just want her to be happy and safe. If you're the man to do that, then . . ."

Athos left the rest of the sentence unsaid, and Ian could see the defeat in his expression. He crossed his arms over his chest and leaned against the dining table where the remnants of everyone's lunch still sat. He studied the other man for a minute. "Does she know?"

Athos looked at him in confusion. "Does she know . . . what?"

"That you're in love with her?"

The question was obviously the last thing Athos expected him to ask. Mirroring Ian's stance, he leaned against the back of the couch and stared at something over Ian's shoulder. "To love someone the way she deserves, you have to have not only a heart but a soul as well. I lost both of those a long time ago. I've been trying to get even for my mother's and sister's deaths for so long . . ." He shook his head sadly. "I have nothing left to give her, which is why I stay away from her as much as I can, yet still hold on because she's all I've got."

He paused and regarded Ian a moment. "So, right back at you, Sawyer. Does she know you're in love with her? Because I'm not blind either, man."

Before Ian could respond, although he wasn't sure what his answer would've been, Brody came barreling down the stairs from the den with his laptop in hand. He placed it on the dining table so both men could see the screen. "We've got big trouble."

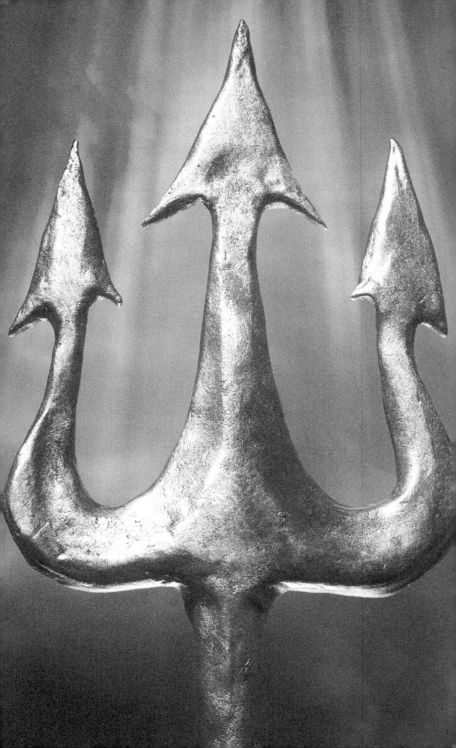

CHAPTER SEVENTEEN

Ian and Athos closed in on the table to read the news brief from Atlanta's CBS website, and both started cursing. Athos' handler, Arthur Giles, Special Agent in Charge of the Atlanta DEA office, had been killed in a drive-by shooting. He had been gunned down as he exited his vehicle at his home on the city's outskirts around a quarter after seven last night. There were no reported suspects, but the police and feds were looking at a local gang of drug runners.

"Fuck! God damn it!" Athos plunged both hands through his hair again and spun around, looking for something to vent his anger on. Not finding anything other than a wall, he punched it, and the pain didn't even register as his knuckles began to swell. "His daughter had his first grandchild a month ago. And now he's dead because of my fucking need to get even with those bastards."

"You don't know that for sure." Ian didn't believe his own words but needed to calm the man down. Athos rounded on him, getting in his face, but Ian didn't back down.

"Don't I? Come on, Sawyer, don't fucking patronize me. You know how this fucking goes. They're cleaning house after the cartel found two DEA agents from the same office had infiltrated them. Someone found out who our fucking handler was and stopped any more interference from him. No one from Atlanta was supposed to know where Artie sent us. Fuck, no one in Atlanta was even supposed to know who the hell Aaron was."

Ian didn't say anything more because they both knew the likelihood of Athos being wrong was slim to none. There were very few coincidences in their line of work, and he doubted this was one of them. Carter had heard the commotion and returned to see what was wrong. Ian pointed to the still-open laptop, and the operative walked over to read it, adding his own curses to the ones they'd spouted out earlier.

He pinned the DEA agent with an understanding stare, having overheard his last rant. "Don't beat yourself up, A-man. If you didn't volunteer, Artie would've sent in someone else, and the result would've been the same. Put the blame where it belongs—on the dirty agents and the cartel." He paused and let his words sink into the man's brain. "Artie was the only one who knew you went under, wasn't he?"

The agitated man nodded. It meant he had no one he could trust in his department. They knew two of his fellow agents were dirty and had no idea who else at the Atlanta office was on the take. He couldn't risk contacting anyone until he knew it was safe. For now, Carter and the Trident team were his only backup.

Ian arched an eyebrow at Carter. "Where's Angie?"

"She took a walk with Jake. She's still pissed off, and I

wasn't stupid enough to stay in the line of fire. That woman is a firecracker."

Brody had been quiet since he first came down and now took a deep breath. "Okay, so where do we go from here? Athos has no backup from his agency. His handler is dead. We can't take out the whole New Orleans cartel without starting an all-out war or getting ourselves life in prison or worse. Angie's still in danger. Did I miss anything?"

"Nope, and thanks for stating the obvious, Egghead."

"No problem, Carter. Glad I could help keep you in the loop." Turning his sarcasm off, he asked, "Now, does someone have a plan?"

While they all remained silent, trying to think of a way out of this horror story they'd found themselves in, Ian's phone rang. Glancing at the screen, he saw it was the backup phone his brother kept in his car. "Hey, Dev, what's up?"

"Jenn's been kidnapped!"

Ian stiffened in shock, not believing what Devon had just blurted out. Panic assaulted him. "What do you mean Jenn's been kidnapped?"

The other three men also froze in place, wide eyes searching Ian's pale face as if it held all the answers to their questions. He punched the speaker button and set the phone on the table so they could all gather around.

His brother's frantic voice came through loud and clear. "Henderson called. I put him and his partner on Jenn, just in case. They were pulled over by an unmarked car while driving her to the college. From the description he gave me before I lost him, it sounds like the two agents who tried to get Angie. Henderson took a bullet to the chest, and his partner was shot in the head. I think Henderson passed out, but the line is still open—it's why I'm on the backup. I'm on the way to the scene now and just heard the cops and paramedics arrive."

"Was Jenn hurt?"

"I don't know, Ian. All I know is she's gone. I'm about five minutes away. I'll call you back as soon as I know anything. Marco called about twenty minutes ago and said they landed and are on the road."

"I'll call them and have them turn around, then make sure CC's ready to take off again. Keep me posted." Ian disconnected the phone.

"Don't turn them around." Brody rushed up the stairs to get his gear from the den. He raised his voice so he could be heard without stopping. "If they're already on the road, we can have CC do a quick hop to the airport in Ashville. It's about halfway between us. We can meet them there, and it'll save us some time."

"Good. Call him and get him in the air." Ian jerked his chin at Carter. "Can you go get Jake and Angie? We're out of here in five."

Without an answer, the man jogged out the door. Once he was out of sight, Ian grabbed Athos by the neck and shoved him up against the wall. The agent grabbed his wrists but wisely didn't resist. Ian let out a low growl. "If anything happens to my goddaughter because of you, you won't have to fucking worry about the cartel. You hear me?"

Regret filled Athos' eyes. "I hear you and wouldn't expect anything less from you. For what it's worth, I'm sorry."

"I don't give a shit about your fucking apology. Just help us get Jenn back, then we finish this and guarantee Angie's safety."

HIS ANGEL

Without waiting for a response, Ian released him and moved toward his bedroom. "Let's grab what we need and get the hell out of here. I'll call Marco from the road."

* * *

A few minutes after they were all in the air, Brody held out his hand to Boomer. "Did you bring my new toy?"

The man reached into the pocket of his jeans and handed the geek the piece of jewelry he'd asked him to grab from the war-room. Walking from the couch area to where Angie was sitting alone in the same seat she'd occupied on their first flight, Brody sat beside her and asked her to hold out her left arm for him. She was still pissed about everything and now terrified that Jenn had been kidnapped and possibly hurt or worse.

When he finished attaching the gold bracelet to her wrist, she stared at it in confusion. "Um, Brody, I don't have any allergies, and I'm not a diabetic or anything, so what's with the medical alert bracelet?"

"It just says you're allergic to bees, sweetheart. Nothing serious. In the meantime, if something happens, which we'll avoid at all costs, I can track you with the GPS in there. If I'm close enough, there's also a one-way hidden microphone so I can listen in on what's going on around you through a receiver in my laptop. It's short range, but the GPS is long range. If I need to, I can always," he coughed the word "hack" before continuing, "into a satellite to track you. No one wears ID bracelets anymore, and I needed the room inside, so I figured a fake medical alert was the best thing to use. It's a prototype, and you're my guinea pig . . . sorry, figure of speech."

Still holding her hand, he hesitated a moment as if struggling with what he wanted to say next. "Are you and I okay? I know you're still pissed over us bugging your house, but, sweetheart, my friendship with you was . . . *is* the real thing."

She nodded and saw his tense body relax. Her voice was forgiving but tired. "I know, Brody. It's just that everything hit me at once, you know? I've been independent for so long, and I hate being left out of things that concern me. I'll get over it, but you better get your ass over to my house as soon as this is all over and take out every single one of those cameras and bugs." She glared at him to let him know she meant business. "Understand?"

"Yes, ma'am!" He grinned at her with his famous flirtatious expression. "You know, if I didn't know better, I'd think you were a Domme at times. That's called a switch, by the way. But don't tell Ian I told you. He'll shoot me for putting ideas in your head."

"Hmm. Maybe I can have Jake train me to be a Whip Master."

He looked at her in feigned horror, and they both laughed, glad they had a chance to clear the last bit of friction still between them. When he stood to go back to the rest of the group, she got up and followed, then took the seat at the end of the couch between Boomer and Ian's recliner, which was in its upright position. Ian smiled at her, but it didn't reach his eyes, which were filled with worry. Angie leaned over, linked her right fingers with his left, and set their joined hands on the couch's armrest.

His other hand was holding the jet's phone to his ear as he got the update from Devon. "Okay. Do what you can, call in whoever you need, and keep me updated."

Disconnecting the call, he looked up and told them what he knew, which wasn't much. "There's been no word

HIS ANGEL

from the kidnappers yet, or agents, or whatever you want to call those assholes. No leads either. An APB was put out on the agency vehicle. Dev called in a few favors with the locals, and so far, they've agreed to keep the DEA out of the loop despite the connection. He also put a call into Keon just in case we need to override the local law enforcement."

Their contact in the FBI, Larry Keon, was the Deputy Director, otherwise known as the number two man in the agency, and would help them with whatever they needed. "Henderson is alive but still unconscious. He lost a lot of blood, and they took him into surgery. His partner didn't make it. Dev's pulling in everyone he can and using our local contacts and snitches. Nothing so far."

"Why did they take her? I mean, Jimmy has never even met Jenn."

Angie wasn't seeing the big picture, but the men were. Ian squeezed her hand. "Angel, they obviously don't know you well enough yet. Otherwise, they would've gone after one of your friends. It would've taken them a while to figure out who you would run to save. You have no other family except for Athos and vice versa. The only connection they could figure out fast is Brody since he helped you. Brody's trail led them to Trident. Their best chance to get you, and ultimately Athos, was to take either Kristen or Jenn. Kristen hasn't left the compound, so Jenn was taken. We'll get her back, but for now, we wait until they contact us."

Her bottom lip trembled, but she didn't break down. "They want you to trade me for Jenn, don't they?"

Ian tugged on her hand until she stood, and he pulled her down on his lap. Wrapping one arm around her hips and holding her to him, he cupped her chin with his other hand and ensured she was looking into his eyes. "That's not

239

going to happen, Angel. I'm scared to death for Jenn's safety, but I'll throw myself on the gates of Hell before I trade your life for hers. Once we find out where they're holding her, we're going to get her back . . . alive. It's what we do, sweetheart. Dev's called in some former team members who can get to Tampa fast. Boomer's dad is already on his way to help along with a few others. These bastards will rue the day they ever messed with Jennifer Mullins. I can guarantee you that."

Tiny chimed in. "Don't worry, Miss Angie. We got this covered."

Angie's gaze moved to each brave man's face, and she saw their determination. She nodded but knew it was evident she was still terrified for Jenn's safety. Climbing off Ian's lap, she headed to the jet's bathroom, which was twice the size of regular airplane facilities, and shut the door. It wasn't until she was alone that she allowed her tears to fall. She didn't want the men to know how upset she was because they had enough to deal with without her breaking down in front of them.

It was a few minutes before she got herself back under control and began to splash some water on her face. There was a knock at the door, and she did a pat-dry of her hands and face before tossing the paper towel into the trash. When she opened the door, she was surprised to see Jimmy, and instead of standing aside to let her out, he stepped into the small space with her and closed the door behind him. "What are you doing?"

He took her hands in his. "I wanted a moment alone with you, and this was the only option. I'm sorry, Ang. You have no idea how sorry I am that you and Ian's niece are in jeopardy because of me. I'm sorry I put my need to avenge

HIS ANGEL

Mom's and Ruthie's deaths before my relationship with you."

He stared at their joined hands. Swallowing hard, he struggled to find the right words. "Before I got called into my CO's office and was told they'd been murdered, I was planning to finish my tour and get out. I was going to come home and ask you out on a real date." Angie gaped at her best friend while he lifted his sad eyes and shrugged his shoulder. "I know, crazy, right? But being away from you, so far away, I realized how much you meant to me. Somewhere in the middle of our letters, phone calls, and my rotations home, I fell in love with my best friend. Hell, I'd been in love with you long before that but refused to admit it to myself."

"Oh, Jimmy. Why didn't you ever say anything?"

"In the beginning, before . . . I was just plain scared. Here I was in Special Ops, and a cute, sassy little blonde, who means the world to me, had me scared shitless, thinking she wouldn't say yes to a date. Besides, I wanted to tell you face to face. I didn't want to give you time to overthink things. Then, my world fell apart, and I was so bent on revenge. When Artie approached me with a way to get even with the dirtbags who sold drugs to my sister and millions of other kids like her, I took it. And I didn't like who I'd become afterward. I couldn't expect you to fall for a man who'd become so bloodthirsty he was willing to throw away the best thing that ever happened to him. You. You have been my world since the day I met you in ninth grade English and picked up the book you'd knocked off your desk and gave it back to you."

She gave him a sad smile. "I felt that way too, but I thought you didn't want to ruin our friendship for something that might not work out."

"I didn't. I thought if it didn't work out, I'd lose you altogether. And when I was finally ready to face my fear . . ." He took a deep breath and let it out again. "Sawyer is good for you. I watch him watch you. You come before everything else for him. I can't say the same, and you have no idea how sorry I am for that. At one point in my life, I thought we were soulmates, you know? Now, I think you may have been mine, but I was never yours. But if he ever hurts you, there will be hell to pay."

She started to say something, but he shook his head, stopping her. "I want you to be happy, baby, and despite everything going on, I see how you look at him too. I know you're in love with him, and I'm okay with it. Well, maybe not at the moment, but I'll get there. Maybe when this is all over, I'll start looking for my true soulmate if she's out there. But honestly, Ang, you'll be a tough act to follow."

By the time Athos finished talking, Angie was crying again. He pulled her into his arms and held her until the tears stopped a second time. Then he let her go, but not before he placed a lingering kiss on her forehead. "I love you, Ang. I always will."

"I love you, too, Jimmy Andrews. You'll always be my best friend."

When the two of them stepped out of the bathroom together, Ian saw her swollen, red eyes, and she could sense the anger blasting through him as his stare shifted to the man who'd made her cry. Before he could say or do anything, Angie hurried over to him, climbed back into his lap, and wrapped her arms around him, needing to soothe him and herself. She felt his body relax when she whispered in his ear, "It's okay, Ian. He had some things he wanted to tell me, but it's you I want to be with. He'll always be my friend, but it's you I'm in love with."

HIS ANGEL

Ian tugged her hair, pulling her head back until he could look into her eyes. He had to see the truth there—she *was* in love with him. Her heart belonged to him and only him. He leaned down so his mouth was next to her ear and spoke so no one else would hear. "And I'm in love with you, my sweet angel."

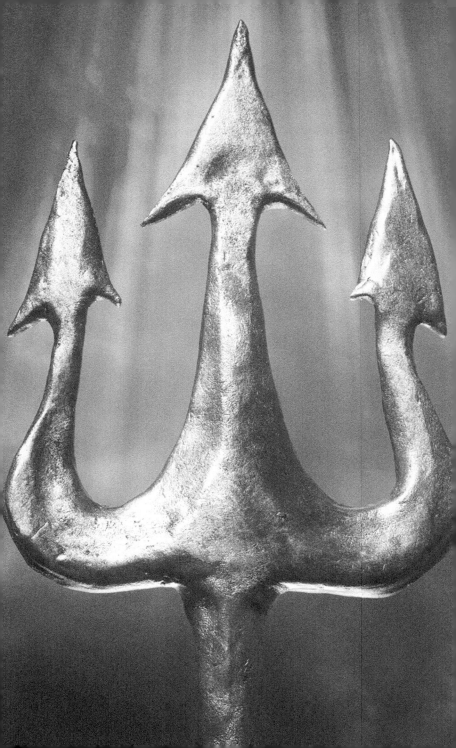

CHAPTER EIGHTEEN

When they arrived back at the compound, they were met with a nearly full parking area outside the Trident building. There were several government-issued cars, marked Tampa P.D. units, and personal vehicles belonging to whoever Devon had managed to contact. Jenn had about forty surrogate uncles from SEAL Team Four, all of whom would drop everything for Baby-girl, but only a few were close enough to Tampa to get there within a short time frame. Even Beau knew he was "on duty" and had attached himself to Angie's side as if knowing she was the human who needed him the most. Boomer's father, Rick Michaelson, and Devon approached Marco and Ian's vehicles, which they had driven home from the small airstrip.

As Boomer greeted his dad, who was also a former SEAL, Devon got down to business and filled them all in. "Still no word from the kidnappers, and we can't figure out why because it's been over three hours. They've gotta still be in Tampa somewhere because Angie's their objective. In addition to Rick, we've got Bannerman, Rad, and Urkel inside the conference room doing what they can to coordinate everything and try to figure out where they may have her. We also called Chase and asked him to spare whoever he had on hand, which was only five guys with the experience we need."

When necessary, Trident contracted additional manpower from Chase Dixon, who owned Blackhawk Security. It was his two men who'd been assigned to protect Jenn. "But he'll have more tomorrow if it goes that long. He's at the hospital with Henderson, who's still in surgery. His folks are on their way from Jacksonville. I told Chase to book them a room at the Hilton up the street from the hospital and bill it to me. He told me to fuck off—he's got it covered.

"We're keeping the DEA out of the loop until we know who we can trust. Instead, I called Keon. He's stuck in D.C. but contacted the local office and told them to help us however they could. Unfortunately, it means Frank Stonewall is here, and he ain't happy about it."

The local FBI Special Agent in Charge had been far from thrilled with his supervisor, Trident, and Carter after he was shut out of the investigation when Carter killed the hit-man targeting the team several months ago. While the rest of the team groaned at Devon's announcement, Carter smirked. The last time he and Stonewall met, the SAC almost crapped his pants when the pissed-off operative lit into him. The fed's reaction to seeing him again should be interesting.

"Angie!" All heads turned as Kristen came running from the residence building, straight into the other woman's arms, and held her tight. The two of them tried hard not to crumble, but they couldn't stop the few tears that fell down both their faces.

Ian strode over and stood beside them, rubbing his

hands up and down their backs in comfort. "Kristen, why don't you take Angie to your apartment for now, *hmmm*? Too many people are in the offices, and you'll just be in the way. Take Beau with you, and we'll let you know when we hear something." Facing Angie, he added, "We're doing everything possible. We'll find her and bring her home. I promise."

The two women nodded, neither trusting themselves to speak at the moment. Ian kissed them both on the head, lingering longer on Angie's. Then he watched as they staggered back to the apartments, arms around each other in mutual support as Beau trotted beside them. Taking a deep breath, he focused on his now extended team and gestured for them to head into the offices. It was time to make good on his promise.

Inside, Colleen sat at her reception desk, calling in an order for pizzas and two cases of bottled water for the men now occupying the conference room. Devon's office and two vacant desks in a small bullpen area behind her were also in use. The young secretary's eyes were red, and she'd clearly been crying earlier. As they walked by her, she gave them a watery smile filled with trust, as if she had no doubt the Doms would do everything they could to save Jenn's life.

Brody went straight to his war-room, unlocked it, and started booting up the computers he needed. Curt Bannerman, their backup computer specialist on Team Four, joined him, taking a spare chair and rolling it over to assist his fellow geek. Neil 'Rad' Radovsky and Steve 'Urkel' Romanelli gave Ian and the rest of the team lazy salutes while staying on their respective phones with their contacts, trying to find where Jenn might be being held.

Inside Devon's office, the five men borrowed from

Chase were checking their weapons and waiting to be called to duty. One was on the phone, and from the sound of it, he was talking to his boss and checking on Henderson. Ian would have to find out about the slain bodyguard later to see what they could do to help the man's family deal with their loss. Earlier on the plane, Ian had told Devon, who agreed, that they would take care of all costs for the funeral and burial. If he had a wife and children, they would ensure they were well cared for. It was the least they could do for a man who had given his life trying to protect Jenn.

The conference room was filled with three FBI agents, including a scowling Stonewall, two uniformed policemen, and two plainclothes detectives from the local P.D. If the situation wasn't so serious, Ian might have laughed when Stonewall paled at the sight of Carter walking into the room. As it was, he heard Boomer chuckle behind him when the kid noticed the same thing. Carter, in turn, gave the SAC his best Dom glare, then ignored the man and got to work, calling his own contacts.

Also present in the room were Colleen's Dom, Reggie Helm, and Ian's cousin, Mitch Sawyer, who shook Ian's hand and offered them whatever help they could give. Mitch asked, "What should we do about the club? Do you want me to shut it down for the night?"

Ian glanced at the clock on the wall and sighed. They still had about three hours before the club opened at nineteen-thirty hours. "Yeah, the fewer people here at the compound, the better. We don't know how long this is going to last. Whatever you do, don't let the members know about Jenn. Otherwise, every Dom will be showing up to help, and while I'd appreciate it, they'll be in the way. We have enough personnel here as is."

HIS ANGEL

Mitch nodded. "I'll send out the mass text from my office." He turned to Tiny. "Do you mind helping me call the staff? I want to make sure everyone knows not to show, and the phones will probably start ringing off the hook when the members find out we're closed, wanting to see what the problem is."

Ian spoke in a low tone to Reggie so he couldn't be overheard, "Take Colleen home with you. She doesn't need to be here for this, and the less you know, the better. We may need you after this is all over."

Reggie was one of Trident's lawyers, and this was Ian's way of keeping the man out of the loop for when the shit hit the fan. If Reggie needed to defend them in court for any reason, like for a murder charge, it gave him plausible deniability. When lawyers spoke to their clients accused of crimes, they rarely asked them outright if they were guilty. They didn't need to know to defend their clients and usually didn't *want* to know.

Right after the two Doms and Tiny left with Colleen in tow, the company phone rang, and Ian picked up the line on one of the conference room phones sitting on the table. When he heard the computer-altered voice, he rapidly waved his other hand and snapped his fingers to alert everyone in the room that the kidnappers were making contact. Everyone stopped in mid-sentence and remained silent. Marco ran out the door toward the war-room to tell Brody to start tracing the call as Ian hit the speaker button so they could all hear.

". . . see her again. Tomorrow morning at eight o'clock, you'll receive a text. Have Agent Andrews bring Angelina Beckett to the address, and we'll release your pretty niece, although she may not be too pretty anymore if you don't do as you're told."

The hair on the back of Ian's neck tingled as his fear and anger intensified. Leaning against his two hands on the conference table, he growled at the person on the other end of the phone. "Listen, you fucking bastard, if you hurt one fucking hair on that girl's head, there won't be anywhere on this fucking earth where you can hide that I won't find you. And when I'm done with you, you'll be fucking begging me to kill you to end your suffering! You hear me, you piece of shit!"

He'd been in such a blind rage and was yelling by the end of his rant that he didn't realize the call had been disconnected until a hand gripped Ian's bicep.

"He hung up." Devon's voice was low, trying to calm his brother down, but it didn't work. Ian grabbed the office phone, ripped out the cord, and threw it against the wall, where it shattered.

The flying debris didn't hurt anyone, although several men were hit. Not a word was spoken as the usually unflappable man stormed out of the room and made his way to his office, passing a stone-faced Marco. He slammed the door behind him, and they heard a roar of frustration and anguish. The men all knew the call time was far too short for a trace. They were equally frustrated because despite all the missions and cases they'd been on over the years, this time, it was personal.

Devon glanced around the room. "Give him a few minutes. In the meantime, get back to harassing your contacts."

* * *

Angie was in Ian's bedroom after telling Kristen she'd be up in a few minutes. Brody had programmed her hand print for the lock scanners at Ian's request earlier in the week, so she'd been able to let herself in as Beau followed

Kristen upstairs to her and Devon's apartment. This was the first time Angie had a moment to herself since Jimmy had shown up, her brief time in the plane's bathroom notwithstanding. She needed some time to come to terms with a few things. In addition to her worry about Jenn, she was still reeling from Jimmy's confession and the fact that she'd told Ian she was in love with him. She hadn't expected him to say the words back to her, and although she knew he meant them, she couldn't help but think he was still holding himself back from her. His ex-fiancée must have done a number on him, and she was glad the woman didn't live nearby because she might have gone looking for her and pounded on her for hurting him.

Entering the bathroom, she rewashed her face, then brushed her teeth with the spare toothbrush Ian had given her to use after her first overnight stay. When she returned to the bedroom, she pulled the pieces of her disassembled cell phone out of the sweatshirt Ian had given her to wear when she started shaking at the news of the kidnapping. She'd retrieved the phone parts from the backseat of his SUV, where he'd tossed it yesterday, and shoved them in her pockets.

God, was it only yesterday afternoon when she and Brody had been running for their lives? So much had changed in less than thirty-six hours.

Putting the SIM card in, followed by the battery, she closed the cover and powered the phone up. At once, it began alerting her to missed texts and calls. Checking the call log first, she saw four voicemails from her friend Mandy, Shelby from the club, Red Rose Books, and one other client. Then she checked her texts and saw more of the same, but one *Unknown* message caught her eye.

When she opened it, Angie was horrified to see a photo

of Jenn, and her blood ran cold. The girl had been bound, gagged, and blindfolded. The message accompanying the photo told her to contact the sender immediately without telling the cops or the Trident team, or they were going to kill Jenn. Checking the time stamp, she saw the message had only been received twenty minutes ago. She sent a return text as fast as she could.

> I'm here. Tell me what I should do.

Less than fifteen seconds later, the phone rang in her hand, and she'd been so startled that she almost dropped it. The screen read *Unknown Caller*. After punching the connect button, she brought the phone to her ear. "H-hello?"

A computer-disguised voice came over the line, and Angie's hands began to tremble. "Come alone to the address I'm going to text you. If I see your boyfriend, the cops, or anyone else, I'll kill her. You have fifteen minutes."

Before she could respond, the call was disconnected. She stared at the phone until a text message alert sounded.

UNKNOWN CALLER

> 1795 Route 301 . . . Alone!

Frantic, she ran out to the living room and began to search for her purse and car keys before remembering her car wasn't there. It was still in the driveway at her house. She spotted Ian's spare set of keys sitting on a shelf of his entertainment center. Snatching them, she ran out the front door and jumped into his Audi, pushing the keyless start button as she grabbed the seat belt. She couldn't risk telling Kristen where she was going, or anyone else for that matter. But she wasn't stupid, though. When she reached the destination, she would text Ian to tell him where she and Jenn were.

Relieved to see no one was outside except two security guards, whom she barely knew, she put the car in drive and accelerated as fast as she dared without alerting them something was wrong. The gates had been left open to allow the police and feds to come and go as needed, and Angie drove out of the compound, heading for the main road. Ian and Jimmy would kill her if the drug dealers didn't do it for them, but she knew they wouldn't exchange her life for Jenn's, and she refused to be responsible for the girl's death.

It didn't take her long to get to Route 301, but she didn't know if she needed to go north or south. She programmed her phone's GPS with the address and turned north when the annoyingly cheerful woman's voice told her to. A few minutes later, the same voice spoke again. "You're approaching your destination on the right."

Pulling to the shoulder, Angie viewed the structure set back from the road. It was similar to Ian's compound but had fewer trees, no fence, and only two warehouse buildings, the only ones in sight on the unpopulated strip of highway. From where she sat, she could only see two vehicles—a black SUV and a plain, four-door sedan, which she assumed belonged to the DEA agents who'd been at her house. Grabbing her phone, she typed a text to Ian.

> Kidnappers called. They're at 1795 Route 301. I'm trading myself for Jenn. Hurry.

After pressing the send button, Angie tossed the phone on the passenger seat. She put the car back in drive and eased forward, turning onto the long driveway leading to the buildings. She parked next to the SUV and climbed out of the car, leaving the engine running with the key fob in the center console so Jenn could escape. Angie glanced back and forth between the two buildings, trying to figure out which she was supposed to go into, when the door to the one on the left opened. Agent Jackson was standing inside the door jamb, pointing his gun at her. "Inside. Now!"

Angie trudged toward him with trembling knees and heavy feet, praying Ian got there before it was too late.

CHAPTER NINETEEN

Devon was about to knock on the still-closed door when it swung open, and he took in Ian's wild expression. He knew immediately what he saw in the blue eyes so similar to his own—terror . . . sheer terror. "What's wrong?"

Instead of telling him, his brother shoved his phone in Devon's face, so he could read the text Ian had received seconds earlier.

ANGEL

Kidnappers called. They're at 1795 Route 301. I'm trading myself for Jenn. Hurry.

"Ah, fuck!"

Ian ran to the reception area. "We gotta move! Now!"

The team, former SEALs, Chase's men, Carter, Athos, the feds, and cops came running and followed the Sawyer brothers into the parking lot. "We've got an address. Not only do they have Jenn," Ian paused and looked directly at Athos, "but they contacted Angie on her cell, and she decided to play Wonder Woman. She's on her way to trade herself for Jenn."

Athos' eyes mirrored the same fear which was in Ian's. Around them was a chorus of curses and frustrated groans. The men knew there was no way the kidnappers would let Jenn go, even if they had Angie. Not meaning to, Ian's little angel had made their job twice as hard, and when he got a hold of her, she wouldn't be able to sit for a month. He'd make sure of it, but first, they had to rescue the two women he loved.

"Where are they?"

The question came from Stonewall, and Ian looked at Carter, who gave him a slight shake of the head. Ian agreed. They were doing this without the local law enforcement's involvement. This is what his team did best. If they let the cops and feds show up at the scene, it would become a cluster-fuck in the first degree, with Jenn and Angie's lives on the line. The FBI and Tampa P.D. had protocols that, by law, they had to follow. Trident didn't have those restraints, and it was better to apologize later than ask permission before they acted. Carter pulled out his cell phone, one of his many throwaways, and dialed a number from memory while stepping away from the group.

Stonewall saw Ian's hesitation, turned bright red, and yelled, "Oh, no, Sawyer! Not again! You're keeping us in the loop on this, or I'll arrest all of you right here, right now!"

As much as Ian wanted to race to save the two women, he knew if he took off, the feds and locals would be right on his tail. He assumed Carter was calling Keon and forced himself to wait a moment.

While the SAC continued to rant, his two subordinates and the local police didn't look too thrilled about trying to arrest seventeen hyped-up men. Men who'd killed plenty of terrorists and criminals while in the military and were currently out for blood.

Most of the specially trained operatives ignored the irate agent and gathered around Marco's vehicle. The communications specialist was handing out headsets so they could all talk with each other without needing their hands. Weapons were being double-checked, and Jake loaded up his favorite sniper rifle and backup MK11, which he would loan to Carter if needed.

Amid the commotion, Kristen came running down from the residences with Beau on her heels. She ran straight to Devon and blurted out that Angie was missing. He explained what had happened, and a look of shock came over her face. He grabbed her chin for her attention. "I need to know you're safe. Tiny and Mitch are in the club office. You're to go directly there and do everything they tell you, Pet. I can't do my job if I'm worried about you. If you give them trouble, you'll get a public spanking you'll never forget. Understand?"

She knew he was serious when he'd said the word 'public' because, while she loved to watch other subs be disciplined in front of everyone at the club, she wasn't thrilled when it was her ass on display. "Yes, Sir. I love you. Be safe."

He kissed her on the lips. "I love you too. Now go. Beau is coming with us. I'll call you as soon as we have them safe."

Devon ordered Beau to heel as his fiancée headed straight for the building that housed the club. The dog's rear end spun around, and he attached himself to Devon's right leg, not looking happy to see his previous protection detail walk away without him. His human reached down and scratched behind his furry ear. "It's all right, boy. She's fine. We need to rescue Jenn and Angie and maybe even give you someone to sink your teeth into."

While Dev knew the dog should understand very little of what was being said to him, the canine seemed to know exactly what he meant. Beau barked excitedly at the prospect of biting someone who deserved it.

In the meantime, Carter had stopped talking on his cell and approached Stonewall. With a glare that had made some men tremble in their boots, Carter handed him the phone. The fed blanched and looked confused but took the device. Trying to salvage his authority, he barked into the speaker. "This is FBI Special Agent in Charge Stonewall. Who the hell is this?"

Ian, Devon, and Athos watched as the last of the man's blood drained from his face. "Yes, Director Moran, sir . . . I understand, sir . . . no problem, sir . . ."

Without waiting for the SAC to finish getting his ass handed to him by his boss, the men, minus the law enforcement, scrambled for their vehicles and flew out of the compound single file behind Ian's SUV. Carter and Athos sat in the back, behind the Sawyer brothers, with Beau between them. The dog seemed to be anticipating the upcoming mission as his tongue hung from his panting mouth.

Ian drove while Devon sat in the passenger seat, bringing up the GPS coordinates. After that, he dialed his cell phone and waited for Tiny to pick up. When the head security guard did, he told him, "I need you to take Kristen and lock her down in the panic room until further notice. Tell Mitch to stay locked inside the club if he doesn't want to go with you, but make sure he's armed. Shut down the gates whether the cops leave or not."

When the big man confirmed the orders, Devon discon-

HIS ANGEL

nected the phone and looked over his shoulder at Carter. "Did you really use one of your get-out-of-jail-free calls to Mr. Big? Why didn't you just call Keon?"

The spy shrugged, but his face remained expressionless. He rarely contacted Director Moran unless necessary, preferring to deal with the deputy director instead—fewer politics. "Actually, I tried calling Larry, but he didn't pick up, so I went up the ladder. The director was already in a foul mood and all too happy to threaten the jackass with a transfer. I think he might've mentioned some town in Alaska with a population of two."

Devon let out a sharp bark of laughter and shook his head in disbelief before Brody's voice came over everyone's headsets. On his laptop was a live stream from one of the many satellites orbiting the Earth, and it was zoomed in on their destination. "Don't ask whose SAT I'm using because you don't want to know." A few chuckles came through the headsets. "Ian, when you get to 301, you're going north. Four-point-three miles up, there's a dirt road on your right. Take it about a hundred yards in and approach from the south on foot with a two-minute ETA.

"The address has two warehouses on it running west to east. There are three vehicles—it looks like your Audi is one of them, and I think another is the DEA sedan from yesterday, but I can't be positive without seeing the plates. The other vehicle is a dark SUV. From their parking jobs, I can't tell which building they're in, so we need to check both. A second team can drive past without suspicion, pull off about a half mile up the road, and come in from the north."

Ian acknowledged the information and asked for a breakdown of who was in which vehicle. When he had the info, he broke them down into three teams. Marco would lead Team Two while Ian took Team One. Marco had Jake,

Brody, Rick, Bannerman, and Rad with him. Ian's team consisted of the three men in his vehicle, along with Boomer, Urkel, and one of Chase's men, Tanner. And, of course, Beau. The remaining four contract agents would take position across the highway, storm the driveway after the entry teams breached whichever building held the hostages, and intercept anyone trying to run for it.

Less than ten minutes later, the vehicles were in position, and the men poured out of them. While waiting for information back at the compound, Dev had instructed Chase's men to load up the vehicles with equipment they would all need to stage a rescue. The men had worked with Trident on several missions and knew what was needed. Now, all three teams were suiting up with bullet-proof vests, KA-BAR knives, sidearms, and flash-bang grenades. Colt M4 Carbines or HK MP5s would be used, depending on each man's preference for their assault rifles.

Jake and Carter would carry their sniper rifles. Individuals grabbed other equipment that the team needed but wasn't necessary for each member to carry. Beau was outfitted with a harness and specially designed canine bullet-proof vest. The dog's ears and tail twitched excitedly while his paws eagerly danced, but he remained silent. There would be no need to worry about him barking and alerting anyone to their presence since he'd been trained well, and the team often practiced different drills with him. Beau would do his job as precisely as his human counterparts did theirs.

"Team Two, Team Three, ready?" Ian spoke into the headset attached to his right ear as he handed Beau's short lead to Boomer. When the responses came back affirmative, he told them to move out. He didn't have to worry about the men who weren't part of Trident's core

HIS ANGEL

six. They all had Special Ops experience, including Athos, so they knew how each man and team would work in unison.

Team One approached, bounding as two sections, which meant while half the team moved forward to the next tree or object to hide behind, the others covered them, ready to fire their weapons if needed.

They silently reached the southernmost building, and Ian signaled for Urkel and Tanner to check the structure. While Tanner covered him, Urkel scanned the exterior wall with a heat-seeking hand-held device and came up negative for warm-bodied occupants other than a few rodents along the floor line. With hand signals, he gestured all clear to Team One, and the rest of them joined the two operatives, using the building as cover. Brody's whisper broke through the intercoms. "Teams, hold position. I have audio coming through from Angie's bracelet. Hot damn, it works. Stand-by."

Ian tamped down his urge to rush into the other building and gun down everyone inside who wasn't a female in his life.

* * *

Angie tried her best to speak in a calm voice. She didn't want to upset Jenn any more than she already was. While Jenn could hear everything, the gag and blindfold remained. But, apparently, the dirty DEA agents and three other men, who looked like gang members, didn't bring a second set so Angie could still see and talk. She was sitting on a chair in the middle of the cavernous warehouse, which was half-full with boxes and crates. Her wrists were handcuffed behind her, and it had taken her a while to remember that the GPS bracelet Brody had given her also had a microphone. Grateful for the thing, she ignored that it was hurting her since it was digging into her flesh under the metal handcuff.

She prayed the tech geek was listening as she began asking questions to the men holding them hostage. "I'm who you want. Why won't you let Jenn go?"

One of the dirtbag gang-bangers with a knife scar on his face looked up from the three-man poker game and sneered. "Because I like the hot little mama. She and I will have some fun after that pig shows up, and we get paid."

"Shut up, asshole," Agent Holstein snarled at Scarface, who shrugged and made a vulgar gesture toward Jenn. Angie was grateful the younger woman couldn't see it, as she was already trembling enough.

"So, it takes five of you to kidnap two women and handcuff them to chairs in the middle of a warehouse? We're helpless and not going anywhere, so please put away your handguns."

Please, Brody, be out there somewhere with Ian.

She changed subjects, not wanting the kidnappers to catch on that she was hopefully giving Trident information. "How did you find out about Jimmy and me, anyway?"

While the pacing Holstein didn't want any of the gang-bangers to answer her questions, the same didn't seem to apply to his partner. Agent Jackson was sitting on a crate about fifteen feet in front of her. "Saw the prick talking on one of those burner phones he used a lot and figured there was a good reason behind them. When I tried to get closer to hear what he was saying, he hung up and tossed it in his drawer when an 'agent down' came in, courtesy of an anonymous call, of course.

"After he tore out of there with the rest of the squad, I picked the lock on his desk, checked the phone, and copied your number. Figured it would come in handy someday.

HIS ANGEL

Andrews, or Athos, or fucking asshole, take your pick, was never the type of guy who could stay away from U/C. I knew he'd go back under again someday, and I was right. Traced the number and found you. When our connections from New Orleans called to see if we knew the new guy who was making them nervous and sent me a picture of him . . . well, let's just say I wasn't surprised to see your boyfriend."

"So, you're the one who told the drug dealers who Jimmy and the other agent who was murdered were?" The man shrugged without a verbal response, but the cruel expression on his face confirmed what she'd asked. "So now what happens?"

"Now we wait a little while, and when we're ready, you'll call your boyfriend and tell him where to meet us. If he comes alone, you both die. If he doesn't, then you die, he dies, and whoever he brings dies. Then we collect the money owed to us for this fucked up operation . . . simple enough?"

She didn't answer him.

"By the way, which one is really your boyfriend? Andrews or the hick who you escaped with?" He leered at her. "Or are you banging them both?"

She realized he still thought Brody was her boyfriend and knew nothing about her relationship with Ian.

The man jumped off the crate, stepped toward her, and squatted in front of her chair. "Maybe I'll see what has all these assholes beating a path to your door, *hmm*? You that good in bed, darlin'?"

He imitated the Texas drawl Brody had used on him. She shuddered when he dragged a finger down her face and neck to her chest. Instinctively kicking out her leg, she missed connecting her shin with his balls by mere inches.

263

He shifted in time, then backhanded her across the face, sending her and her chair toppling. "You fucking bitch!"

Seconds after she hit the ground, the metal doors on both ends of the warehouse were kicked in, followed by flashes of blinding light and loud booms. Gunfire and pandemonium broke out, and Angie pushed her legs against the cement floor, forcing her upper body toward where Jenn sat, frantically straining against her restraints. At the same time, muffled screams emerged from around her gag. Unlike Angie, she was tied to the chair and couldn't escape the line of fire.

As the shooting continued, Angie managed to get to her knees and, using her upper body, knocked Jenn sideways, chair and all, to the ground, then covered the helpless woman's body with her own the best she could.

"Sit-rep," Ian demanded.

They were still in a holding pattern. Brody listened with one ear to a headset plugged into his portable tablet, which ran the same program as his laptop, while his com-set was in his other ear. Angie's voice came in loud and clear with occasional scratching noises, and he could make out the male voices in the distance.

He hit the record icon when Angie started to ask the questions the team needed answers to. "Way to go, sweetheart. Teams, standby, our girl is giving us info . . . five tangos . . . principles are handcuffed to chairs in the middle of structure . . . handguns at ready. No hints at any other weapons . . . she's off-topic. Your call, Boss-man."

"Team One, taking west end. Team Two, take the east

end. Get me heat confirmation, Two." Ian signaled for his men to circumvent the empty warehouse they were still behind toward the front entrances for both buildings. The other team would work their way toward the back. He also indicated for Carter to find a way to the roof to see if he could get eyes into the northern building. High windows would run along the south side of the other structure if they were the same. "

Reverend, south sniper looking for a position, do the same on north if you can." After Ian's teammate acknowledged him, he asked. "Heat signatures?"

Rad's voice came through as a low whisper since he needed to stand close to the target building. "Affirm. Looks like three sitting at a small table—two others in chairs about twenty feet to my left, possibly our principles. One pacing east to west looks like he's southeast of principles. One more sitting between duo and trio, maybe on a crate or something."

"Windows, doors?"

The men in the best positions to answer did so, starting with Rad on the north side and going clockwise. "Second-story windows on North, no entry."

Marco's voice came next. "East, one kick-in door, no windows."

"South, windows, no doors," stated Devon, who was first in line along the front of the unoccupied building and could see the last two sides from where he stood. "West, one kick-in, one overhead, no windows."

Carter reported in. "Sniper position on top of south structure. Partial line of sight. Best I can do. Can get head-shots on everyone but Pacer—he's too close to my side. Lots of hiding spots, boys. A bunch of wooden crates and boxes in there. Princess A sitting in chair, hands behind back.

Princess J, five feet east, hands same, also blindfolded and gagged."

"I've got Pacer in sight from north position." Jake was straddling a limb in the tall tree he'd managed to climb about fifteen yards from the target building. It wasn't the greatest spot because he couldn't rest his sniper rifle against anything, so it would have to be a holding shot without a spotter. As long as the branch didn't break under his weight, he'd be okay.

Ian acknowledged all transmissions. "Team One, breach west. Team Two, breach east. Team Three, standby for intercepts. On my go."

Marco took the remainder of his team, rounded the building to the back door, and stated they were in position while Ian's team took the front. Before Ian gave Devon the word to use the mobile ram to breach the front door and Bannerman to do the same at the back, Carter spoke into his headset from his elevated roost. "Crate tango hopped down, walking toward Principle A. Right in front of her, no weapon threat, lost headshot. . . smacked her, she's on the floor."

"Breach!"

Simultaneously, the east and west doors were banged open, and two flash-bang grenades were tossed through each, far enough for them to cause the most confusion among the building's occupants. Explosions, screams, yelled orders, Beau's barking, and sounds of gunfire filled the air as the members of both teams made their entries —some going left, others right—and took cover. Jake's calm voice penetrated the headsets. "Pacer down, headshot."

The trio from the poker table and Agent Jackson scrambled for cover while firing their weapons toward the doorways. Thanks to Carter, one of the gang members went down with a hole in his head.

Devon and Tanner had moved to the left after entry, while Boomer and Urkel went with Ian to the right. They worked their way around a maze of crates and boxes as the two remaining gang-bangers tried to make a run for the front door using whatever they could find as cover. Boomer released Beau with an order to attack, and the dog lunged for the nearest bad guy, clamping his jaw down on the man's arm. The suspect screamed in pain and tried to throw the dog loose but only succeeded in falling to the ground with the angry beast on top of him. He brought his gun up to shoot, but Boomer was there, kicking the weapon from his hand and shoving his own gun in the dirtbag's face. "Don't fucking move, asshole."

Ian and Urkel worked their way in further as the other team approached from the other side of the long warehouse. A final gunshot sounded as Devon took out the last gang member who'd still been firing his weapon while heading for the door. All was silent except for heavy breathing heard through the headsets and Beau's barking as the teams searched for the missing tango, Agent Jackson.

From Ian's spot behind a crate, he could see Angie's prone body lying on Jenn's. His niece was thrashing against her restraints, and he couldn't tell if Angie was moving because she was also struggling or if Jenn's actions were causing the body on top of her to move. Seeing no sign of the last suspect, and with Urkel covering his six, he ran low toward the women and knelt beside them, relieved when his angel turned her head to face him. "Ian!"

He put his assault rifle on the ground at his feet and reached to help her off Jenn. But the sound of near-simultaneous shots had him drawing his sidearm and spinning toward where they came from on the other side of several large crates. Both teams converged on the spot, and Ian heard curses and Tanner, their medic, telling someone to call for an ambulance.

From where Ian was still covering the women, he could only see some team members and wasn't sure who'd been hit. Marco gave the "All clear, suspects all accounted for," then Brody appeared at Ian's side and handed him a handcuff key before turning to set Jenn free.

Ian released Angie's wrists, and she threw her arms around his neck, hugging him as hard as possible. "Thank God you're here."

"It's over, sweetheart. I've got you, but you've got one hell of a punishment coming to you, Angel."

Returning her embrace, he watched his teammate remove Jenn's blindfold and gag, then cut through the ropes that bound her to the chair. Like Angie, she was crying and shaking but appeared unharmed, aside from a few bruises. Adrenaline, fueled by Ian's anger, fear, and relief, had him trembling as he held Angie tight, but he stiffened as his brother's voice came through the earpiece.

Angie cried out and scrambled to stand after she heard Devon say, "Come on, Athos. Stay with us." Her ear had been pressed against Ian's as the lowly spoken words had come over his headset.

Ian helped her stand and wrapped his arm around her shoulders as they hurried to the other side of the crates. Marco stood over Agent Jackson's dead body while Tanner and Devon worked on slowing the blood pouring from the side of Athos's chest.

The dirty agent had rounded the tall shipping crates and encountered the other agent's blindside. Jackson had fired a millisecond before Rick Michaelson spotted him and

HIS ANGEL

could get his own shot off, hitting the bastard in the head. But the damage had been done. The bullet had entered Athos' chest from the left side, in the thin area under his arm, which wasn't covered by the bullet-proof material. It was one of the worst places to get hit while wearing a vest.

Regret filled Rick's face that he hadn't seen the suspect two seconds earlier. 'What if' was something they'd all learned to deal with since their first moments in combat, but it never made it any easier. Jake and Carter appeared and cursed when they saw what had happened.

Angie rushed forward, falling to her knees as Devon made room for her at Athos's head. She grabbed her best friend's right hand while Dev leaned over his chest, holding pressure on the wound. Tanner quickly started an IV in the injured man's left arm. Athos's eyes fluttered open at Angie's voice, begging him to look at her. Struggling to breathe, his voice came out as a hoarse whisper. "Ang, you okay?"

"I'm fine. You are, too, Jimmy. They're going to fix you up good as new." She wiped the sweat from his brow and the blood seeping out of the corners of his mouth, but it kept coming. His face was pale, and his lips blue. Tanner looked up at Ian, standing behind Angie, and gave him a slight shake of his head. It wasn't good, and unless a miracle happened within the next five minutes, the man would bleed to death, and there was nothing any of them could do. The bullet had caused too much internal damage, probably nicking the heart or aorta before lodging somewhere in the lungs.

"Promise me something, baby." The wounded agent was fading fast. His labored breathing increased, and the blood filling his lungs made him cough. "Promise me you'll be happy, and remember I love you."

"I love you too, and you're not going anywhere, damn it! You stay here with me. That's what will make me happy! Stay with me!" Tears poured down her cheeks, and her lips trembled as she pleaded with him.

Athos' eyes shifted and met Ian's. "Take her. Take her out . . ."

The rest of his words were lost to a coughing fit. He used the last of his strength to lift the hand that Angie was holding and gestured to the man he was entrusting her life to.

Ian understood. Athos knew he only had a few minutes of life left in him, maybe even less, and he didn't want his best friend, the woman they both loved, to see his final moments.

Ian nodded and took hold of Angie's shoulders, pulling her to her feet. She began to fight him, struggling to stay where she was, but her friend whispered, "Love you, baby. Go."

"No . . . no, Jimmy!" Angie became hysterical, and Ian had no choice but to force her from the scene. "Let go, Ian! Put me down! I have to save him! Please, someone save him!"

Ian lifted her into his arms and cradled her to his chest as she struggled and screamed. He tried to offer words of comfort, but she wasn't listening to him. As much as it hurt her to be forced to leave–she might even think he was cruel–he knew it would be worse if she stayed.

As death neared, Athos would begin to cough up a lot more blood, and it wasn't a sight she needed to see. She also didn't need to hear the death rattle as the man took his last few breaths. Ian could hear the sounds of the approaching sirens as he carried her to the door. Urkel and

HIS ANGEL

Boomer had the one remaining suspect, whom Beau had caught, in handcuffs. The others were all confirmed dead.

He brought her outside to where the paramedics, police, and a very pissed-off Agent Stonewall had just arrived. After the gunfight, Carter had informed Ian that he'd contacted Keon. The deputy director would ensure the scene was cleaned up and no one, other than the surviving gang-banger, would be in trouble over the incident. Chase's men had secured the area and began to talk to the agents and officers in an attempt to give Ian and his team some breathing room.

Brody had also taken Jenn outside, putting her into the front seat of Ian's still-running Audi. One EMT ran over to check on her and Angie while the others rushed into the warehouse where they were most needed. Angie finally stopped fighting Ian, and he set her down on her feet but refused to let her go, embracing her as she sobbed and mumbled into his chest. "He's going to die, isn't he?"

The painful acceptance in her voice caused a lump in his throat, so instead of responding, he just held her tighter. A few minutes later, they both raised their heads when Carter approached. Placing a hand on Angie's neck, he leaned in and kissed the top of her head, whispering, "I'm sorry, little one. He's gone."

Her wail of grief was heard by all.

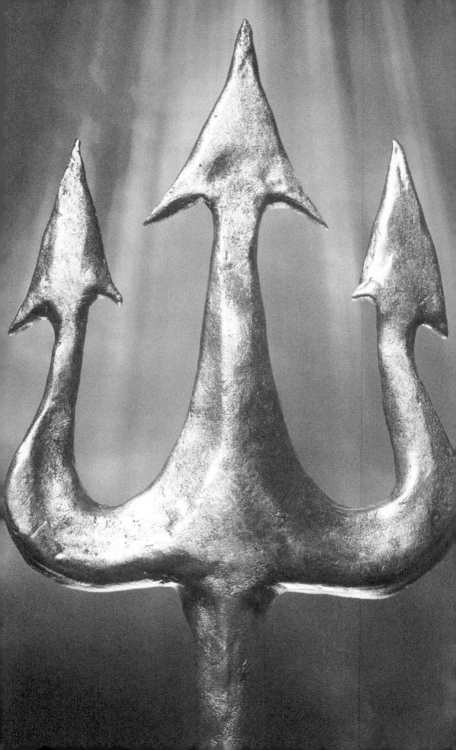

CHAPTER TWENTY

Ian sat in the passenger seat of Jake's Chevy Suburban as his friend drove Angie and him home to the compound from the airport, and he was less at ease now than he'd been before they left. It was three months since they'd buried her best friend next to his mother and sister in upstate New York. Brody's recording of Agent Jackson's bragging had ensured James Andrews was put to rest following a full federal government and military ceremony. A U.S. Marines honor guard had carried his coffin in and out of the Lake George church where he'd been baptized as a baby and made his First Communion and Confirmation. DEA agents and other members of law enforcement, fellow Marines, high school friends, and the Trident Security extended family had filled the church pews to capacity for the hometown hero's funeral. Flower arrangements covered the altar and, later again, the gravesite. Some of the colorful memorial displays were from Will Anders, Roxy and Kayla London, Tiny and The Covenant staff, Shelby Whitman, several of Angie's friends from Florida, and one from Red Rose Books. Kristen must've told her editor about their new graphic designer's loss.

Ian had spotted Carter, with dark sunglasses on, standing at the back of the church and, again, off to the side at the cemetery. The spy never approached them and disappeared after catching his and Angie's eyes, giving them a single somber nod.

At the gravesite, three volleys of seven rifles were fired in salute, and Ian held a weeping Angie as Taps was played. A sharply dressed Marine Corps captain knelt and handed her the U.S. flag, which had been draped over the coffin and then folded with expert precision. He softly told her the President of the United States, the United States Marines, and the United States Drug Enforcement Administration were grateful for her loved one's honorable and faithful service to his nation.

With Jimmy's death, what was left of the drug cartel in New Orleans had no reason to come after Angie. Besides the fact she could no longer be used as leverage for anything, they were too busy trying to keep themselves from getting life-without-parole prison sentences. The ensuing investigations led to Manny Melendez being killed during a raid and subsequent shoot-out with the feds and local police. Three of his minions were killed as well.

There had also been a city-wide round-up of suspects, including two DEA agents from the New Orleans office, three local cops, and thirty-seven other people. For now, the Diaz connections in New Orleans were either in jail, on the run, or dead. The large incoming shipment of drugs had been seized from the transport cargo ship in a joint operation between the DEA, FBI, and Coast Guard.

Henderson had survived the bullet wound to his chest but was out of commission for a few months while he

HIS ANGEL

recovered. Ian and Devon had kept their vow and paid for his partner's funeral, along with Chase Dixon. The team, Angie, Kristen, and Jenn had also attended that burial before flying to New York for Jimmy's funeral later in the same week.

Jenn's bruises had healed, and with the help of her psychologist, who'd counseled her following her parents' murders, she was getting past the memories of the kidnapping. Now, she had to convince her uncles to ease up on their over-protectiveness, which had increased ten-fold since the incident. They were back to arguing with her about running background checks on her prospective boyfriends, among other ridiculous precautions.

Angie still had moments when her grief would hit her. Ian did everything he could to help her through those rough times and decided to take her away for a while. It took longer than he'd expected, but they managed to clear their schedules and workloads a little over two weeks ago. They flew to the Philippines to meet his folks for ten days, followed by four days as guests of King Rajeemh, the ruler of the small North African country of Timasur near Mali. The king owned a home on Clearwater Beach near Tampa and used Trident Security to offset his protective detail whenever he and his family visited. He'd been inviting Ian and the team to his country for the past two years, and this was the first time any of them had a chance to take His Highness up on his generous offer.

Introducing Angie to his parents had been a breeze. As he'd expected, they fell in love with her instantly. His mother had taken them on a tour of the facility where she'd been performing surgery and even showed Angie first-hand examples of before and after surgery on two of her patients. His angel had been in complete awe of the work his mother was doing and told her so, much to the older woman's embarrassment. His mom was proud of the work she did. However, she didn't do it for the accolades but for the smiles of the children she helped.

Any reservations Angie may have had about meeting his billionaire father were quickly forgotten after the man had given her one of his big bear hugs. He'd worked side by side with them as they helped build a new school on one of the many Philippine islands while Marie Sawyer was busy at the local hospital. Within the first twenty-four hours of their visit, both parents had voiced their approval of Ian and Angie's relationship. Ian just wished he felt as certain about it as they did.

He wasn't worried about the connection he felt with Angie because the woman was one hundred and ten percent perfect for him in every way. She loved him–he was sure of it–and they were a good fit. She liked trying all sorts of new things with him—in and out of the bedroom—and she obviously enjoyed the sex as she was very vocal about it. And, like him, she couldn't get enough of it.

What worried Ian was, could he continue to make her happy for the rest of their lives? Was he good enough for her? Because the woman deserved the very best and then some. Yes, he had plenty of money for them to be financially comfortable, and yes, he made her smile . . . laugh . . . and come, over and over. He would give her the moon if he could, but what if she got tired of him sometime down the road? What if one day she woke up and decided she didn't want to be with him anymore, took off his collar, and walked out the door? Ian knew his heart would never recover from the loss and never love another woman like he loved his angel. His fear of losing her was why he was so scared to ask her to move in with him and eventually marry him.

When they'd been in Timasur, they'd been the king's guests at the main palace—a beautiful eighty-room castle on twenty-five acres of manicured lawns and maze-like gardens where they were always getting lost. After the first day, Ian began to joke he needed to save some breadcrumbs from each of their meals to lay down a trail. That way, they could return to their opulent suite without wandering around for an hour looking for it.

The country was beautiful, and they had spent their days with a guide who took them to many of the tiny nation's historical and natural sights. Kael had been full of history and wit, making them laugh often while showing them the wonders of his little corner of the world. Each night, Ian and Angie had been exhausted, falling asleep in each other's arms after a round or two of amazing love-making.

He would never tire of this woman, but would she eventually tire of him like Kaliope? Granted, he wasn't disappearing for months as he had been during his time in the Navy, but still, his thoughts kept nagging at him. He couldn't get himself past his distrust of "forever" relationships.

Early the morning of their last day in Timasur, Ian took advantage of the complete gym in the palace's east wing while Angie slept in. By seven o'clock, he'd been on the treadmill for over forty minutes, pacing himself at a comfortable ten-minute mile on his way to a seven-mile goal. His running workouts had been limited while on their trip, so he'd pushed himself a little more that morning.

As he was in the middle of his fifth mile, Princess Tahira walked in and jumped on the treadmill next to him. The twenty-

three-year-old tended to drive the Trident team crazy on her visits to Florida, where they were contracted to be her security detail. While the king, queen, and Prince Raj were very laid-back people who treated their employees with respect and gratitude, the princess came across as a spoiled brat—plain and simple.

She also had a thing for American men, especially her physically fit bodyguards, whom she always found ways to touch. While none of them had taken her up on her numerous offers of afternoon delights, it hadn't stopped her from trying. And when they still didn't give in, she would find a way to torture them for denying her what she wanted. Her usual form of revenge involved a credit card, a mall, and five or six hours of trying on everything in sight, particularly shoes.

Ian had been taken aback by how different Her Highness had acted during their visit to her homeland. She'd been polite and pleasant toward Angie and him and never once put the moves on him, which was so out of character. He spent most of his time in her presence waiting for the affable façade to drop and the real princess to emerge.

After five minutes of silence, while he ran and she walked on their respective treadmills, he couldn't take it anymore and slammed his hand on the stop button. When his feet came to a halt, he grabbed his towel from the machine's handle and wiped the sweat from his face before turning his body toward her. "All right, Princess, what gives?"

She didn't stop or slow down her pace as she glanced over at him with a confused expression on her face. She looked innocent, and he wasn't buying it for a minute.

"What do you mean, Ian Sawyer?"

He'd gotten used to how she called most Americans by their first and last names. "Well, since Angie and I have gotten here, you've gone out of your way to be pleasant and cordial. You

HIS ANGEL

haven't come on to me once, which isn't like you, so what are you up to?"

She hit the red button on her treadmill and slowed to a full stop before turning to face him with a wry grin. "In spite of what you think about me, what you think you know about me, the one thing I don't do, Ian Sawyer, is . . . what is the word you Americans use? Oh, yes, I don't . . . poach . . . on another woman's man, no matter how attractive I find him."

After her last words, he'd expected her to place her hand on his bare chest despite his sweat, but she didn't, which surprised him. He thought back to when she'd been in Florida and realized the only men who hadn't complained about her constant advances were the few contract guards who wore wedding rings.

"I envy you, Ian Sawyer. You and Angelina Beckett have found something I have only dreamed about."

He tilted his head and stared at the gorgeous young woman like he'd never seen her before. "What's that, Princess?"

She grinned at him. "I'm a firm believer in soulmates. But I also believe not everyone is lucky enough to find theirs. You two have—in each other. You have something between the two of you I have never had the privilege to see before up close."

Ian shrugged and took a drink of water. "Your parents have been happily married for a long time, haven't they?"

She paused long enough to take a sip out of her own water bottle. "Not always, no."

At his raised eyebrow, she chuckled. As long as Ian had known the royals, they had been an affectionate couple with each other, and if they did argue about anything, it was never in view of others. "Yes, my parents are very happy now, but it wasn't always the way. As with my grandparents and great-grandparents, my mother and father were the result of an arranged marriage when they were eighteen, and neither one was happy about it at first. The way my mother tells it, although

279

they thought each other was attractive, they . . . what is it you say . . . scrubbed each other the wrong way?"

He smiled at her flubbed cliché. *"It's rubbed each other the wrong way, but I understood what you meant. I had no idea your parent's marriage was arranged. Wow, I can't imagine what it was like to have your spouse picked out for you with no input."*

"Thankfully, my parents decided not to force the same tradition on my brother and me long ago. We are free to marry whomever we choose." She started her treadmill up again and began walking. "As I said earlier, I envy what you and Angelina Beckett have. You have found your one true love, the person you were destined to spend the rest of your life with. I'm worried I will not find mine, but if it is written in the stars, I will have to wait. In the meantime, I'm going to enjoy myself."

She glanced at him before facing forward again. "I'm also jealous of the babies you will have. You are very handsome, and she is a stunning woman. I'm sure your babies will be beautiful."

He couldn't help the panic which had settled in his chest. Him? A father? Could he be a good one? Could he be a good husband? He knew the answer was yes in his heart, but he still couldn't help but feel that one day, it would all disappear when Angie walked out the door on him.

Tahira seemed to be done talking to him, so foregoing the rest of his workout, he started for the door to return to his suite but then spun around and strode back to her treadmill. When she continued to walk but looked at him inquisitively, he told her, "I hope someday you find who you're looking for, Princess. Your soulmate. You deserve it as much as everyone else does."

"Thank you, Ian Sawyer. I hope he is as handsome as you."

. . .

HIS ANGEL

Ian didn't realize they'd pulled up to the compound's outer gate and stopped before Angie leaned forward from the backseat and placed her hand on his shoulder. He looked at her and then at a grinning Jake, neither of whom said anything as the man handed Angie something. Darting back and forth between the two, his eyes narrowed. It was obvious they were up to something. "What?"

Jake remained silent as Angie held up what he'd given her. A blindfold. "Put this on."

"Uh, not without a good reason, Angel."

She sighed dramatically, and his mouth curved upward. "Please? It's a surprise for your birthday."

His chuckle and expression were filled with lewdness, which made her blush. "You gave me my present on my birthday a week ago."

And what a present it'd been. For once, he'd let her completely take over the blowjob she'd given him while she was dressed in a frilly bra and panties. She'd also worn a garter, sheer hose, and his favorite pair of fuck-me heels, which she'd packed without his knowledge. He hadn't been allowed to touch her with his hands, and she wouldn't let him orgasm until she said so. It was an hour of the sweetest torture he'd ever been subjected to, and he thought his heart would stop when she finally allowed him to blast his cum down her throat. Thank God he had been lying on a bed because it'd taken him a good fifteen minutes before his legs stopped quivering afterward.

She held out the blindfold. "Please, Sir, for me?"

How could he resist her? The answer was easy—he couldn't. Taking the blindfold with its elastic band, he slid it over his head and eyes, then sighed. "This better be quick because I feel ridiculous."

281

SAMANTHA COLE

She giggled as Jake put the SUV in drive again and accelerated. "Now you know how I feel sometimes."

He knew she was kidding. His little angel loved being tied up and blindfolded while he had his wicked way with her, sometimes in public and sometimes in private.

Ian felt the car slow a bit as they approached the second gate, and when they didn't stop for Jake to have his hand scanned, he knew someone else had opened it for them. When the vehicle stopped, he estimated they were near the residential building. He heard the two of them exit the vehicle and shut their doors before his door was opened. Angie took his hand in hers and guided him carefully out of the car.

She told him to take three steps forward and stop. When he did, she grabbed his shoulders and turned him a little to the right before releasing him. "Okay, on the count of three, you can take it off. One . . . two . . . three!"

A chorus of "Happy birthday!" greeted him.

Holy shit! Ian's mouth fell open, and he couldn't believe his eyes. *What the hell have they done?*

It was beautiful . . . beyond beautiful. He stepped toward the ample space between the third and fourth buildings and tried to take everything in at once. The area was wide enough to have three tractor-trailers side by side and long enough for two of them to be bumper to bumper, so it was the size of a residential backyard . . . and now, it looked like one. Since he and Angie had left over two weeks ago, someone had transformed the paved, ugly, unused space into a garden of sorts. It was complete with grass, trees, shrubs, flowers, sitting areas, a fire-pit, and even . . . was that a waterfall spilling into a small pond at the far end?

For the first time he could ever remember, Ian was

HIS ANGEL

speechless. He had a knot in his throat and, *crap* . . . tears filled his eyes, and he wasn't ashamed of a single one of them. He took a few more steps, not knowing where to look and seeing something new with each pass. A bar and outdoor kitchen blended well with the landscaping, along with a giant barbecue and a weather-proof flat-screen TV.

Beau was rolling around on his back in the grass a few feet away, looking like he was in heaven. *I'm right there with you, dog,* Ian thought to himself. A small wooden sign two feet inside the grass line caught his eye—*Ian's Oasis.*

Okay, now he had to wipe away the few tears that had started to fall. He stared at Angie standing next to him with her hands clasped together at her chest, waiting anxiously for him to say something. His gaze then turned toward his team, Mitch, Jenn, Kristen, and Tiny sitting around the oblong fire pit. "Who . . . how?"

He cleared his choked-up throat. "Shit, I can't talk."

They all laughed, and Angie clapped her hands in glee. His brother stood and stepped toward him, grinning like a fool. He shook Ian's hand and tilted his head toward Angie. "Happy birthday, bro. This was your lady's idea–she designed it all on paper for us. While you were away, we dug up the asphalt and had some people bring in the sod and landscaping and install the kitchen and koi pond.

"We all helped as much as we could because we wanted you to know this came from our hearts. Angie picked out everything, and while you were away, Jenn and Ninja-girl took the list and went on shopping sprees for the furniture, barbecue, TV, and kitchen stuff. By the way, they did some major damage to the Trident credit card."

Ian laughed and wiped away a few more tears, which insisted on falling, before looking at his beautiful angel. "This was what you three were doing a few weeks ago?"

One day, he left the office to join her for lunch. When he didn't find her in his apartment as they had planned, he went upstairs looking for her, knowing she was most likely chatting with Kristen. He'd interrupted a pow-wow between the two of them, along with Jenn, and they'd clammed up when they saw him while Angie tried to hide the sketchbook she'd been holding. When he had attempted to find out what the little brats were up to, despite his best efforts, they all remained mum and broke up their little meeting. He'd forgotten all about it until now.

Angie nodded. "I wanted to do something special for your birthday, and I remembered what you said up at the safe house about wanting your own little oasis in the middle of nowhere. This isn't exactly in the middle of nowhere, but it's close enough until you're old enough to retire. I was going to suggest we go up to Maggie Valley for the week so they could get this done without you knowing, and then you suggested we visit your folks. We couldn't believe we kept it a secret from you. You, Sir, are a very good interrogator."

"Ha! Apparently, not good enough."

Everyone else stood, and there was a round of hugs from the women followed by handshakes and back-slapping from the men. After he finished with the reception line, he pulled Angie into his arms and kissed her senselessly. When the whistles and cat-calls faded, he ended the kiss, leaving them both breathless.

She placed her hands on his cheeks and looked at him with all the love in her heart. "I love you, Ian. I love you now and will love you when you're old and gray. I will never walk away from you, even if you push me, without trying everything to stay by your side. And if you leave this world before me, I will look forward to the day I join you in the

HIS ANGEL

afterlife because you're it for me. You're my heart, friend, Dom, lover, and soulmate, and I will love you forever."

Ian stared into the eyes of this incredible woman, and like a light bulb going on, everything clicked into place for him. She wasn't Kaliope or any other woman he'd been with over the years. She was the woman his heart had been searching for, and if any of those other relationships had worked out, he wouldn't be standing here next to his destiny.

A line from one of his brother's country songs came to mind—something about God blessing a broken road leading him to this point and to her—and he knew it would be his mantra to her for the rest of his life. He took her hands from his face and kissed her knuckles once but didn't release them. With a deep breath, he took a leap of faith. "Marry me."

"W-what?" Angie was stunned. "Say–say that again."

Ian barely heard the other women squeal and the men chuckle and groan over his heart pounding in his ears. "I'm not perfect. I'm not even a romantic. I'm not a flowers-and-perfume kind of guy. I don't spout poems out of my mouth or break out into songs. Hell, I don't even have a ring for you—yet. I will probably drive you crazy with my demands. We'll argue, we'll fight, but then we'll make up, and that's what I'm looking forward to the most. But the one thing I know is . . . I love you, Angel, and I will love you long after the day I die. You are my soulmate. Marry me. Have beautiful babies with me. Please."

He waited for a heartbeat and then a few more—hell, he'd wait forever—for her answer before her mouth turned up in a sexy grin. "Who says you're not a romantic? Because you most definitely are one, and yes, Sir, I will marry you."

Overjoyed, Ian grabbed her by the waist and swung her

around before capturing her mouth with his and kissing her like crazy again. From the group surrounding them came a chorus of cheers and clapping, but for him, his angel was the only person there.

Continue the adventure in *Waiting For Him: Trident Security Book 3* - now available.

Want to know what the Trident Security compound looks like? Check out the map on my website!

Also, look for the best reading order for the Trident Security series and its spinoff series also on my website.

PREVIEW

WAITING FOR HIM
Trident Security Book 3

Boomer sat at his office desk, his eyes narrowing as he studied the paper before him. The answers should be easy, but for the life of him, he couldn't come up with the solution. He glanced at his cell phone to check the time and noted it was eighteen-twenty hours. The six-thirty appointment Colleen had scheduled for him was later than normal, but she'd told him the new client had requested the evening hour, so here he was, trying to kill a few more minutes.

Mondays and Tuesdays were the only evenings it wasn't a problem for Trident clients to come to the compound where their offices were. The rest of the week, Ian and Devon Sawyer's other venture, The Covenant, was open, and Trident clients might be a little shocked to see the BDSM club's members in varying stages of undress walking through the parking lot.

The fenced-in compound consisted of four warehouses and was off the beaten path on the outskirts of Tampa, Florida. The first building after the guarded gate was home to the club. Beyond that was another gate leading to the remaining three buildings. Trident's offices, bunk rooms, firing range, training areas, gym, and vehicle garage occupied the next two structures, and the final one had been renovated into two large apartments. The bottom one belonged to Ian and his fiancée, Angie, while Devon and his fiancée, Kristen, lived on the second floor.

The rest of the building was empty space, and plans were being drawn up to construct two more apartments. One would be home to Ian's god-daughter, Jennifer Mullins when she wasn't at college. The men of Trident were her surrogate uncles, having served under her father in the teams. Ian had taken over her guardianship after her parents were killed in a home invasion the year before. The last unit would be offered to the youngest Sawyer brother, Nick, whenever he decided to opt out of the Navy. He'd made it through BUD/s, the SEALs' intensive training three years ago and was now with Team Three in Coronado, California so the twenty-five-year-old wouldn't be joining them anytime soon.

As Boomer tapped his pen on the desk, he looked over the hints available to him and became more frustrated because he still couldn't figure it out. He glanced up as Ian walked in and sat in one of the two guest chairs on the other side of the desk. "What's a nine-letter word for vague? Starts with an 'A' and the fifth letter is a 'G.'"

"Ambiguous." Ian rolled his eyes. "And if you're going to

HIS ANGEL

keep asking me for help with the daily crossword puzzles, then I'm getting you a fucking thesaurus for Christmas this year instead of your bonus."

Boomer gave his boss a smirk as he filled in the blank spaces of the puzzle. "You do, Boss-man, and I'm signing you up for an anchovy-of-the-month club."

Even though he knew his friend and employee was joking, Ian got a queasy look on his face. Boomer always found it funny how, out of six retired SEALs, he was the only one who liked the oily yet salty fish, considering how much time they'd spent in and on the ocean while in the Navy. Well, maybe that *was* the reason.

"Not funny, Baby Boomer." Ian picked up the stress squeeze ball the other man kept on his desk and tossed it back and forth between both hands. "So, did you find out any information on this new client?"

Boomer threw the pen down on the newspaper and leaned back in his chair. "Nope. Colleen said the woman, a Kate Zimmerman, needed to hire Trident, but she wouldn't deal with anyone except me. I've racked my brain and can't recall ever meeting anyone by that name. I tried calling the phone number she'd left but got the standard computerized voice telling me to leave a message. It comes back to a throwaway cell."

"One-night stand?"

He snorted but didn't take offense since all the guys on the team had participated in more one-night stands over the years than any of them cared to admit. Their time in the military and then the security business hadn't given them many opportunities for long-term relationships. Even if it did, Boomer wasn't interested. "I'd be lying if I said I remembered the first and last name of every woman I've ever slept with or scened with. But I'd like to think it would ring some sort of bell. Maybe she's a friend of a friend or something."

"Could be." They both knew a lot of their business was gained by word of mouth. "Guess we'll know in a few minutes. If she has no objections, and even if she does, I'll sit in on the meeting until we find out what she needs from us. If it's a bullshit my-husband's-cheating-on-me thing, I'll leave you to it."

"Fine with me. Are we the only two left in the office?"

Both men's phones chimed a text. The guard at the front gate was alerting them to their new client's arrival. Murray would buzz her through the second gate and instruct her where to park. They stood, and Boomer grabbed a legal-sized yellow pad and his pen while Ian headed for the door. "Yeah. Colleen left. Polo and Egghead are on their way to New York to escort a shipment of diamonds from a dealer to the buyer here in Tampa.

"Jake is trying to track down one of his informants who he's worried about—hasn't seen the guy in about two months, which he says is unusual. And my lucky brother is wedding venue shopping with Kristen and picking out pink tablecloths with matching napkins as we speak."

"Ha!" Boomer barked and shook his head. "I wouldn't fuck with him, Boss-man. You're right behind him, and karma's a bitch. Angie will be dragging your ass through the same tablecloths and napkins someday soon."

"Don't I know it. I'm trying to talk her into eloping, but I'm not having much success."

The pained look on his face was mostly false since Boomer knew he'd give his woman the world if she asked for it. Well, if he didn't have to help pick out matching flowers, cummerbunds, and bridesmaids' dresses, he would. "I'll go get your client and meet you in the conference room."

"K. Just going to hit the head really quick."

While Boomer headed in one direction for the bathroom, Ian walked in the other toward the reception area. The front door could only be opened from the inside by a lock-release behind Colleen's desk or by a hand scanner which unlocked the door for only those whose prints had been programmed into the system.

He pulled the door open and found himself looking at a brown-haired beauty who seemed to be about Boomer's age of thirty. Wearing a pair of jeans and a short-sleeved, navy blouse, she stood about five-foot-five in her flat, off-white shoes, which matched the belt at her slim waist. Her slender build made the shirt and pants look a little big on her as if she'd recently lost some weight but had yet to find clothes to fit her new frame. In Ian's opinion, she looked too thin.

She took off her sunglasses and peered up at him with big chestnut-colored eyes. "Hi, my name's Kate Zimmerman. I'm looking for Ben Michaelson. I have an appointment with him, and the guard told me he was in this building."

When she glanced over her shoulder to where Murray was keeping watch at the front gate, Ian's eyes didn't follow hers. Instead, he briefly stared with interest at Beau, who was sitting near the driver's door of Ms. Zimmerman's Ford

Focus. The goofy-faced dog was panting, but something about his posture and the fact that he seemed to be in a "stay" position had Ian eyeballing the woman in front of him. She saw where his gaze had been, and the corners of her mouth curved upward a tad as he raised a curious eyebrow at her.

Her smile didn't quite meet her anxious eyes, and when he got no answer to his unasked question, he opened the door wider. "Please come in, Ms. Zimmerman. I'm Ben's boss, Ian Sawyer. It's nice to meet you. If you don't mind, I'll be sitting in on your appointment."

Her smile faltered a little before she recovered. "Um, no. I mean, it's fine. I don't mind. It might be better that way."

Ian's curiosity was now further piqued, but he wasn't getting any bad vibes from her other than her nervousness, so he let her last comment slide for the moment. He glanced back at Beau, who was still sitting there with his tongue hanging out of his mouth and seemed to be waiting for a command. Ian tapped his leg. "Beau, *heir*."

The dog rushed over to his master, stopped, and when he received a slight hand signal, trotted past him on the way to the darkened conference room. Ian had discovered the dog when it was a young puppy. Its dying mother had dug under the compound's perimeter fence to find a human who would care for the little guy. When Beau was old enough, Ian took him to a friend who trained dogs for police departments and private security firms. Now, the silly-looking mutt was trained as an aggressive tracking and guard dog. All his commands were given in German since it wasn't a common language in the States.

"He's beautiful. Lab and Staffordshire Terrier, correct?"

"We think so. I found him as a pup . . . well, actually, he

found me." He shut the door and gestured her toward the conference room. "The vet thinks there may be something else mixed in there, maybe Great Dane, because his legs are a little longer than normal for the two breeds."

He turned on the overhead lights to the room as they entered. "Please have a seat. Boomer will be here in a moment.

"Boomer?" she queried as she placed her large purse on a chair while he pulled out the one next to it for her to sit in.

Ian sat across from her, leaving his usual chair on the end empty. Although this was his company, he trusted his employee to take the lead in the unknown case. The client had requested him specifically, and Ian was willing to cede his authority for the moment, therefore giving Boomer the "head" seat at the table.

He studied the woman for a few seconds before answering her. "Sorry, I meant Ben. Boomer is his call sign from the Navy. No one uses his first name around here, but it's out of habit."

He heard the man in question come down the hallway and saw him enter the room a second later. Ms. Zimmerman's back was to the door, but Ian knew the moment she realized Boomer was there without having seen him. Her body stiffened.

"Sorry to keep you waiting, Ms. Zimmerman. I . . ." Boomer walked over, peered down at the woman's face, and froze. Confusion in his eyes turned to pure shock, and Ian watched as the blood drained from his teammate's face. His normally strong voice dropped to a hoarse whisper. "Katerina?"

And with that, Benjamin Thomas "Boomer" Michaelson did something he'd never done before in his life. He fainted.

Waiting For Him is available now!

There had been many a night he'd cursed her for leaving him, the universe for taking her, and himself for loving her.

Thirty-six hours was all it took for eighteen-year-old Ben to go from being the happiest man alive to having his world fall apart.

Kat was his best friend's sister and the only woman ever to hold the key to Ben's heart. Then she and her family were gone in an instant, killed in a devastating accident.

Twelve years later, Kat emerges from the shadows of the Witness Protection Program, only to find the danger her father had placed them in was still out there. The last thing she wants to do is put her high-school sweetheart in danger, but he's the only person she trusts with her life.

Working for a private-security firm, Ben is shocked when his evening appointment is a ghost from the past. He knows he can't refuse to help Kat, but when it's over, he knows he'll have to let her go—she deserves better than the man he's become.

Will Ben and Kat survive, or will he once again have to bury the only woman he's ever loved?

For the best reading order of the Trident Security series and its spinoffs, check out the printable list on my website!

Also by

***Denotes titles/series that are available on select digital sites only. Paperbacks and audiobooks are available on most book sites.

***THE TRIDENT SECURITY SERIES

Leather & Lace

His Angel

Waiting For Him

Not Negotiable: A Novella

Topping The Alpha

Watching From the Shadows

Whiskey Tribute: A Novella

Tickle His Fancy

No Way in Hell: A Steel Corp/Trident Security Crossover (co-authored with J.B. Havens)

Absolving His Sins

Option Number Three: A Novella

Salvaging His Soul

Trident Security Field Manual

Torn In Half: A Novella

***Heels, Rhymes, & Nursery Crimes Series

(with 13 other authors)

Jack Be Nimble: A Trident Security-Related Short Story

***The Deimos Series

Handling Haven: Special Forces: Operation Alpha

Cheating the Devil: Special Forces: Operation Alpha

***The Trident Security Omega Team Series

Mountain of Evil

A Dead Man's Pulse

Forty Days & One Knight

***The Doms of The Covenant Series

Double Down & Dirty

Entertaining Distraction

Knot a Chance

***The Blackhawk Security Series

Tuff Enough

Blood Bound

***Master Key Series

Master Key Resort

Master Cordell

Hazard Falls Series

Don't Fight It

Don't Shoot the Messenger

The Malone Brothers Series

*Her Secret (*Formerly, *Take the Money and Run)*

Her Sleuth (Formerly *The Devil's Spare Change*)

Largo Ridge Series

Cold Feet

Antelope Rock Series

(co-authored with J.B. Havens)

Wannabe in Wyoming

Wistful in Wyoming

Award-Winning Standalone Books

The Road to Solace

Scattered Moments in Time: A Collection of Short Stories & More

***The Bid on Love Series

(with 7 other authors!)

Going, Going, Gone: Book 2

***The Collective: Season Two

(with 7 other authors!)

Angst: Book 7

***Special Collections

Trident Security Series: Volume I

Trident Security Series: Volume II

Trident Security Series: Volume III

Trident Security Series: Volume IV

Trident Security Series: Volume V

Trident Security Series: Volume VI

About

USA Today Bestselling Author and Award-Winning Author Samantha Cole is a retired policewoman and former paramedic. Using her life experiences and training, she strives to find the perfect mix of suspense and romance for her readers to enjoy.

Awards:

Wannabe in Wyoming (co-authored by J.B. Havens) won the bronze medal in the 2021 Readers' Favorite Awards in the General Romance category.

Scattered Moments in Time, won the gold medal in the 2020 Readers' Favorite Awards in the Fiction Anthology category.

The Road to Solace (formerly *The Friar*), won the silver medal in the 2017 Readers' Favorite Awards in the Contemporary Romance category.

Samantha has over thirty-five books published throughout several different series as well as a few standalone novels. A full list can be found on her website.

Sexy Six-Pack's Sirens Group on Facebook
Website: www.samanthacoleauthor.com
Newsletter: www.geni.us/SCNews

facebook.com/SamanthaColeAuthor

twitter.com/SamanthaCole222

instagram.com/samanthacoleauthor

amazon.com/Samantha-A-Cole/e/B00X53K3X8

bookbub.com/profile/samantha-a-cole

goodreads.com/SamanthaCole

pinterest.com/samanthacoleaut

Made in the USA
Coppell, TX
05 October 2023

22456311R00175